THE LAST HOUSE

—•—

MATTHEW SPEAK

SHADOW WOODS PUBLISHING

First Edition

Published by Shadow Woods Publishing

Visit our website at www.shadowwoodspublishing.com

ISBN: 979-8-9866339-0-9

Cover art by BCZ

Contents

This book was inspired by actual events that happened in and around Maquoketa, Iowa, in October of 2017. Names have been changed to respect the innocent and the dead.

For Scott and Valerie

I beheld him gazing upon vacancy for long hours, in an attitude of the profoundest attention, as if listening to some imaginary sound.

-*The Fall of the House of Usher* by Edgar Allan Poe

Chapter One

Something moved, quiet and gray, out in the trees and weeds—a blur of contrast lost in Don Loomis's vision. A whisper of movement, nothing more, sets the skin on his neck on fire. He had seen something earlier, just after lunch.

"You see that?" Don asks, his voice cracking like an ice cube dropped in warm water.

"See what?" Lou says, packing the last of his tools. Sweat beads dot the entirety of his sun-wrinkled forehead, though the October afternoon is a crisp forty-five degrees.

"Never mind."

Lou stares at him, mouth open, then scans the trees, making a thoughtful sound with his lips. With a dismissive grunt, Lou pulls a sack over his shoulder, turning his back to the forest and craning his neck to the house. "Yep, we did good," he says.

Don follows his gaze to the giant windows covering the back of the house. He nods. "Yeah, they'll have a pleasant view out into the gulley."

"They call it a ravine, numbskull." Lou chokes out a guffaw that turns into a ten second coughing fit.

"It's a real marvelous piece of property," Don says. Crunching sounds whisper behind him, as if someone were stepping through fallen leaves. Ignoring the panic in his chest, Don keeps his eyes trained on the house.

That tingling sensation on his neck has spread across his shoulders and down his back like a rash.

Like everyone else in Maquoketa, Iowa, Don had heard the stories about these woods, stretching several acres south and another twenty north, past highway 61, almost to the edge of town. He'd turned down several offers to hunt these parts, and now he wished he turned down the building job. It had been several months of nervousness. Weeks and weeks of strange noises, whispers in the trees, and missing tools.

Lou wipes his mouth with a dirty handkerchief, then folds it over once and shoves it into his pocket. "Yeah, it sure is. The buyers spent enough money on this damn thing, and they ain't no spring chickens."

"How old're they?"

Lou shrugs. "Gotta be in their fifties."

"Hell, that ain't old."

"To take on a thirty-year mortgage and all this damned property? Must have cost them three hundred, four hundred thousand? Hell—"

"Well, it's a nice place, anyway." Don twitches. A light prickling tickles his neck again.

"You got that right," Lou says. "Once they lay the sod and clear the dead wood, it'll be great. Nothing more to do for us. Concrete's set and the inside's finished. Needs people now." Lou glances behind him. "Welp. Let's get this shit out of here before it gets dark." What was that in Lou's voice? A slight break in his cadence? That glance behind him! What was that?

"When are they moving in?" Don says, grabbing his gear in a hurry.

"Tomorrow or the next day. Movers come first thing tomorrow morning."

The sensation of being watched tickles at him once again. Though still nothing is visible but gnarled oaks and leaf-covered ground, the darkening sky sets off warning bells. Lou touches his shoulder and Don flinches.

"Damn, buddy. You OK?"

"Yeah," Don says. "I thought a deer ran by."

"Oh yeah. This land must be full of them. The owner's a hunter, bow hunter, and a big shot lawyer. Steve Spain. His wife is real nice—a southern girl."

Don grunts. "Big shot? In Maquoketa?"

"Course not. He's a partner in a firm in Davenport. Hey, what do ya say we celebrate a job well done? We'll get a beer at Perzactly's. I'm buying." Lou steps off the concrete stairs, meandering up the hill, trying to avoid the rocks and dried crevices in the dirt.

Don lowers his head and follows. "Yeah, real good."

They trudge through the mud around the garage. A breeze blows hundreds of red, orange, brown, yellow leaves across the dirt yard. Lou's pickup sits in the driveway, covered in dust from the miles of gravel roads.

Come back. You forgot something—

As Lou tosses his stuff into the back of the truck and fiddles with his keys, Don stares at his reflection in the passenger window. His eyes are wide and red in the dim reflection. At last, the door unlocks, and Don pulls himself on to the seat, staring at the dashboard, holding his breath.

"Ah shit," Lou says.

"What?" Don's heart skips with a dull palpitation.

"I left my lunchbox on the back steps. Stupid. Can you go grab it? I need to call Ben and fill him in. Let him know we're done."

Don runs his thumb on the stitching at the edge of the passenger seat. The day's light has faded further, so everything has a grainy, almost black and white appearance. "You sure you didn't bring it with you?"

As he finishes dialing a number, Lou places the ancient flip phone to his ear. "Yeah, yeah. I left it by the back steps. Hurry, so we don't miss happy hour."

"Why can't you go?"

A muffled voice speaks over the receiver. "Hey, Ben. One sec." Lou shoves the phone against his chest. "What the hell's wrong with you? Will you just go get it?"

"Why can't you? It's *your* goddamn lunch box."

"I got Ben on the line. You kidding me?"

"No, I'm not."

"Jesus, Don. Quit bein' a pussy." Lou puts the phone back to his ear, turning his back on Don. "Hey Ben, sorry. Yeah, we just now finished."

Don tunes him out and stares out the windshield at the front hood, his eyes watering. The word pussy echoes in his mind. He sighs. Moments later, he's hustling back the way he came, his skin tingling in nervous anticipation.

There it is again. From the woods, a flash, a blur, hovering an inch beyond his sight. Motion—silent and quick—dances at the far corners of his vision with only a hint of movement to betray a presence.

Don gives a quick glance around him. The back steps are empty, no sign of the lunchbox, only dirt and fallen leaves. "Lou, goddamn you. Where the hell is it?" Don steps to the edge of the freshly cemented patio and kicks a rock into the trees. "Lou, you goddamn idiot! If you had it with you the whole time."

Leaves crunch several yards away in the darkened trees. A coldness seizes him as if small icy fingers are digging through his skull into his brain. Squeezing his eyes shut, he prays for protection.

Eyes open, he stumbles a step. He spots something that immediately sets his nerves on end. Set in the penumbra of two giant oaks, several yards beyond the tree line, is Lou's lunch box. A dim shaft of light illuminates it, as if daring him. They'd never stepped foot in the woods the entire day, so how did it get there? Don shivers again.

In a matter of minutes, the daylight has faded considerably. Don's breath catches and his palms are oily with sweat as he steps down the hill, his head on a swivel for any sign of movement. The smell of burning leaves floats on a cool October breeze and Don almost scurries away, leaving the box right where it is. Let Lou go down there into the gulley, or ravine—whatever the fuck it's called.

What would Lou tell everyone? Could Don risk wearing the pussy label for the rest of his life? How long would that story circulate? Lou's a dick, they all are. They'd never let him live this down.

This place—these woods.

Lou's car horn blares from the front of the house, startling him. "God dammit!" he says over his shoulder, then glowers back at the lunch box. "Fuck this."

Head down, fists clenched, Don Loomis marches down the slight slope of the dirt yard. As soon as he steps past the first silver maple and into the cool shadows beneath the changing leaves, he hears whispering, as if a hundred people were lurking somewhere just past his vision, watching him, judging him.

As fast as his feet can take him, he crosses the ten yards to the small black metal container, leaves crunching loud enough to wake the living, reaches down and grasps the plastic handle which lets out a small squeak as he pulls it. As Don stands, his eyes catch another hint of movement behind one of the many old oaks reigning over the forest like frozen wood giants.

At first, he can't place what he's seeing. Is it part of a branch? Maybe another tree growing around the trunk? His eyes focus and a tightness spreads across his back, his neck, and over his scalp. He stumbles into a fit of coughing. In retreat, eyes forward, he holds his hand over his chest as the thing comes into view. A strand of hair falls loosely over dirty skin, followed by a cheekbone and one pale hand.

Run, you idiot! Turn and run! His mind screams in warning, but his body cannot comply. He's got two choices—high tail it like a fearful kid, or stay and face whatever haunts these woods.

Twenty seconds later, he's back in the truck's cab as the F-150 peels out of the driveway. Gravel ricochets off the new garage door, leaving a dozen slight dents in the aluminum. That'll cost them, cost them plenty, but Don doesn't care, and neither does Lou—not after seeing Don's face and hearing what he saw.

Once back on Highway 64, they fly back to town, neither speaking. They don't slow until they're parked in the tiny lot of Perzactly's Bar and Grill, breathing prayers of thanks and laughing despite themselves.

Chapter Two

— · —

1.

"Breathe—just breathe."

Steve Spain takes a left down highway 64 as the Iowa cornfields explode yellow-gold in the October dawn's first light. Normally he'd be gaping at the autumn scene, but not now. Now, he feels like someone's holding a fist against his sternum—at least it's the fist, not the knife. As anxiety attacks go, this one's bearable. Manageable. Temporary.

Check lists, breathing exercises, self-talk—that's the routine. "Stuff out of the old house? Check. Movers putting stuff in the new house? Check. Money in the bank? Check. Bills paid? Check. Firm doing fine without me? Check. Loving, supportive wife? Check."

Mara's black Honda Pilot follows some distance behind. Her brown hair reflects in the light through the windshield in his review mirror. Behind her, Rocky's tail curls up, swishing side to side. Like Steve's Midnight Blue Land Rover, they filled the Pilot to the roof with items too precious to trust with the movers.

"Our things are safer with them than with us," Steve had said.

"Maybe, but I couldn't live with myself if anyone else broke them," Mara had replied in her lilting South Carolina accent, still thick after years in the Midwest.

They hadn't been naïve about the prospect of building a home, but the job turned out to be far more involved than either of them had expected. All the water lines, electric, gas, regulations, permits, and septic stuff, not to mention figuring out how to run TV and internet into the house from miles away. The ten months of stops and starts, victories and setbacks—it was enough to drive them crazy, or drive them back to Davenport.

Steve places a hand over his chest, sucking a deep breath of air through his lips. "Push through. Everything's good. You're good," Steve says between breaths. "You're good."

Ahead, the road curls right, cutting through the same endless cornfields and rolling hills that inspired Grant Wood to paint his *American Gothic*. Winters will chill to the bone with wicked winds driving mountainous snow drifts across roads and bridges. Summers will be humid and hot. Spring will feel two weeks long. Fall will be the only sympathetic season, but it won't last long enough. Soon, winter will make them question why they moved to a place without public services like road graders and snow plows.

But the serenity? The quiet? The dark nights glowing with millions of stars, thousands of fireflies, and a view of the Milky Way you can only get in the country? All worth it, for the occasional inconvenience. Or so they tell themselves now.

Steve adjusts his hands on the wheel as he approaches the turn onto the gravel of 241st Avenue, an appropriate name for such a remote locale. The Land Rover shifts side to side as it rolls along on new-laid gravel, kicking up a plume of grayish-yellowish dust, obscuring Mara's car in the mirror.

When they pull into the driveway, Steve cuts around a massive green moving truck and parks on the far right of the three-car garage. Mara coasts down the drive, stopping just behind him. A stream of workers hustle back and forth with boxes, furniture, appliances and bags of clothes—every bit of their past and future lives.

As Rocky takes off around the corner, his nose lowered, sniffing every inch of dirt, Steve and Mara meet in the middle of what will be their front lawn, sighing in unison, hands clasped, eyes scanning the entryway. It's a ranch-style modular home with four bedrooms, one of which they'll turn into an office. The property slants downward from front to back so the basement opens onto a large stone patio with steps leading down into their seven acres of woods.

A pickup pulls into the drive and a gruff man with a dirty John Deere cap steps out, hurrying over to them. "Steve Spain?" he asks, eyeing him.

"That's me."

"Don Loomis—with Reynolds construction." The guy's eyes dart left and right, never making eye contact with either of them.

"Oh, yeah," Steve says. "How's it going?"

"Good, good. Lou asked me to give you this." Loomis hands him an envelope like he's dropping a potato into a pot of boiling water. "It's an estimate on the garage door. We had an accident with the gravel yesterday and we dinged it up good. Lou'll get it fixed or replaced. His cost."

"Ah, I see—"

Mara gives Steve's waist a slight squeeze. "Well, that's awful kind of him. Tell him thanks," she says.

The man's face twists into a funny expression. He opens his mouth to say something, then closes it again. Wiping his brow, he glances past the garage into the trees, mesmerized.

"That all?" Steve asks.

As if awakened from a dream, Loomis's blue eyes dart back and forth at their foreheads. "Uh, yeah. Yeah. Sorry, I just—nevermind. Anyway, we hope you enjoy your place. We'll get the garage door fixed in the next couple of weeks. Sorry it can't be sooner."

"No problem." Loomis jerks away nervously, then climbs back into his pickup. When he backs up the drive, he peels out on the loose rock, kicking a few stones back down toward the moving truck.

"Well, that explains the dents on the garage door, I suppose. He looked like he'd seen a devil. Nervous guy, I guess."

Mara laughs and they turn their attention to the home. She says, "We need to tell the kids to come visit as soon as possible. I swear they're gonna love it here."

Steve smiles. "Maybe give them reason to drive from Chicago to visit more often."

"There's plenty of room."

"That's for sure. A *lot* of room. Oh, dear god. What did we do?" Steve gives a melodramatic moan.

"We? This was your idea, Mister," Mara says, laying her head on his shoulder. "I was just fine in our little haunted house in Davenport. Can we move back now?"

Steve laughs. "I suppose it *was* my idea. But you went along with it."

She squeezes him again. "Hey, I'm teasing. Don't you worry—everything will be lovely. We don't have the fuss of maintaining an old house anymore. It's all brand new."

"I loved that old house," Steve says.

"I did too. But we're choosing a simple life now, remember? Old houses are fussy—new houses are simple. No leaks; no cranky furnace; no foundation cracks."

"Etcetera, etcetera. That's true. *And* a new house has no ghosts."

"Only the ones we bring with us."

Steve shivers. "What do you say we go inside and put our lives back together?"

2.

Steve's Phone Video Recording - Saturday, October 21, 5:08 pm.

We see a view of the front entry—tan siding with four small pillars in front of a large dark oak door with two leaded glass windows. We hear Steve's footsteps walking on gravel. The camera approaches the house, then stops. It pans right and left, and continues three hundred sixty degrees, revealing the front yard and driveway until the front door returns into view.

Steve's voice (off screen) says, "Well, here we are. Brand new house. The last house we'll ever buy, so help me god."

His arm comes into the shot as he reaches for the doorknob and opens the door. It's darker inside and the phone's camera takes a second to adjust. The view bobs up and down, offering the wood floor one moment, the ceiling the next, the top of Steve's forehead next, then a wall. Finally, the camera centers on the entryway. We see new wood floors and white plain drywall walls. We proceed down the hallway and into the central living space.

There is a broad rock fireplace to the left, with a sizable flat-screen TV mounted in the corner beyond. A leather sofa and chair face the fireplace, cutting the room in half. To the right is a large open-concept kitchen with an L-shaped granite countertop that's buried in moving boxes. A farmhouse-style dining room table and chairs sits just past the jutting L-shaped counter, all of it framed by a tall A-frame wall with windows from floor to ceiling, looking onto a vast back yard and a dense forest of colorful trees. To the far right, next to the dining table, French doors lead to a narrow deck. On the left is a door to the master suite and a staircase leading down to a furnished basement living room and three spare bedrooms.

Rocky lumbers into the shot, his tail wagging. A long line of drool hangs from the side of his mouth.

Steve's voice says, "Rocky! Who's a good boy?"

"Not him." The camera spins to Mara at the kitchen counter next to a stainless-steel refrigerator, pulling dinner plates from an open crate. She's half-laughing and shaking her head. "You should see what your dog did to the doorknob downstairs."

"Is it wrecked?"

"Mmm hm."

The camera jostles as Steve pets the colossal mastiff. "Ah, poor guy. He's tense."

"He's bad," she reiterates, yet her voice belies a lack of gravity. "Brand new door knob—looks like the Hulk smashed it. And he's got slobber all over the walls already. Had to wipe them down. Huh, doofus?"

The camera floats into the kitchen until we are close behind Mara as she takes out a china plate covered in newspaper from a short cardboard box. She peers over her shoulder with a raised eyebrow, her long brown hair in messy strands around her face, almost covering her blue-green eyes. "Don't be comin' over here with that. We've got boxes to unload."

"Borrrrrriiiinnnng," says Steve as he advances. The camera goes left and we hear a kiss followed by a sigh.

"Yeah, well, I do not wish to be living in boxes forever, hun. So finish up your scene, Mr. Spielberg, and get back in here and support your wife."

"Oh, I'll support my wahfe," Steve says, imitating Mara's southern inflection. Sound of a quick spank.

"Stop that!" Mara laughs.

The camera shifts back across the kitchen toward the wall of windows. It is sunny outside, with an Autumn mid-afternoon tint to the outside light. Colorful leaves flap in a slight breeze. "Yeah, yeah. I'll get to it. But look at this back yard. It's marvelous! And it's ours."

"Yep, all ten acres."

Steve puts on a mock regal tone. "Yes, shrubs and leaves and critters. We own you. You are—*ours*. We declare the place Spain-tonia!" Sound of Mara giggling. "And here we shall remain until the conclusion of our days, so help us God."

The camera pans over the yard, then cuts to black.

3.

Steve sets two plates of barbequed ribs and sweet corn in front of Mara. The corn they bought earlier from a farmer in his pickup outside Delmar, invariably the finest corn you can get. Mara dishes two bowls with a caesar salad she started earlier, then they take their supper to the deck to escape the mountains of boxes. Rocky snores at the far edge of the deck, his saucer-sized front paws hanging from the top step.

Mara peers into the backyard as Steve tears into a short rib, struggling to avoid painting his beard with Sweet Baby Ray's sauce.

He looks at her. "You're not hungry?"

"I am," Mara says. "I'm just relishing the scenery."

"Fantastic, huh? Will be even better once we get the dead wood thinned. You know—I was considering..."

"Oh, no."

"Hear me out. See that patch of land near the gas tank? Perfect spot for a shed. And I was thinking once we get things settled a bit—maybe Spring or Summer—we raise some chicks."

Mara reaches to her plate, seizes the corncob, and takes a bite. "Steve. What do we need chicks for?"

"Eggs."

"And we can't get eggs at the market like everybody else?"

Steve sets down his rib and dabs his face with a napkin. He settles back in his chair, takes a swig of beer, shaking his head. "Where's the fun in that?"

"You know chicks turn into chickens, right? Where will we keep them? I bet coyotes run all over these woods."

"We'll get a coop! Build a little pen with heat for the winter."

"I guess you've figured all of this out already," Mara says, eyebrow raised.

"Yep."

13

"Have you ever raised chickens before?"

Steve points to her. "Nope, but you have."

"Yeah, I have, and they're a lot of work. Chickens are filthy and hungry all the time. They shit on everything and stink to high heaven. You've got to clean the coop, and one of them always gets sick, which if you're not careful, spreads to all the other chickens. And just like that, every dang chicken in your coop is dead." Mara lifts her hands in the air and shakes her head.

Steve nods, emphatically. "I've read up on it."

"Oh, you've read up on it, huh?"

"I have. Fresh eggs forever—the freshest eggs. It's not like we don't have the room."

Mara smirks and rolls her eyes. "You're something else, Mister Spain. You know you will do it anyway, so why do you even ask?"

Ignoring the accusation, Steve continues. "I promise it'll be fun. And I'll do all the work. You don't have to do anything."

Mara glances at Rocky, shaking her head, then back at Steve. "Yeah right."

"I promise, I'll do all the cleaning and egg stuff. All the raising and feeding and everything else."

"No, you won't, mister! If we do this, we do it together like everything else." Mara sits back and frowns at him with a reluctant grin. "Fine. But one condition."

"Anything!"

"We don't eat them."

"The eggs?"

"The chickens."

Steve pauses. "They only lay eggs for a couple years. That's when you're supposed to—"

"No way," Mara says. "I will not name the damn birds and feed them and look after them and nurse them to health when they get sick—and, oh, they will get sick—only to chop off their heads when they stop laying eggs. That's a deal-breaker." Mara crosses her arms.

Steve raises an eyebrow. "OK, fine. When we get to that point, we keep them as pets or return them to the farm." Steve extends a hand to her.

"Deal." They shake.

"Yes!" Steve shakes a fist at the ceiling. "I can't wait to taste the first batch of scrambled eggs—bacon, too!"

"We are NOT raising pigs," Mara says.

Steve laughs. After dinner, they remove to the side deck with their drinks as the last sunlight streaks across the sky above the trees in orange and pink and light blue and every shade in between. Steve looks at Mara, who is sitting with a cup of hot cocoa close to her lips, staring out into the trees.

"What are you thinking?" he asks.

"Oh, nothing," Mara says with a hesitation. "What vibe do you get from here? From this house?"

Steve takes another swig of beer. "New house vibe. Why do you ask?"

"Not the house, exactly. The property. You get any kind of impression from it?"

Steve gives her a sideways glance, then peers out over the front of the deck. "It's pretty and secluded. Peaceful. That's the vibe I get. Why? Are you feeling something—*other*?"

As if following their discussion, Rocky lifts his head and stares at the timbers, his floppy ears pulled up at the crease and his head inclined to the left. He lifts his snout into the breeze for a few moments, then plops his enormous head between his paws with a grumble.

Mara tips the mug back and finishes the last of her cocoa. "Nothing. Just nervous, I suppose."

"I know it's a change, but the rough part's over. We're here now. And no more strange noises in the night. No ghosts in a brand new home."

"Yeah, I appreciate all of that. I'm glad we're here now; I mean it."

Steve takes her by the hand. "I hope so. It's what we needed—what I needed, anyway. City life isn't for us."

Mara laughs. "Your brother would mock you, calling Davenport *the city*."

Steve scoffs. "Yeah, well, when you live in Los Angeles, anyplace seems small. But Max will concur with me. This place is ideal for us. You'll see."

"Is he still coming to visit?"

"Yep, he'll be here a week from today. I could use the help to chop up some of this wood. Babe, we'll have plenty of firewood for a while." Steve smiles again as he surveys the rows of downed oaks and maples resting at the other end of the yard.

Mara gathers her plate and utensils. "Let's clean up and search for the comforter. If I have any say in the matter, we're crashing early tonight."

Chapter Three

Steve wakes with a jerk. The last images of a vivid dream recede from his mind—standing on a frozen river, the body of a girl floating silently past him under the ice, her red coat shining at him through the frozen river like a beacon.

Awake now, he covers his face with his hands, weeping great sobs without a sound, as Mara breathes beside him. Rocky lies on his side next to the bed, his claws scraping against the wood floor, fluttering in a dog dream. Steve checks the time on his phone. It's 2:17 a.m. He stretches back, settling his eyes on the ceiling, letting the last of his tears run down the sides of his face, soaking into the pillow beneath him.

What have we done? A thirty-year mortgage at this stage in our lives. Are we insane? How can she sleep through this?

Before he knows it, the phone shows 2:37 a.m. Sighing, he removes the blankets, swings his exposed feet onto the icy floor, and sits on the side of his bed, staring at Rocky as he waits for his eyes to focus. Rocky's ribs expand and contract as his front paws continue to twitch. Steve smiles and endeavors to get out of bed.

Stumbling into the bathroom, mindful not to stub his toes on any stray obstacles, he proceeds to the toilet and raises the lid. His nighttime erection stands there like a stubborn teenager, refusing to do what's expected of him. There's nothing to do but wait for it to give up the fight. Once he's peed and washed his hands, Steve re-enters the bedroom then turns to the open door and peers into the kitchen. How long will it take to get used to the ambient noises of this place? A month? A year? It's been so long since he last moved, it's hard to remember.

Ten acres. Why did we need ten acres? He shakes his head and breathes a heavy sigh.

Stumbling through the living room to the kitchen, he hunts through the cabinets until he spots a rocks glass. Steve pours two fingers of Cody Rye—the liquor tastes rich and bitter, but smooth. Pressing his lips together and shuffling over to the wall of windows, he squints into the darkness. The moon's light, though brighter than usual, does not illuminate the woods enough to see much.

A white blur races across his vision, and Steve's eyes catch sight of movement just below the rock steps. His skin tightens. It's a woman in a silver gown with her back to the house. Steve leans closer to the glass, wiping his eyes in confusion. Brown hair flows just past the woman's shoulders and her bare feet are pale in the moonlight. Steve realizes that the woman's gown is familiar.

"Not again," Steve says.

Running to the bedroom door, he sees their bed is empty. Rocky, now awake, lifts his head and blinks up at him, then stands and shakes his entire body, his collar and tags jangling together.

Steve pulls on his slippers, then cuts through the house, out to the deck and down the slope, doing his utmost not to step on any of the many rocks and sticks littered all over the ground. Despite the effort, he rams his big toe into a massive rock. The shock of the pain almost sends him tumbling into the dirt. Cursing, he corrects himself and proceeds until he gets to Mara, who is still swaying just outside the bleak timbers.

He holds her face in his hands. "Mara? What are you doing out here?"

She doesn't reply. In the shadowy light, her eyes are half-closed as she continues swaying side to side. She makes no sound but for the slight crackling of leaves and sticks beneath her bare feet. Steve snaps his fingers, but she offers no response, then he brings his arms around her and whispers.

"Hun, let's get you inside. It's chilly out."

Rocky barrels toward them, startling Steve as he peels into a torrent of violent barking and growling, his front paws spread wide, glaring into the woods. Steve pats Rocky's furrowed head. "It's OK, boy. It's OK."

Groggily, Mara says, "Babe?"

"Yeah, Mar. You awake?"

"Yes," she says. "How did I get here?"

"You're sleepwalking again. I saw you from the window."

Rocky's barking ceases, but the dog remains fixated on the woods, the fur between his shoulders standing on point. Steve follows the mastiff's gaze, but sees nothing but trees and leaves and shadows. Then, just as he turns, Steve hears something stirring. *A deer or a squirrel*, he tells himself. The sounds continue, and Rocky rumbles low, scowling into the ravine. As if reacting to Rocky's threats, the movement ceases.

Mara, oblivious and still half asleep, gestures to the house and trudges up the slope. "I'm going back to bed," she says, her voice barely audible.

Steve stares into the trees for several moments, his eyes playing tricks on him with the shadows of bending branches and flapping leaves, creating the illusion of gray figures creeping closer and closer to the edge of the treeline. *Are they illusions?* As he waits there, he's suddenly not so sure.

Rocky whines, his ears twitching, then follows faithfully behind Mara. With a struggle, Steve breaks his gaze and pursues the two of them back to the house, mindful to keep from twisting an ankle on the cracked soil and tree debris. When he gets inside, he checks the doors and windows while finishing his drink, and reluctantly returns to bed.

Morning. Mara leans against the counter with one hand as she scrambles a skillet of eggs with the other. She glances out the window and shivers once, then pulls her coffee cup from the Keurig, pops another K-cup into the machine, and sets a navy blue and orange Chicago Bears coffee cup under the nozzle. Relieved Steve was still asleep when she woke, Mara snuck out of bed without making a sound. He'll have questions for her when he does wake—questions she's not quite ready to answer.

When she hears the sounds of him stirring in the bedroom, she hits the brew button and takes two plates from the cabinet next to her. Just as their toast pops up from the toaster, Steve shuffles into the living room, yawning and stretching. He stands next to the sofa and looks outside, blinking. He glances at her, then back outside.

His blonde hair, short-cropped in a "gentlemen's cut," as he calls it, from one of those trendy hipster barbershops—the ones with *guy movies* playing on a big screen, and prints of the Rat Pack, The Godfather, and Miles Davis adorning the walls, and a quality selection of bourbon to drink while you're waiting—is speckled with grays on the sides. His glasses are thick and nerdy, and his neatly trimmed beard is a light gray, grayer even than his hair. If he could get away with it as a lawyer, he'd have a long ZZ Top beard, or a handlebar mustache, but the demands of business keep him conservative. Sometimes Mara forgets how tall he is—six foot three inches, barefoot—but she's always loved his height. Watching him move through the living room, Mara wonders how he keeps getting more handsome the older he gets.

Breakfast is silent. The only sounds emanate from their forks scraping against the stoneware and their butter knives crunching on the toast. She glances at Steve, who keeps his eyes fixed on his plate. After several minutes like this, he sighs, sitting back in his chair and fixing his eyes on her, as he takes a sip of coffee.

"You OK?" he says.

Mara shrugs, irritated. "I'm fine."

"What was that last night?"

Mara hides behind her coffee cup. Taking a quick look at him, she sees his eyes are red. "I don't know."

"What do you remember?"

She sets her cup on the table and runs her eyes along the dark grains on the wood surface. "I remember falling asleep and then nothing until you woke me up outside. I guess it was just one of those things, you know?"

Lines cut across his forehead. She hates herself for adding to his stress. She feels his eyes searching her.

He says, "Don't worry about me, Mar. I'm fine. But if it's happening again, I need you to tell me. Don't keep me in the dark; that won't help matters."

"No, it's not happening again. It can't be—this feels different from before. I was just sleepwalking."

"You sure?"

"Mm hm."

Mara doesn't think he believes her, but Steve mercifully drops the subject with a wave of the hand and motions toward the yard. "It is beautiful, isn't it?"

"Oh, yes. It's as pretty as a pie." The way she says pie, with her South Carolina accent, brings a smile to his face. She smiles back at him and the lines on his forehead fade back to normal, replaced by a hint of crow's feet. She gets an idea. "Why don't we go into the town to check stuff out? I think there's a little quilt shop downtown—I'd love to check it out."

Steve nods, thinking. "I could stop by the feed store, maybe ask about the chicks."

She sighs with mock-annoyance, though in reality she's happy for the diversion. Anything to keep him happy and calm. "I suppose there's no stopping you?"

"Only some fact-gathering. That's it."

"Steven Spain, you realize I know you better than that, right?"

He chuckles and swigs his coffee. A shadow seems to pass over his face. Mara thinks about asking what's wrong, but turns her focus back to the surroundings. *Find another distraction.* "Wow, that tree sure is big," she says, pointing to a massive gnarled specimen directly across the backyard. "Look how tall it is, and its branches. They seem to go on and on. I hadn't noticed it before. It's huge."

Steve grunts in agreement. "Must be two hundred years old."

"Oak?"

"Yep. Black oak. Maybe red."

"When did you become such a tree expert?"

Steve shrugs. "I've always loved them, but oaks above all. There's something relaxing about an oak tree, I guess. The thick bark and crooked branches and the colorful leaves."

"Well, you're in luck because this place has a mess of them."

"That's what drew me here—the trees. So many oaks out there. Oaks upon oaks. Oaks and oaks," he says, almost absently. He sets his cup next to the empty plate and bows his head.

The worry lines have returned to his forehead, interrupted only by three great veins protruding under the skin. Mara exhales slowly, trying not to overthink things.

Rocky sits behind Steve, watching.

Chapter Four

1.

Mara's Phone Video Recording #1 - Sunday, October 22, 11:15 a.m.

We see a shifting series of wood floors, a giant dog head, bare feet, flashes of daylight, drywall, and kitchen cabinets. Off camera, Mara says, "I'm coming, hold your horses, *Sarg*."

The camera cuts out, then back on.

We are now staring out the front windshield of Steve's Land Rover at a blacktop road, book ended by yellow cornfields on either side, as they drive along. The camera pans left to show Steve sitting behind the wheel, staring straight ahead.

"What's the population in Maquoketa?" Mara says.

Steve glances at her and winks. "A touch under six thousand, I think."

"Six thousand. Goodness, that's small."

"Sounds perfect," Steve says.

"Mmm hm! And we're heading into town to see the Maquoketa sights."

"We may have to visit the caves soon. Maybe next weekend," Steve says to the camera, with a raised eyebrow.

"Oh, yeah, I heard about them. But you realize I hate caves. I'm not about to traipse into some weird, old, dank cave. No way."

Steve laughs. The camera cuts out and back in.

We are looking out the front window at a small town. Steve clears his throat. The town is quaint, with white picket fences, tree-covered streets, and children riding bikes along crumbling sidewalks. We pull up to a stop sign and turn left onto a small main street with lines of old brick store-fronts.

The camera cuts out.

2.

A bell jingles as Mara pulls open the wood and glass door to Jamies' Quilting Emporium. As she steps foot into the shabby-chic room, a short plump woman wearing glasses the thickness of Coke bottle bottoms walks into the room from behind a cloth drapery. She's in her fifties, at least, with tight curly graying hair and a small mouth with full lips that look constantly in a state of friendly amusement. A brief expression of bewilderment passes over her face as she sees Mara.

"Oh, why, hello there," the woman says. "Welcome. You in town visiting?"

"No, my husband and I moved here yesterday."

"Oh, did you? From where?"

"Davenport. Not too far away."

"Why, don't you have a sweetest accent! Where you from, hun?"

"South Carolina, born and raised."

"Charleston?"

Mara smiles. "Yes, a little suburb outside Charleston."

The woman claps her hands, giggling. "Oh, Charleston is lovely. My oldest brother lives there. He's a surgeon, of all things."

"Ah. Yes, it's a lovely city."

"Well, I'm Jamie and this is my little quilt store. Well, mine and my sister's." Jamie turns her head and calls into the back. "Jame, come out here.

We got a new patron. Jame's my twin. We run this place together, even though she didn't want her name on the sign."

"You have the same name?"

"Our parents weren't terribly creative folk, God rest them. There's no 'i' in her name, so at least they did that for us." Jamie rumbles again with amusement.

"Must get confusing," Mara says.

"How so?" Jamie says, sounding as if Mara had pulled a rabbit out of her ear.

Mara raises an eyebrow. "The same name?"

"Oh, that's not confusing at all. Makes things simpler."

Mara fears she's hurt the woman's feelings, but before she can answer one way or the other, a carbon copy of the first Jamie steps into the room with the same bemused half-smile, stretching a hand to Mara. "Why, hello there."

"Pleased to meet you, ma'am. I'm Mara," she replies, shaking the woman's hand.

"Pleased to meet you too," Jame says. "Oh my, what a splendid accent. And aren't you a charming thing?"

"She's from Charleston, Jame," Jamie says.

"Oh, heavens, our brother lives there!"

"I told her," Jamie says.

"He's a surgeon in Charleston."

"Told her that too."

Jame sighs. "Well, you didn't leave me anything to talk about, did you?" They giggle together and Mara joins them, though she's not clear why it's as amusing as they seem to think. There's something contagious about these two.

"And which house did you purchase?" Jame says, still chuckling.

Mara says, "We built a home on some land a mile or two west of here."

"Oh? Whose property did you buy?"

"We bought ten acres from a fellow named Jensen," Mara says.

All at once, the twins go mute, glancing at each other, clearing their throats. They remain there gawking at Mara for several moments, as if checking her eyes for a joke. The room cools and Mara fears she's said the wrong thing.

Jame says, "Well, that's nice. Mr. Jensen has lovely property out that way. Was it farmland you bought?"

"No, woodland. It's like a little forest all our own." Mara clears her throat.

"Well, that's—*lovely*," Jamie says, though her eyes tell a different story.

Mara's eyes jump from one to the other. She shifts on her feet and stares around the shop. "So, do you make all these quilts?"

Jame says, "Oh heavens, no. Only half, maybe."

"Our mom is the one who does the lion's share, though she can't do as much as she used to—you know, old age and all." Jamie tilts her head back to face the ceiling. "She lives up there in the apartment above the shop. She owns the building. We run the business down here. At one time, it was a general store, if you can believe it. But when the Casey's chain opened on Main, they kinda killed things for us. So we decided we ought to come up with something different. Since our family has been so crafty all our lives, a quilting shop seemed like the obvious choice."

Jame nods.

Mara touches a blue and white quilt lying on the table next to her. "And you do enough business to stay open? That's remarkable."

"Oh, yes, we get along pretty well. Our quilts are the best value this side of Des Moines. That's a fact. Plus, we get traffic in town on weekends. People from Cedar Rapids, Cedar Falls, Iowa City, even Ames, come here to shop or see a show at Codfish Hollow. Do you like live music, hun?"

"Oh, I do! Steve and I used to go to shows a lot," Mara says.

Jamie says, "Well, then Codfish Hollow is the place for you. They get all kinds of acts. We don't much care for places like that, but it's very popular."

Mara likes Jamie and Jame, with their polite demeanor and midwestern charm. They remind her of family friends back in Charleston. For a moment she thinks she might fit right in with this bunch, their odd reaction at the Jensen property aside.

"Do you quilt?" Jamie says.

"Oh, no. Not yet. I've been learning to knit a little. But I love a nice quilt, and these are breathtaking. Y'all do incredible work."

The Jamies giggle at each other. Jame says, "Why thank you so much."

"Could I bother you with a question? Is there a good place to eat lunch?"

"There is a Mexican place down the street. They've got darn good tacos, though I can't say they're *authentic*. And there's Dimitri's—"

"No Jamie, he's closed up for the weekend," Jame says. "Death in the family."

Jamie clicks her tongue. "Oh, yes, that's right. Heavens, where's my brain? There is a new little diner; they serve old-style greasy spoon type food. Opened about six months ago by a young couple who moved into town. He's got a long scraggly beard that hangs down to his chest and she's got bright pink and black hair—both all covered up in tattoos and those awful piercings. A little strange if you ask me, but to each her own. I must admit the food's not half bad, for a couple hippies."

"Hipsters, Jamie. Not hippies. Oh my," Jame says, and the two of them peel into another round of giggling.

"Well, whatever you call them. It's a tad expensive for what it is, you ask me," Jamie says.

"That's true. Dimitri's is reasonable, but he's not open this weekend, like I said. There's Perzactly's over on Olive—that's a fun little dive. But it's more of a bar and grill."

Mara lifts a blue and brown blanket from a table and says, "That diner you mentioned sounds good. Steve enjoys a good greasy spoon, and he *loves* hipsters. He might have been one in a former life, but don't you tell him I said so."

The Jamies stare at her for a moment, their faces blank. Mara gives a wink and the twins double over with laughter.

Mara smiles, delighted, and removes a delicate blue and pink quilt with hand-stitched birds on every panel. "I'll take this one," she says.

3.

A bell jingles as Steve steps into the musty Maquoketa Feed Store. From the back end, a gruff voice says, "Be out in a minute!"

"No problem," Steve says.

The store is wide and dim, warehouse-like, with only scattered light provided by fluorescents hanging from the ceiling, giving the store an ethereal quality. The dark exposed brick walls almost fade out of view, so each glowing aisle looks like an island amid nothingness. Steve rubs his eyes, willing them to adjust to the peculiar lighting, but nothing he does diminishes the strangeness.

Steve scans the aisles for anything resembling chicken stuff. Most of the products on the shelves are dusty and faded, as if it's been ages since the store has received a customer. A noise, like a hiccup, sounds out from his right. An old man, slim and frail, with dark-rimmed trifocals set halfway down the bridge of his snout and a large John Deere cap pulled down above his eyes, sits by the cash register. He goes off again with an abrupt "Pip," that pops his head up, and Steve wonders if the sound isn't some kind of verbal tic, rather than a hiccup. Steve watches the old fellow for a moment, hesitant to offer a blessing.

"Don't pay Pops no mind," says the voice from the back.

Two men appear from a rear office. The first is short with skinny legs and an immense gut. He saunters into the shop in jeans and a worn polo that carries the store's name above one breast and his first name, Buck, on the other. The second guy is lanky, perhaps six-three or six-four, in jeans and a dingy flannel shirt, with a long face and sunken green eyes that glare out from under his wiry graying eyebrows. He waits in the doorway.

"Pip," the old man erupts again, startling Steve.

"Ah, hello there. Steve Spain." Steve holds out his hand.

"Buck," the chubby man replies, ignoring the gesture. "You passing through?"

"Pip!"

Steve lowers his hand. "No, I'm new to town. Built a place outside town some ways."

"Is that so?" Buck glances toward the man in the back. "You the couple who bought property from Jensen?"

"Yeah, that's us. Moved in yesterday."

"You don't say. Welcome to Maquoketa. What can I do ya for?" Buck crosses his arms, giving Steve the once-over.

"Pip!" Steve jerks again in response.

"Oh, don't mind old Pops. He pops now and then. Pops and pips, pips and pops!" Buck crouches over Pops with his palms on his knees, his face a few inches from the old man's face, mimicking his vocalizations, though his impression is loud and cruel. "Pip, pop, pip!"

"Pip!"

"Now what did you say you're looking for, mister?" Buck asks.

"Oh, well, I was figuring I might raise hens. Raise them up from chicks and whatnot—"

"Chicks ain't whatnot."

"What's that?" Steve says.

Buck raises his voice louder than he needs to. "I said, chicks ain't whatnot! They're a lot of work. Understand?"

Steve clears his throat. "Yes, I gather that. I—"

"Pip!"

Steve coughs out a shaky laugh, glancing at Pops, whose eyes remain fixated on nothing specific. "I meant I'd like—I mean, that's my hope. To raise chicks into hens."

"Chickens are damn nasty things—dirty."

Steve smiles. "So I hear. But I'd like to give it a go."

"Sorry, we ain't got any." Buck walks behind the counter and flips through some mail stacked on the formica.

"Do you know where I can get some?"

"Sure, sure. You can order them online nowadays, or Scott County Feed in Davenport should have plenty for ya. Sorry, but we stopped carrying those cursed things a few years ago. Kept dying on us."

"Pip!"

A heart palpitation sends a jolt through Steve's chest. "I see. You have anything else for chickens?"

"Oh, sure, sure. We have a couple coops back in the corner. You'll need to hit Home Depot for the fencing if you plan to let them roam. But our coops are nice. How you like your new property?"

Surprised by the abrupt social skills, Steve says, "It's great, what we've seen so far. I used to camp up here with my dad when I was a kid, and kept up the tradition as an adult. Maybe not as much the last several years. But with the building and all these past few months, we've gotten to know the place a lot better."

"Have you now?" Buck's icy stare offers no welcome. "I still can't believe Wendell sold that land."

"Pip!"

The overt unfriendliness of these fellows has taken Steve off his guard. "Oh, yeah? Why is that?"

"Dunno." Buck shrugs. "Didn't think he would. Not to someone like you."

"It is a beautiful property—wood-covered and all," Steve says, ignoring the passive insult. "We're sure glad he sold it, at any rate."

Buck looks up from the mail, eyes narrowed. "Gets dark in those timbers. Lotta tree cover in that ravine—a lot of upkeep. Pops wouldn't enjoy it one bit."

"Pip!"

"Yeah, well." Steve shuffles on his feet from side to side.

"Could be you're right," Buck says. "Still, it's a wonder. You must have made old Jensen one hell of an offer."

"Only the asking price. Seemed reasonable to us."

Buck chuckles and shakes his head with a wink toward the dour man at the back of the shop. "Anyhow, the coop is back there off aisle one."

"Pip!"

Steve contemplates asking Buck a question. But, thinking better of it, he turns and heads toward aisle one, his heart quivering.

4.

Mara enters the coffee shop and sees Steve sitting at a booth across from a long counter running practically the length of the place. Everything is neo-vintage, chrome and tile, black and white, fluorescent and neon, with the sound and smell of sizzling bacon buzzing in the background like the hum of bees. Clanking plates from the kitchen and tinkling silverware on plates cut through it all as the place is roughly three-quarters full with a lively mix of locals sitting at the counter, and young out-of-towners recovering from hangovers. Steve sips a mug of coffee, his hand shaking, staring out the window next to him. *Is his face red?* Mara crosses to him and slides into the seat opposite him.

"Hey," he says, glancing at her. His face is red—his eyes bloodshot.

"You OK?" she says.

He nods and takes another sip.

Gently, "Is that decaf?"

"It is," he says.

"What happened?"

He shakes his head and waves his hand. "Oh, nothing. I panicked for a second. It's nothing."

"Did something happen?"

"No, I said, no. It's only anxiety."

"Did you bring your Xanax?"

"No. It's at home."

"OK," she says. She tilts her head, struggling not to push.

"I don't want to take too much of that stuff."

"Dr. Nguyen said it's fine as long as you're under 10 milligrams a day—two tablets a day—as required."

"Yeah."

"Only when you need it, right?"

"True."

She nods with him and promptly a server is at their table, flipping pages on a small order pad. She's in her early thirties, with dyed black and pink hair and a full sleeve of tattoos covering the whole of her left arm. A white gold band adorns her ring finger, set next to an identical band with an immense black gem. Her right arm is bare, showing the natural pale translucence of her pure skin tone. Her oval face is almost cherubic in contradiction to her overall style. Crystal blue eyes peek out through a pair of vintage horn-rimmed glasses set under a straight line of pitch black bangs. "Hi there," the waitress says, with a casual friendliness. "Welcome to The Last Diner on Earth. Can I bring you something to drink? Coffee? Tea? Organic juice?"

"I'll have a coffee, regular, praise you," Mara says.

"Need a minute with the menu?"

"Uh, yes, please."

"You got it." The waitress bustles back behind the counter and seizes a coffee mug.

Mara returns her attention to Steve. "It came out of nowhere?"

Steve rubs his eyes, raising his glasses onto his knuckles. "Yeah, I guess."

"Steve." Mara takes his free hand in hers. "Talk."

"Sorry. Yeah, it kinda came on out of nowhere. I went to the feed store, and it was strange in there. Made me nervous."

Mara looks into his eyes and says, "How was it strange?"

"You'd have to see these guys, real small town types. One of them, a guy named Buck, what a charmer. Seemed like he knew I was the one who bought the property from Jensen."

"How would he know that?"

"Beats me. But as soon as I told him we moved here, he asked if I bought from Jensen, and like he knew the answer. Weirded me out, even though it shouldn't have. So fucking frustrating, this crap. Anxiety—" Steve puts his face back in his hands.

"Hey, it's OK," Mara says, caressing his forearms.

"No, it's not OK. I can't break down every time I'm in an uncomfortable situation. I can't—what the hell is wrong with me?"

Mara takes his hand and kisses it as the waitress drops off the coffee. She pauses, then returns to the kitchen. "Look, you have anxiety, OK? That's all. Anxiety. Millions of people—"

"Yeah, yeah, millions of people go through it. I know," Steve says, verbally rolling his eyes.

"It's true."

"But *why*? Why now, at this point in my life? It makes no sense."

"You know why. It's why you've taken a leave of absence from the firm this fall. It's why we moved out here to the sticks. You require time, some space. That's all."

"But I can't—I wish I could—I can't put my finger on it. It's a problem I can't solve." Steve points a finger down to the tabletop.

"I understand." Mara kisses his hand again.

"I want to understand, but I can't. That's the problem, you know? I'll be like, hey everything's good. It's been three days, four days—a week! Am I right? And *boom!* I'm back to square one."

"Yeah."

"And you know what takes the cake? It's like this is my life now. This is me—Mr. Panic Attack. Pleased to meet me. How am I supposed to go back to the firm like this? When the new year hits, what I am I supposed to do?"

"We'll figure it out."

"What about the house? We bought this fucking house. And all that land, all those trees." Steve's eyes are ringed with tears and his lower lip quivers.

"Let's not worry about it, Steve. We're fine. We're fine. If it comes to that, we sell your part in the firm. You can work from home—private practice—anything you want. Heck, I can support us on my salary. And you only have like ten years until retirement. Ten years is nothing. Nothing, Steve! And our 401K's have plenty already. It's all fine."

Steve squeezes his eyes closed. "I know."

"See? We're fine. Better than most people. You've made good money. Money goes a long way here in Iowa, especially the money we make. We're solid."

"The worst part is, I'm aware of all that. And that's the dilemma, isn't it? I mean, I recognize all the stuff you're telling me is true. We're better off than most, better off than my dad was, better off than your dad, better off than Max, who's living out there in California paying what? Two thousand a month for a one-bedroom apartment? I get all that, but I can't stop this shit. And that's the problem—none of it makes any sense. The worries still come. It's like I'm in crisis mode, but there's nothing going on."

"Well, to be fair, it's not nothing, Steve. I mean, we did just buy a house and an enormous property. It's OK being stressed about that—it's justifiable. But we're solid. Keep telling yourself that." Mara rubs his palm.

"See? There's no reason for it. No reason at all, and somehow that makes it worse. Like part of the anxiety comes from the anxiety. It's crazy-making." Steve pulls his hands away and sits back in the booth, shaking his head as he stares out the window, his eyelids lined with water and ringed with redness. "I'm sorry," he says.

"Steve, please do not apologize. You know you don't have to apologize."

"No, no, not about this. I'm sorry I was short with you this morning—about the sleep-walking thing. I should have been more sympathetic. After all my shit? Christ."

Mara smiles. "Steve, it's fine. You were fine."

"No, I was irritable. I'm sorry."

"It's OK."

"No, it's not. But thank you for saying it." Steve takes a big breath and holds it for a few moments before closing his eyes and exhaling. He repeats this exercise three more times.

"Yes, breathe. Good, that's good. How do you feel?" Mara says.

"Over the hump. Thanks." He squeezes her hand, and they sit quietly for several minutes.

When the waitress returns, Mara notices her name tag and reads it aloud. "Rose. That's a lovely name, my granny's name."

"Thank you. That's a pretty accent. Where you from?" Rose says.

"I'm from South Carolina," Mara says with a broad grin.

"Oh, I hear it's nice there. Never been myself."

"It is lovely, yes."

Rose glances at Steve and says, "I'm from Chicago, and so is my husband back there in the kitchen. That's Rob." She points behind her to a guy in a small order window reading order slips, wearing a white apron. He's got a long brown beard and thick black-rimmed glasses. Full sleeve tattoos cover both his arms.

"My. Do you two own this place?" Mara says, glancing at Steve—the redness has subsided just a little.

"Yep. Bought it about a year ago and opened last March. It's going great, so far. It gets pretty busy on weekends, especially in the summer. You guys live around here?"

"Yes," Mara says. "We moved here from Davenport. Bought a little piece of property and built a house on it. Just moved in this past weekend."

"What made you choose to live in Maquoketa?"

Steve says, "My parents had a little cabin out here when I was growing up."

"And you just couldn't help but move here permanently?" Rose says.

"Something like that." Steve smiles and looks out the window.

"Ah, that's great. Small town life takes some getting used to—or at least it did for us. Most of the people are nice."

Rose takes their order and heads back behind the counter.

Mara squeezes Steve's hand and says, "You feeling better?"

"Yeah. Thanks. Much better. Don't know what happened there." He blinks several times and wipes his green eyes with the back of his flannel sleeve, then runs his fingers through his hair.

From a distance, it's hard to see the gray on his head because of his blond hair, but close up in the light of day, Mara sees he's covered with them. Her heart warms as she thinks how unfair it is that men can look so good as they age. She sips her coffee and stares out the window, thinking, until their food arrives.

They eat in silence.

5.

As they pull the car into the driveway, they spot an antique Ford pickup parked in front of the garage, empty save for a white lab panting in the cab. The truck is one they've seen several times over the previous months, owned by Wendell Jensen, the man from whom they purchased the property almost a year ago.

Wendell appears at the corner of the garage, making his way towards them. He nods, and Steve steps out, waving back. "Hey there Wendell!"

"Howdy, folks."

"Hello, Mr. Wendell," Mara says.

"You all out seeing the Maquoketa sights?"

Steve laughs. "Yep, that's just what we were doing. Everything OK?"

Wendell crosses to them, keeping his hands in his pocket. "Oh, yeah. But I actually came here to ask you guys the same thing."

"Us?" Mara asks, glancing at Steve.

"What do you mean?" Steve says.

"I heard some yelling last night. Don't mean to be a nosy neighbor—believe me, I hate that shit. But I felt like I needed to check in. Just to be sure."

Steve says, "Yes, it's all fine. We just—"

"Rocky went after a coyote. You must have heard us calling him."

Steve swallows, happy for Mara's impromptu tale. "Yes! Sorry to wake you. I'm actually surprised you could hear us all the way down at your place. Aren't you half a mile away?"

Nodding, Wendell says, "That we are! But the ravine carries sound quite a way, especially this time of year."

"Interesting," Steve says.

"People say things about this property. Sometimes I let it get to me."

Mara and Steve look at each other. "What kinds of things?" Steve asks.

"Oh, nothing but nonsense. Nonsense and superstition. Nothing to bother you with." Wendell removes his hat and wipes his forehead.

"Like what?" Mara asks.

"You'll hear some people claim there are spirits out here in these woods. I know it sounds nuts, but they say it all the time. But I tell you, there's nothing out there but coyotes and deer. It gets dark out here, way darker than you get in town. And sometimes the eyes play tricks on you. That's all it is."

Mara says, "Well..."

"Thanks for the information. Nothing to worry about here."

Shaking his head and moving away to the driver's door of his pickup, Wendell gives a wave. "Thanks a bunch. I'll get out of your hair. If you need anything, just call us, ya hear?" He opens the truck's door and pauses as if waiting for a reply.

"Sure, sure. No problem, Wendell. Thanks for stopping."

Steve and Mara watch as Wendell Jensen backs out and drives off.

CHAPTER FIVE

Steve wakes with a start again. His breathing strained, his hands numb. The dream, shrinking from his memory, was a nightmare filled with chasing wolves and creatures with black skin, short and flabby like adult toddlers, rushing along behind and snickering, shrieking after him until Steve slams into a tree trunk, waking himself.

In the irrational moments between dreaming and waking, he hears a quiet voice, a girl's voice, appealing to him. *"What's that sound?"*

Reality pushes through the dream as Steve blinks into the shadows. There is a hush over the house, save for the sounds of Mara and Rocky breathing. Steve watches them, envious. As he takes several deep, rhythmic breaths to calm himself, his eyes adapt to the darkness. The moon, which had shone through their window like a nosey neighbor at bedtime, has made its way past the trees on its nocturnal wandering. Steve reaches to the nightstand and flips the face of his phone toward him like a poker player peeking at his hand. It's 2:30.

A feeling comes over him, bitter and smothering, like being dragged under the surface of a deep lagoon. Each heartbeat thrums heavy in his breast, and drops of sweat rise on his forehead. A gulp of air catches in his throat as anxiety tickles up his forearms.

Something's in the house.

Steve stops breathing. The skin at the back of his neck stiffens. His hearing sharpens, and his pupils enlarge, absorbing what little light there is in the room. Here, in the middle of nowhere, darkness is a presence. Peering out the bedroom door, he chokes.

There is something out there by the sofa. It's frozen. It's watching me.

He clutches the side of the bed. Rocky whines in his sleep, his paws twitching back and forth, as he runs through a field of some glorious dog dream. A still voice whispers to him, barely audible.

"It's—"

Steve's eyes swell with tears. His heart drums in his chest with a force that unnerves him, and he tilts his head to listen better. The bed springs moan and Steve senses the attention attracted to him by the thing. He holds his breath for what seems like minutes as he listens for another sound.

"It's—"

The vibrations of heavy and labored breathing roll in through the bedroom door. The shadowy silhouette moves lower, crouching. Steve opens his mouth to cry out, but he can't produce a sound, whether from fear or cottonmouth. Instead, he swallows hard, and resolves to glimpse back at Mara. He reaches a hand to her, flashing a look at the thing which, in the moments he'd turned away, had crept closer. In the softness of night, Steve thinks he sees two gleaming eyes peering from the shadows.

"It's—"

Steve touches his wife's leg again and whispers, "Mara," making little better than a crackling noise. As the thing comes closer, step by step, fear weighs down on him until he's almost paralyzed by it. "Mara," he squeaks again, this time slightly stronger, but she doesn't stir. He leans back and grasps her thigh in his hand. Then, to his relief, the jangling of dog tags cuts through the tension and the black figure freezes only feet from the doorway. From the other side of the bed, a low growl vibrates the mattress.

"Rocky, stay," he says, but his loyal protector rises to a crouched position, hackles risen, as the shadow creature sways back and forth. Steve's heart beats forcefully in his chest and a light-sensation comes over him.

"It's—"

The room swirls around him like a carnival ride. He grips the side of the bed with both fists, trying fruitlessly to steady himself as the darkness in the other room moves toward him, threatening to consume him. Steve tries to stand but falls back onto the bed as the world goes black.

When he wakes again, a chill wind blows across his face, and his legs shiver. He is outside, staring at a giant oak in the ravine behind his house. Confused, he looks all around. He's in the woods, just below his house, about fifty yards. Rocky's low ruff of a bark echoes through the trees behind him. Steve's head is cloudy—like waking from a heavy sleep—as if someone packed his ears with balls of cotton. He turns to peer deeper into the thicket as Rocky's booming threats echo across the night sky, reverberating through the forest. Steve opens his mouth, but can't find his voice. He clears his throat. "Rocky," he finally says, choking out the word.

The barking stops and soon, the sound of huge paws padding across the dead leaves draws closer until he spots the mastiff galloping toward him like a bear. The dog glances behind him into the shadows once or twice, but continues loping through the forest until he is sitting at his master's feet, his tongue hanging several inches from his mouth.

"Hey boy, what's going on?" Steve says. "How did we wind up out here?"

The dog stares into his eyes, but heavy panting is his only response. His ears, lifted at the top, twitch back and forth. Steve looks past Rocky, feeling a presence just beyond his vision, somewhere deep in the blackest part of the woods. His breath catches as he looks straight into the blackness formed between a trio of trees about a hundred yards to the West. Something is coming from that dark place. It's coming for him.

He looks to the house. Its windows give no reflection, black as night, like a barricade of black holes from which no light can escape. For a moment, he can't determine which darkness holds greater dread, the house or the woods.

Rocky growls, then looks at Steve again and offers a slight squeal of a whimper as if to ask, *"Can we go home now?"*

"It's ok, boy. Let's get back inside."

Fixing his eyes on the deeper woods, Steve backs away in the house's direction. To his dread, he sees it now—a black mass about fifty yards out, stretching from one side of his vision to the other, moving towards him like a colossal wave of an abyss. Moving through the woods, silent—stalking him like a hunter.

Fascinated and terrified by equal measure, his heart slows to a dull beat, the sound of it echoing in his ears. The darkness continues toward him, now picking up speed, and something inside his mind screams for him to snap out of it.

Rocky lopes up the slope a dozen yards, then glances back at his master, panting, no doubt dreaming of the massive stainless steel bowl of water in the kitchen, but loyalty keeps him in pace with his owner.

With monumental effort, Steve peels his attention from the wave of darkness and walks back up the hill, patting Rocky on the head as he goes, when a sharp cracking sound rings out from the woods behind him. He freezes and Rocky's head cranes upward. His floppy ears are tensed, his brow furrowed and creased in deep furrows. Another low growl rumbles from his barrel chest, followed by one sharp bark. Steve squeezes his eyes closed, then draws a deep breath to keep the hysteria at bay. Picking up his pace, he calls for Rocky to follow, which his companion does, though with some hesitancy.

Then he hears it—whispering—soft at first, but unmistakable. At first it's only one voice, a child's voice calling from the gloom. But soon it spreads through the woods as if hundreds of people are whispering in unison. He cannot make out the words—whether English or some alternative dialect, he cannot tell. But the words seem to be meant for him.

His quickened pace now swings to a full sprint, with Rocky doing his best to keep up. When they hit the house, Steve slams the door behind them and drives the bolt home with enough force to wake Mara from her slumber.

Chapter Six

—·—

1.

The phone rings. Steve looks at the screen and groans. He touches the screen and sets it to his ear as he sits on the massive leather living room armchair, staring out the rear window. "Hey, Mike."

"Steve-O. How are you doing?" says a metallic-sounding voice on the line.

"Good, good. How are you?"

"I'm great. How's the house?" There's a tone in Mike Goodwin's voice, though he's working hard to suppress it.

"The house is perfect, thanks."

"And Mara?"

"She's good."

A pause lingers for several moments. Mike says, "So—I understand you called a few times this morning. Left some messages last week. Everything OK?"

"Yeah, yeah. Everything's good. I was just checking in." Steve stands and paces behind the sofa—head down, eyes clamped shut, fingers tracing the worry lines on his forehead.

"Checking in?"

"I—"

"Steve..."

"No, I—"

"You don't need to call."

"No, I get that. I was sitting here, running over the Dawson situation. The suit." Steve turns to the stairs and descends into the basement.

"Yeah, that's all under control. I talked to the other lawyer this past weekend—they will settle. It's done. But you don't worry yourself about that baloney. You're on a *leave of absence*. It means you *leave*; that's why they call it that."

"Yeah, yeah. I—" He stares into the basement den, furnished with a brand new leather sofa and chair matching the ones upstairs.

"Look, buddy. This place will get through without you. Debra's got the Dawson thing, and she's wonderful. Hell, you hand picked her—and with all the material you left for her, she'll be great. Besides, it's not your problem even if she's not fine. I'll support her, or Ray can step in. We've got options. As for your other clients, we've got them handled too. You read me?"

"Oh, sure, sure."

"*Sure, sure,*" Mike says. They've been friends and business partners for twenty years. In fact, it was Mike's idea to start the firm back in the nineties, an enterprise that turned out to be more profitable than either of them ever fantasized. "I'm serious, Steve. Just focus on yourself. We'll be fine. Your firm will be here whenever you're ready to come back. Got it?"

"OK, yeah. It's just one of those things."

"Is Mara with you?"

"She's meeting with a client in Dubuque this morning."

"You have a psych appointment this week?"

"Yeah, every other day. Have one this afternoon."

"That's good. Talk to him. Learn to relax."

"Her."

"What?"

"It's a woman. The psychologist, I mean."

"Well, whatever. Just take your time and figure this shit out. In fact, you want my advice?"

Steve snorts. "Sure."

"You should have this therapist explain to you what *leave of absence* means, then have her tell you how to make the most of one. If you keep calling me every day, worrying about shit you need not worry about. Well, you'll be shooting yourself in the foot—self-fulfilling prophecy and all that. Am I right?"

"Yeah, you're right. It's just tough for me to relax."

"I get that. But you need to figure that out. You're no good to anybody acting like you've been the past few—" Mike's voice cuts off abruptly.

Steve cringes. "Yeah."

After an uncomfortable pause, Mike says, "I'm sorry, that didn't come out right. Your job right now isn't the firm, it's not your clients. It's only one thing, and one thing only. You. For the foreseeable future, *you* are your only job. Client! That's it. You are your own client, and I want you to take care of yourself. We've got everything else, everything else in the world. You handle you. You hear?"

"Yeah, yeah, I hear."

"Good. Start by sitting down and having a coffee—you still drink coffee, right?"

"Yeah. Well, decaf."

"That's good, that's fine. Any coffee is better than no coffee. Am I right? You sit down with your Cubs mug full of decaf and stare out all those windows out there in the middle of Quoke-town and relax. Don't read the news. Don't turn on the news—fucking Fox News, CNN—or whatever bullshit you watch. That shit'll drive you nuts, especially nowadays. Understood?"

"Understood."

"I might have a heart attack from the extra stress, but don't worry about me."

"Well, shit—"

"I'm kidding! I'm kidding. We're fine here. You get yourself stronger and don't worry about us."

Steve says his goodbyes and turns off his phone. He had hoped talking to Mike would set him more at ease, but the steady thrumming of his heart tells a different story. Mike doesn't understand, no one understands. If you've never experienced a bout of extreme anxiety, you can't appreciate the debilitating horror.

He paces in the den for a full fifteen minutes before cutting into the downstairs bathroom for a shower.

2.

"How do you like your new home?" Dr. Nguyen sits across from him, her legs crossed, hands folded on her lap. This time, she isn't holding a notepad or pen. She appears to be in her late thirties or early forties, or she's one of those people who could be much older or younger than she looks. In their first and only other session, she informed him she was Vietnamese, born here from immigrant parents who had escaped to the US on rickety boats in the seventies.

A simple navy business suit with a knee-length pencil skirt cut just above the knees reveals thin but muscular legs. Steve imagines that she's a runner in her normal life. She's got her hair pulled back from her shoulders, held in place by what looks like a pencil stuck through it.

"It's good. Beautiful property."

"Relaxing?" she asks.

"Yes. Very. My parents had a cabin out there when I was growing up. I always liked that area—rolling hills and endless farmland. Grant Wood did a lot of painting out there, I think."

"I imagine it's calming, being away from traffic and lots of people. Might help your anxiety."

"That's my hope. I had my first blackout at that cabin, oddly enough."

Dr. Nguyen's eyes light up. "Oh? When was that?"

"I don't know—I was in my early thirties, or late twenties, maybe—maybe fifteen, sixteen years ago. Around the time when all this stuff first started. It didn't happen often back then, the panic attacks, but when they did, there was never any reason. I'd just get super anxious for no reason."

"Were Mara and the kids with you at the time?"

"No, I was by myself. Just a weekend getaway. I was cutting wood outside one evening when it hit me out of nowhere. Next thing I knew, I woke up on the ground in the middle of the night. That was the last time I stayed at the cabin, come to think of it. My dad sold the place a couple of months later."

"I see. It must have been a serious episode for you to black out."

"I guess. I don't remember."

She nods, listening.

Steve says, "What made you practice in Davenport? I mean, an Ivy League degree could have gotten you a cushy job in Manhattan or some-place like that, I would think."

"I did my internship there and worked in New York for about ten years, but I grew up in Pleasant Valley. I guess always saw myself as more of a midwestern girl than a big city type. How about you? Did you ever live anyplace else?"

"No. Except for college in Iowa City, I never left. My little brother moved away, though." Steve smoothes the top of his slacks with his hands.

She raises an eyebrow. "Oh? Are the two of you close?"

"Yeah, I guess. We talk on the phone a few times a month. It's not like Mara and her sister—we're guys, so it's a little different. We text a lot more than we talk. But he comes home once or twice a year and stays with me for Christmas or Thanksgiving. We both like whiskeys and IPAs, or whatnot. He lives in Los Angeles now, so it's not as easy to get together. I wish I could see more of him."

"Oh." Dr. Nguyen smiles and lets out a controlled exhale.

"I guess I don't know what I'm supposed to say in these sessions."

"You can talk about whatever's on your mind. That's the only rule, aside from using the time wisely. There is a point to all of this, but I want you to use it however you need to use it. I believe a client's needs will always come to the surface."

Steve nods. "Yeah, I get that. Difficult for me, but I understand."

"But I can start us off this time, if you'd like. You mentioned your brother—what's his name again?"

"Max."

"Yes, thank you. Is Max on your mind?"

Steve thinks about it. "I don't know. I guess maybe."

"When you think of Max, what thoughts come to mind?"

At the suggestion, a picture blazes through his mind like an explosion of light and color, like a video streaming through his memory, delivering Steve to a specific moment in time. But it's not a memory of Max. It's the little girl from his dreams. At first, she's standing a dozen yards away on a white plane of nothingness, staring into Steve's eyes. Her face is a mystery of serenity, no emotion—no fear or anger, no happiness—no nothing. A baby is crying somewhere behind him, a muffled sound, like from inside a house, but the girl sees only Steve. She says nothing, but stands there staring at him until Dr. Nguyen's voice interrupts the image.

"Painful memories?"

Tears rise in Steve's vision. "Yeah. Rotten, to be honest. But not of Max. I mean, it's not a memory of *him*."

"I see." She shifts in her seat and touches her chin with her midnight blue nails. "Is there much of an age difference between you two?"

"Sort of. Seven years."

"Were you close, growing up?" she says.

"Oh, not really. He kind of annoyed me when we were younger, and I wasn't around much after I graduated high school. But we're pretty close now."

"Except for the distance."

Steve nods. "Yeah, California is far. We talk on the phone a lot and text, or whatever."

"And your sister?"

Steve pauses and swallows. He takes a tissue from the box sitting on a small glass-topped table next to him and dabs his eyes. "She was three years younger than me."

"So, when you think of Max—when I bring up his name—what do you see? Do you see a specific memory? Maybe a family trip, or a day at the ballpark?"

"No. None of that," Steve says.

"What is it you see? Close your eyes if you like. Close them and think of Max. What do you see?"

"Liesl."

"When you think of Max, you see Liesl?"

"Not always, but lately I do." Steve dabs his eyes again with the tissue.

"Why?" Dr. Nguyen says.

"Hell if I know. I was hoping you could tell me."

"I could venture a guess, but I'd rather know what *you* think." Her patience sets him at ease, though there is a probing quality to her questions—subtle and efficient. Steve noticed it first in their consultation, which was part of the reason he chose her.

"I don't know."

"How's your father doing?" she says, taking a sip from a tall Starbucks travel mug.

"He's fine. Lives in one of those nice-but-not-too-expensive retirement communities in Bettendorf. I guess he's doing a lot better now. He had a hard time after mom died; I mean, we all did. Max was a mess."

"And you?"

"Me too, for sure."

"How long ago was that?"

"That was 2008. So what, nine years? Shit, it's been that long? Isn't that strange?" He looks out the window again, shaking his head, and sees his mom's face—not the placid mask of her later Parkinson's years—but the vibrant smile of her younger self.

His mother's voice speaks to him through the vision. *"Be careful. You'll catch your death of cold out there."*

Shivering, Steve returns his attention to Dr. Nguyen.

"Are you OK?" she asks.

"Yeah."

"Was your brother with you when your sister died?"

"Yeah. He has no recollection of that day, obviously. He was a baby. Lucky. I only remember him crying."

"He was crying?"

Steve says, "Yeah. No reason. Just crying like babies do, you know? Whenever I think of that day, I hear Max crying in the background. Sort of muffled, from inside the house. Ha! I could hear him all the way out on the river. That kid had quite a voice."

"This was at your house?"

"No. We were visiting friends of my parents. They lived out in Port Byron, I think. Or maybe it was East Moline. Anyway, they lived in a little stone cottage by the river."

"The Mississippi?"

"Yeah. It was January and ice covered the river as far as you could see. We were out there messing around, Liesl and me, laughing and sliding around. What were my parents thinking, letting us go out there with no supervision? I guess that's just the way it was in those days."

She nods.

"Then Liesl fell through the ice and disappeared. Just like that. One moment she was standing there staring at me. Her face—Jesus, her face—the look. I'll never forget it. Fear, you know? She said nothing, but I saw the panic in her blue eyes. Then she fell through the ice, and that was it. Disappeared."

"You say you were playing *by* the river?"

"We were playing *on* the river. Skating around on the ice in our boots, you know? Sliding and laughing our heads off. And then—horrible day."

"I imagine you think about it a lot."

"Every day. Many times a day." He nods and looks at one of the large bookshelves that line the inside walls of the office. A plump tear breaks over his lower lid and trails down his cheek. He thinks about wiping it away, but lets it be. "But what can ya do, ya know?"

"What do *you* do? To cope?"

"I manage."

"How did you manage when you were a child? After it happened?"

"Pushed it out of my mind, I guess. In high school, I'd get drunk every weekend. Do stupid stuff at parties, hook up with random girls. You know. Never kept a girlfriend, or anyone, not until Mara. Ha, and that wasn't until my thirties. In college, I sank myself into my studies and then after law school I sunk myself into the work, the job. When I started my firm, I sank myself into that—didn't give myself time to think."

"Why?"

"Seems obvious."

"And that worked for you?"

"Yeah, for a while. I kept myself busy, but I guess that took a toll. Once things settled down at the firm, the thoughts crept in, little by little, until…"

"Until it overwhelmed you."

"Yeah."

Dr. Nguyen sets her notepad on the table beside her. "Many things cause anxiety. Sometimes the cause is specific, and sometimes it's ambiguous. Sometimes it's related to current events in a person's life, while other times it's more abstract, tied to events from our past—our childhood, for example. Does that make sense?"

"Yes. So my sister's death is at the heart of my anxiety?"

"Well, yes. But it could be more than that. We should have a session on Thursday. I'd like to hear about the dreams too, if you're ready to talk about them. Is morning a good time for you?"

"Uh. Yeah. As good a time as any."

"Good."

Steve pinches the fabric of his slacks and grunts, nodding.

Dr. Nguyen smiles, then stands and leads him to the door.

Chapter Seven

Don Loomis sits in the front of his green '89 F150, staring out the dirty windshield across the little league baseball field, vacant now save for a dozen crows lumbering about in the outfield. The grass, once a vibrant and deep green, now flecked with yellow blades and mostly covered in red, brown, orange, and gold leaves from the trees just beyond the home run fence.

Don remembers hitting a few dingers on this field. Not much has changed since those days—the towering fence behind home plate, rusty from decades of Iowa weather. The wood backstop, bumped up from decades of sharp foul balls, is doubtless the same one too.

Not much changes here.

He's wearing the mesh John Deere baseball cap he's had almost as long as the Ford, pulled down to his eyebrows to block the sun's glare. The pickup and cap are not much to look at, but they do their jobs. Don can afford something better. Work has been strong this year, but there's something about the well-worn and familiar that comforts him.

His kids are growing fast, with high school on the horizon for the eldest. His wife, Rebecca, has big plans for the empty nest. She says having had kids when they were young—he was twenty and she was nineteen—means they'll still be young when the kids are out of the house. Get it done early and enjoy life, just the two of you. Don isn't so sure.

These days, kids don't pick up and fly off like they used to. Nowadays kids need their parents longer, especially the insurance and the money, always the money. Don doesn't mind. He's not as eager for the empty nest days as his wife seems to be. The kids need him and that feels good.

It's almost noon, and the sun casts the world in the golden-hued warmth only fall can deliver. The cornfield stalks beyond the ball diamond, now dried out and swaying in the October breeze, glow like a meadow of gold. The long silky leaves of hundreds of cornstalks flap like a crowd at a sporting event, waving across the park to him, cheering him on. Cheering him for what?

A roaring engine blares behind him and he sees a school bus rumble across his rearview mirror, right to left. In the mirror, he sees a blur of a dozen small heads framed in the rectangular bus windows, some wearing caps and others sporting ponytails or pigtails, some with spikey cropped hair, others with no hair at all. Don squints his eyes closed and squeezes the steering wheel, letting out a slight grunt. It's barely past noon—must be an early day.

Glancing out the side window, his eyes follow the old bus as it proceeds down the narrow lane until it squeals to a stop at the corner just past the park, its turn signal flashing as it waits for traffic. Don's forehead pounds and visions fill his mind—ugly thoughts, unwanted thoughts. Then, as he slides the key into the ignition, the bus lurchers forward with a rattle and a cough of smoke, heading down Main Street.

Across the field, the cornstalks are motionless, like rows upon rows of ghostly soldiers observing him from a distance.

But none of it matters, not the corn or the baseball diamond or the bus full of bouncing heads. All he can think of is that house—the one on the Jensen property. The Spain house. Images flash like a picture book, flipping front to back from a powerful wind.

At first, he sees nothing, just trees and shadows, leaves and acorns dropping in the fall breeze. But then, a figure emerges from behind an old oak, a figure he's seen twice before in his life. Its back is to him, but he knows it's the same.

The first time, he was a teen out riding bikes with some buddies past dark on one of those crisp fall evenings when the entire world appears to be falling sleep. Their bikes had taken them out into the country and down a certain gravel road. That's where he saw it the first time. It was only a moment, but that was long enough.

The second time was just two days ago on the Jensen proper—no, wait. The Spain property. *Spain*. Jensen gave it up. *Why?* That question bothered him almost as much as the images.

The pages flip faster and faster, as the shadowy figure strides through the woods until it comes into a small opening at the trunk of a prodigious willow. The figure stares ahead, scanning the deeper woods, then freezes. To Don's horror, it turns its head until two glowing eyes are radiating out from the flipping pages. They peer through Don's eyes, past his physical self, until they stare into the vast recesses of his empty soul. With great effort, Don shakes the vision away, his heart pounding through his overalls.

Talk to Ronald, he tells himself. *Talk to Ronald. He'll know what to do.*

Don leans his head onto the hand-worn steering wheel and screams.

Chapter Eight

The Last Diner on Earth is quiet. The only customers are an elderly fellow at the counter holding a magazine, and a young couple at a booth towards the back, both focused on their phones.

Steve rubs his forehead, breathing through another exercise. The anxiety is manageable today—only a six, maybe even a five on his one to ten rating scale. *I got this. Today is better. Better than yesterday, for sure.*

It's an ocean. The next wave is always over the horizon, never gone, only managed. Fear of the next wave keeps true serenity at bay. Anxiety about anxiety. Panic over panic. The cycle comes back around, no matter what you do. Dr. Nguyen assured him it would take time—get worse before it got better, and all that.

A woman enters the diner wearing a stained pink hoodie with an Iowa State logo on the front and a ripped knitted shawl, half tied around her shirt. The jeans fit a little too loose on her thin frame. She appears to be in her mid-fifties, though it's hard to tell a specific age. A rat's nest of hair, highlighted here and there by a bright blond, now grown out several inches from the roots. Wrinkles zig-zag across her face and forehead, scars from the knife of time.

She murmurs to herself as she drifts toward the counter, her eyes searching the floor as if she's hunting for a dropped contact lens. Taking her time, she sits on a stool at the middle of the counter and folds her filthy hands in front of her. "Oh, dear. Oh, dear," she says.

Rose returns from the kitchen, order pad in hand, but when she sees who it is sitting at her counter, she tucks the pad back into her apron and approaches the woman. "Hello, Melly. How are you today?"

"Fine, fine," the woman says.

"You want the usual?"

"Huh?"

Rose clears her throat and raises her voice a little. "The usual. Your eggs and bacon?"

"Oh, yes. Yes, please. Thank you, doll." The woman mumbles something unintelligible. "Oh, and can I have a cup of coffee, please? If it's not too much trouble?"

Rose nods, then cuts back into the kitchen. From the kitchen, Steve hears her say to her husband, "It's Melly."

"OK," is the response, followed by the sound of clanging pans.

Steve takes a sip of his decaf, wondering about this unusual new customer. *Is she homeless?*

Caught up in his thoughts, he doesn't realize the woman has taken notice of him. When he finally focuses on her again, she's staring right at him. Her eyes are wide and her mouth opens and closes as she licks her lips. Rose returns and sets a coffee cup next to her.

"Now, Melly, don't go bothering the customers," Rose says, half-joking, but with a glance in Steve's direction that seems to say, *"so sorry."*

"You there," the woman says. Her voice is rough, sounding like several decades of cigarette smoking and loud music.

"Hello," Steve says.

She mumbles to herself a moment or two, then says, "Have you seen her?"

Unsure if he should engage with the woman, or if she's even talking to him, Steve smiles and looks down at his coffee, hoping she'll distract herself with something else. However, in the corner of his eye, he sees she's still turned toward him—her eyes still focused on his face. Still, he keeps his eyes pointed down, like a ninth grader hoping the Algebra teacher calls on someone else.

"Hello! You there," she says.

"Melly, leave the poor guy alone," comes a male voice from the kitchen through the order window.

The woman glances at the kitchen, then slips off the stool and shuffles towards Steve, her hands clasped in front of her. "Mister. You from here?"

"I just moved here this weekend."

"But you not born here."

"No."

"You ain't born Maquoketa, you ain't *from* Maquoketa."

"OK."

"Thing about this town—the shadows move along the highways and byways, by the dirt roads and the deer paths. The oaks—the oaks whisper. You hear it? You hear them out there, whispering?"

"The oaks?"

"Yeah. They are quiet, but you can hear them. All you got to do is listen, and you'll hear them as plain as day. They are full of whispers." She lays her hands on the formica tabletop and leans in toward him, her eyes wide and searching, then slides into the booth across from him. "You deaf?"

"Nope."

"If you don't hear em now, you will. They don't take to being ignored." Steve sits back and looks toward the kitchen.

"Name is Melly, Melly Harmon. You don't have to worry, Mister. I don't bite—*much*." She peels into a fit of laughter that develops into a productive coughing fit, ending with her chewing whatever came up.

"I'm not worried," he says.

"You seen my daughter?"

"Your daughter? I don't think so. Was she in here earlier?"

"No, she wasn't in here. She gone."

Though he feels his heartbeat pick up its pace, Steve doesn't leave the booth. This Melly, absurd as she is, makes for a perfect diversion from his previous thoughts. "She's gone?"

"Yep, gone." She slaps her hand on the table and coughs again.

"What do you mean?"

"Gone! Left me here alone. Never seen her again."

"I'm so sorry. But I'm new here and I know nothing about your daughter." Steve picks up the bill sitting at the end of the table and reads it.

"Only the oaks know where she went. They see everything. But they ain't the only ones who know, I promise you that."

"Mm."

"*Mm*," she mocks. "No use in bluffing. You already dead—dead inside—dead as a doornail. The outside ain't caught up."

"Melly!"

Steve hadn't noticed that Rose had returned from the kitchen and was now on the other side of the counter, holding a plate of food, listening to their conversation.

Melly sits back, flustered. "Sorry, sorry, Rose. I'm sorry, I—I didn't mean that. I—" She covers her mouth with her hand and sobs.

Steve stares wide-eyed at Rose. She shrugs back with a sympathetic glance.

Rose says, "Melly, it's OK. I'm bringing out your food. Eggs and bacon, your favorite. You should return to your seat and get some food in you."

The woman's eyes descend to the greasy breakfast in Rose's hands. She licks her lips and swallows, then looks back at Steve, opens her mouth as if to say something, but leaves it alone. She kicks her legs around and pulls herself out of the booth, making her way back to the steaming dish.

Steve sighs and chuckles as Rose approaches him, winking. "Can I get you anything else, Mr. Spain?" she says.

"Please, call me Steve. I was thinking about that slice of blueberry pie you've got over there in that magnificent old display case."

"Excellent choice, Steve. My husband makes the best blueberry pie in the state of Iowa. Just ask him." She laughs, and Steve joins in.

"In that case, I suppose I'd be foolish not to give it a go. By all means, bring me a slice, please." Steve giggles, though he doesn't know why. Perhaps it simply feels good to feel good. He pushes away the fear, inching its way into his mind—the nervous anticipation for the next bout of panic. For now, he's happy with his pie and his quirky companions, even the bat-shit crazy woman at the counter, and that's enough. That's more than enough.

Rose dances her way back around the counter as her husband, Rob, pokes his head through the order window and calls out to her. "Hey now, no having fun on the job! It's against the rules!"

"Who says?" Rose says as she opens the display case door and pulls out a wide slice of blueberry pie.

"The state of Iowa! Duh!" Rob points a finger at Steve and they all laugh again. The couple's energy is infectious.

"Let the state come in and make me stop having fun. Won't be able to, no way sir-ee. I'm born this way. I'll die this way," Rose says as she glides back around the counter and sets the plate and a fork in front of Steve. "You need another cup of joe to chase it down?"

"I'm OK, thanks," Steve says, still laughing.

As Rose returns to the kitchen, he watches her go. He smiles then looks across the room to Melly, twisted around on her stool to face him, her eyes narrowed in judgment. Did she catch him checking out Rose's behind? He blushes a little and turns his attention to the pie before him.

"Go on, try to hide. You can't hide from me, you know," Melly says.

"What do you mean?" He takes his first bite. The rich tangy sweetness of the blueberry pie rolls over his senses and he closes his eyes in the euphoria that follows. He determines not to let his woman upset this moment.

"Mm hm," she says, then takes up her plate and brings it over to the booth. Without asking, she plops herself down and rips off a bite of bacon, chewing with her mouth full open. "You don't recognize it yet, but I do."

They sit like that for some time, Steve devouring the delicious pie while Melly cleans her plate, all the while watching him. He returns her stare. For no logical reason, her demeanor changes. She bows her head and falls into a fit of weeping. The sounds of water spraying and dishes and pans clanging together still emanate from the kitchen.

"Why are you crying?" Steve says.

"She's gone," she says between sobs. "She's gone."

"Who?"

"My daughter! Don't act like you don't know."

"I'm new to Maquoketa—I don't know your daughter."

This seems to take her off guard, and she gives him a wary look, as if she's doubting herself. Melly grunts, blows her nose in a napkin, folds it, and sets it aside. "She's gone."

"She moved away?"

"No, they took her. Someone took my baby girl. Kidnapped her on that very street." She points out the window. "They took her and they never brung her back."

"Someone kidnapped your daughter?" Steve notices that the water in the kitchen has stopped running and the clang of dishes has ceased.

"Yes! What the hell you think I've been telling you?"

"I'm so sorry, Melly," Steve says, setting his fork next to the plate. "When did this happen?"

Melly inhales and looks at the ceiling. "I don't know. It's been fourteen years, maybe. *Fourteen*? Yes, it happened October twenty-fourth, two-thousand two. That's fourteen, right? I remember the date. Can't do the math."

"You're almost right. That's fifteen years ago."

"Yeah, that's right."

"What was your daughter's name?"

"Her name was Jessica, but I called her Jesse, like Jesse James. A spitfire, that one, with her long blond hair and skinny legs. She'd be tall by now—a damn model, I swear it. Could have been..." Melly's face breaks like a china plate into another deep sob and she bows her head until her chin rests on her chest.

Steve lets her cry like this for a few minutes as he looks down at his clasped hands. The pie, which is half-eaten, doesn't seem so appetizing anymore, and he regrets the judgment he'd had about the woman earlier. The kitchen remains silent, though Steve thinks he hears whispering, barely audible over Melly's crying. Finally, he says, "Did they ever find out what happened?"

She shakes her head and rolls her eyes, now flooded over with glistening tears, "Nope. Cops around here don't recognize their ass from a hole in the ground. You want to kidnap someone? You a serial killer? Come to Maquoketa—they'll never catch you here! They all in on it!"

"Everything OK out here?" Rob says, poking his head through the order window.

Steve says, "Yeah, sure, sure. We're OK."

Rob nods and his eyes bounce back and forth between the two before he says, "OK, just checking." He disappears and the sound of running water returns.

"So, they never found her. She's still missing? No leads?"

"Not much. She grabbed her lunch and headed out the door at her usual time. Kissed me goodbye, like always." Melly's eyes drift off toward the back wall, seemingly lost in her own thoughts.

"Did she walk to school? Melly?"

"Yes. Every day."

"Did anyone see her that morning?"

"Yes. A few people saw her walking to school."

"Who?"

Melly thinks about it. "There used to be a hardware store down there past the stop sign," she says, peeking over her shoulder down the street. "They did good business when it was open. The owner said Jesse walked past the store at around seven forty. And a friend of hers, Liz Kinard, said Jesse stopped by her place to pick up a math book she'd borrowed. And then there was Dan Hampton, our postman. He said she was talking to a guy a block away from the school. He said it looked like they were arguing, but when the police looked into it, they decided he was mistaken. Said it was some other girl. Oh, yeah, and a few kids said they saw her a month later, walking down the old road. The teams of volunteers scoured the forest out there. Nothing."

"Forest?" Steve's skin tightens as gooseflesh spreads across his arms, the hair standing on end. "Which forest?"

"Oh, the woods out there on what's-his-name's property. Jensen!"

"Jensen?" Steve's breath catches and his heart picks up its pace. So much for his relaxing afternoon.

"Yep, Jensen's property. Or was it Tupper's? Anyway, it doesn't matter because one kid said he couldn't be sure if it was her and then after they talked to the cops, they all agreed they'd made a mistake—it was some other girl. That was that. The new chief doesn't know shit."

"What was the name of the hardware store owner?"

"Gil Vernon. He's retired now. Lives out in Camanche, I think. Or Clinton? One of those towns. I've called him a hundred times over the years, but he doesn't answer me anymore. Says he's got nothing more to say about it. All he did was see her walking past his shop—it's not like he saw her get taken. He's a kind man, not like some others."

Steve leans back and lets the weight of her story sit with him for a while as she weeps more. The Jensen property—a forest on the Jensen property. Now his property. Anxiety pulses through him, but he takes a few breaths and closes his eyes. Once it levels out, he opens his eyes again. "Well, I'm so sorry. I wish I could help you."

She wipes her eyes with a new napkin she's pulled from the chrome dispenser at the edge of the table. "You ain't a private detective, are you?" she says.

"No, no. A lawyer, that's all."

Melly clears her throat, and her eyes widen. "Well, that's sort of the same thing, ain't it?"

Steve almost laughs, but seeing the desperate sincerity on her face, he stops himself. "Oh, no, no. You need a detective, not a lawyer."

"Why? You have clients, right? And you try to prove they're innocent, right? Well, this is *kinda* the same thing, ain't it? You find out who *did* it, what happened to her."

"Well, I don't—"

She grabs Steve by the arm and squeezes hard enough to make him wince. "Please, please, help me! I've been searching all these years—I can't focus on anything. Can't keep a job for more than a week because I can't stop thinking about it. I can't do anything. Hell, I'm on disability for anxiety and depression. These goddamn panic attacks hit me and I can't think straight for days. Thank god I have the tiny house my dad left me, or I'd be out on the streets. Please, Mister. Someone has to help me."

Steve drags her hand off his forearm. "OK, just calm down."

"You're probably a busy man, lawyer and all. I can pay you if it's the last thing I do. But, mister, I just have to know." She bows her head. "I'm sorry, I'm sorry. I—"

"No, don't be sorry. I'm on a leave of absence from my firm."

At this, she perks up a little, though her body twitches now and again from random hiccups brought on by the crying fit. "Why? You sick?"

"Oh, no. I took time off."

"I see."

His eyes trace the contours of Melly's face. Years of alcohol and stress may have robbed her of her beauty. Though she's a little younger than Steve, she looks at least ten years older.

Steve says, "Like I said, I'm not an investigator by profession, but in the course of my work, I have done some investigating. And I've hired investigators many times and been around them long enough to understand what's involved, I guess." Steve thrums his fingers on the tabletop, staring out the window at the partly cloudy sky. "I don't mind looking into it, but I can't promise anything."

"Oh! Oh! Do you mean it?" Melly slaps her hands over her mouth hard enough to leave red marks on her chin.

"Yes. But I'm serious, I doubt I can help. I'm not a professional detective and besides that, it's been almost fifteen years."

"Oh bless you, bless you, bless you."

He smiles at her as she weeps yet again, this time with tears of joy. While he accepts her words of thanks, Steve realizes he can no longer hear sounds coming from the kitchen.

CHAPTER NINE

After grabbing a notepad and pen from his car, Steve crosses Main Street and strides past the windows and storefronts of the quaint downtown street to the corner of Niagara and Main, where the now empty hardware store had been located for decades, through three generations of Vernon's until 2012. The paint on the brick exterior still says Vernon's Tru-value Hardware in bright blue and orange, though it's now faded and chipped away.

A sign on the front door says Main Street Bar and Grill—Coming December 2017. Fumbling some loose change and keys in his pockets, Steve scans the blocks on either side of the building.

Images shift from present to past as he imagines that crucial morning when Jesse Harmon, only thirteen years old, took what would be her last walk to school. An image emerges of an All-American teenage girl, thin and awkward, naïve and trusting—strolling down the most American little town of all of small-town Americana.

She turns to look at the storefront window, flipping her hair as the morning sun dances over her, each strand glistening like little waves in a roiling lake of gold. She tosses Mr. Vernon an amiable smile through the window with a nod as she proceeds to the corner. The image of the girl dissolves in the crosswalk, broken by an SUV squealing through the intersection.

Steve spots Maquoketa Police Station a block down Niagra Street. The grand trees, now orange and yellow and red, release their leaves in the October wind like chicks leaving the nest.

He enters the one-story, mid-century-styled brick building. At once, he's hailed by an officer with long, dark hair pulled up and pinned in a bun behind her head. She says, in a friendly tone like a greeter at Walmart, "Hello there. Can I help you?"

Steve pauses for a moment, as if surprised by the mundane question. "Uh. Hello. Officer, Swan—"

"Swanson."

"Yes, Officer Swanson. I'm looking for the chief."

"Oh, sure, Chief Branton just got back from his rounds," she says, picking up a phone. "Are you a lawyer?"

"No. Well, yes, but that's not what this is—I mean, I'd like to ask him a few questions about an old case, if he has the time." Steve pushes away the nagging thought that he's just taken on an investigation, based on the ravings of a madwoman in a diner.

"OK, no problem. I'll see if he's got the time." She covers the receiver and whispers. "Which, yes, he's got the time. Not much going on today." She laughs and dials an extension. "Hey, chief. A man is here to see you. A Mr.—"

"Steve Spain," Steve whispers.

"Spain. Says he'd like to talk to you about an old case. Mhm. Says he's a lawyer. Yeah. OK. OK, no problem. Uh huh, will do." She hangs up the phone and says, "OK, Mr. Spain. He'll be right out. You can wait over there in one of those chairs. He shouldn't be more than a few minutes."

Moments later, Chief Branton arrives in the lobby, extending his hand with a smile. "Hello. Chief Branton." The chief is tall and though Melly described him as a "kid," he's in his early to mid-forties, at least. Dark brown hair with speckled gray patches at the temples frames a handsome face.

With his svelte figure, chiseled features, and deep brown eyes, Steve guesses every woman in Maquoketa dreams of being rescued by him—even issued a speeding ticket or two. There's something thoughtful about him, and perhaps kind, qualities Steve hadn't divined from Melly's description.

Steve takes his hand, matching the firm, business-like handshake offered. "Hi, Steve Spain. Thanks for seeing me."

"No problem. You and your wife settling in OK?"

"Yes, we are. Thanks."

"Good, good. I heard you bought some of Jensen's property. Quite a shock that he sold it."

Steve laughs. "Yeah, so I've heard."

After an uncomfortable moment, Branton says, "So, what can we do you for?"

"Well, I suppose this is unusual, but I hoped I could pick your brain about an old missing person case."

Branton chuckles. "Did old Melly get to you?"

"What's that?" Steve says.

"I'm guessing you were having breakfast at that new diner, and she got ahold of you. Am I right?"

Steve sighs. "Yeah, that's pretty much it. Is none of her story true?"

"Her missing daughter? That part's true, I'm sad to say. And I'm sure she told you some theories she's concocted over the years. We don't get people moving into town all that often, but when we do, she finds them. Sorry to say."

Steve waves the apology away. "Oh, it's OK. I find myself with some extra time these days, so I figure it couldn't hurt to see what I can find out. Not that I'm saying I'd be better at your job than you!"

"Ha! Ah, don't worry about it. Why don't you come back to my office and I can tell you what I remember? Maybe get the file out. I don't mind."

Branton leads him through a security door into a large common room with several messy desks covered in papers. Officers sit at three of them, one with his feet propped on the desk, reading a newspaper. None of them pay much mind to Steve as he and Branton pass through.

"How many officers do you have in this town?" Steve says.

"Oh, we're the county seat, so our station serves Maquoketa and several of the little towns scattered around the area. Sheriff's Department handles the rest. But it's enough area to keep us busy, that's for sure. Don't get a lot of missing persons cases though. None since the Harmon girl." At the far end of the room, they turn left down a hallway.

Branton stops at the end of the hall and leads Steve into a modest office with a desk, a small round conference table, and several half book shelves filled with many hard bound legal texts. His computer is several generations newer than his employees' computers, with a flat screen monitor and ergonomic keyboard. A long line of windows stretch across the opposite wall, and several file cabinets line the wall to the left. A red leather swivel chair sits behind the chief's desk. There's a paperweight facing Steve that says, "*The Buck Stops Here.*"

Branton sits, offering for Steve to do likewise with a quick wave of his hand. "What do you want to know?"

Steve sits. "Well, for starters, how familiar are you with the case? I know you weren't the chief back then."

"Nope. Old Wicker was chief in those days. I was a street officer for six months before the girl went missing. I was part of the search and helped some with the investigation. Small town like this, street officers help investigations a little when something like this happens."

"Which isn't often," Steve says.

"What's that?"

"You said missing person cases aren't common here in Maquoketa."

"Nope. Not since Jesse. Oh, a kid might run off now and again, but we find them before the day is over." Branton leans back and crosses his legs for a moment, then uncrosses them, and sits up. "Hey, can I get you anything? A coffee or tea?"

"No, I'm fine, thanks. Do you remember if anyone had a working theory?"

Branton sits back again and looks up at the ceiling, shaking his head. "Nothing that made it past brainstorming. To be honest, we were all stumped by this case, then haunted by it, especially Old Wicker. Oh, there were leads, but none panned out."

Steve nods. "Melly said someone reported seeing Jesse arguing with someone—a man. The postal worker reported it."

"Yeah, that's true. And she can't get past it, even though that lead didn't pan out either. We found out it wasn't Jesse Harmon, which I'm sure she didn't tell you. It was Natalie Wooten, a girl who looked like Jesse. Natalie and her dad were arguing before school. The postman, Dan Hampton, he admitted to being in a rush that morning and might not have seen what he thought he saw—happens a lot, as I'm sure you know. He was trying to be helpful, but when we pointed out the mistake, he agreed it was Wooten. He felt terrible about it, leading us on a goose chase, and all."

"And this Wooten girl confirmed it was she and her dad?"

Branton nods. "Yep."

"And her dad? Did he confirm?"

"Yep."

Steve taps the pen on his notebook. "OK, good. What about the boys? The ones who said they saw her on some gravel road a month later?"

"Yeah, now that one had us all in a frenzy. We figured we'd gotten an actual break in the case, strange as it was. Had half the county searching those roads past Jensen's property and the Tutters, through all those fields and even into the woods behind your place. Nada."

"How about the caves?"

"For sure. Heck, any time a kid misses their curfew, parents head straight to the caves." Branton laughs.

"Logical."

"You bet."

"Do those boys still live around here?" Steve says and notices a shift in Branton's eyes.

"Uh, yep, I think so—most of 'em, anyway. There were five boys; four still live around here. One died a couple years ago. Rest in peace." Branton coughs and takes a tissue from a box at the edge of his desk. He wipes his mouth.

"So young?"

"Uh, yep. He moved up to Webster City after high school. They found him face down in a creek with a pistol next to him and a note in his pocket."

"Suicide?"

"Mm hm."

"When was this?" Steve asks.

"Oh, a couple years ago. Must have been 2015, I guess?"

"Does his family still live here in Maquoketa?"

"They do. A couple of odd birds, the Miltons, but they're friendly enough."

"Any idea what the suicide note said?"

"Oh, no. I wasn't privy to that. Sad though. So young. Good kid too." Branton's eyes drift away. He shakes his head and looks back at Steve. "Anyway, the others are still around. One works odd jobs around here and the other two live not far away, in Delmar. They work at a garage their family owns."

"Could you tell me their names?"

Branton's eyes narrow. "Why? You're not pursuing this thing, are you?"

"Well, I'd like to help Melly. It'll give me something to do with my time, too. Might be good for me—and her."

Branton rubs his forehead. "The kid who committed suicide was Joey Milton, and the two deadbeats are Frankie and Willy Trillo. I would be cautious around them. They've got themselves mixed up with some unsavory characters around these parts. And Bob Baxter—he was with them. Oh, and Don Loomis, though he claimed he never saw a thing."

"Loomis you say? Don?" Steve says.

"Yep. Why?"

"Pretty sure he worked on my house." The coincidence sends a shiver up Steve's back.

"Is that right? Well, makes sense—small town and all." Branton bites into a fingernail, then puts his hand in his pocket.

"OK, thanks chief. I'll follow up with some of these people and let Melly know I at least tried. Sorry for taking up so much of your time." Steve stands.

Branton stands. "Good luck. And remember. Watch yourself with the Trillos, OK?"

"Gotcha. Thanks."

As Steve heads to his car, he glances back at the building, peering through a window to see Chief Branton on the phone, watching him.

Chapter Ten

Mara kicks a rock down the road unimaginatively named 250th Avenue. Yellowish sandstone gravel covers the lane, with four wheel-width paths winding through it on either side. Though few cars ever pass this way, there's still enough traffic to move the gravel around.

Rocky is off leash, loping ahead near the shoulder, seeking rabbits, squirrels, mice, or any of the myriad of animals too quick for him to have a chance of capturing. Though Rocky is large enough to handle himself in a scuffle, speed does not come with the package.

The late afternoon sun has fallen somewhere off to the west, well below the treetops, lighting the clustering clouds in amber and pink hues. The crickets are starting their high song, building in strength as the day diminishes. Mara looks behind her, expecting to see Steve's Explorer rumbling along toward home, but she finds only a rabbit sitting at the edge of their driveway, on its haunches observing her, or more likely Rocky.

Where are you, Steve? She shifts back to the road ahead. The new dwelling is handsome and all this tranquility is a delightful change, but being alone here isn't peaceful. Each timber sways to its own rhythm, but together they seem to move toward her.

In the last house, you were never alone. Something was always hovering about in the room next to you, or in the corridor, or upstairs walking about, creaking the floorboards. The many presences in that old Craftsman home were active at all times. Their friends and family would either relish an evening in that house, or decline to even step foot in it. Though the frequent sleepless nights wore on the Spains over time, part of Mara still misses the thrill.

Yep, I miss it. Even if it almost drove me crazy.

Steve worries her more than the house or the woods. His anxiety—it's worse now than before. That's expected after an immense purchase like a house and ten acres. Perhaps he needs time.

She kicks these concerns around in her brain as they ramble along the lane. Rocky trots ahead, picking up his pace until he is practically out of sight around a curl in the road. Mara is about to call to him when he freezes, his floppy ears tipped upwards, right paw hanging a few inches above the gravel. His tail stands up as tense as the rest of his body.

"Rocky?" Mara says, halting for a moment. She waits for Rocky to relax and continue on his way. The mastiff remains frozen in his tracks, only breaking the pose long enough to glance back at her, his brow furrowed with deep grooves of worry. "Hey, doofus! What do you see?"

As she approaches, Rocky rumbles out a low growl, and his tail rises, stiff as a tree branch. She pats him on the head and stares down the darkening road. At first she sees nothing but an old mailbox fixed to a wood post at the end of a driveway on the opposite side of the road from their own. Her body jerks with shock as she realizes a man is standing in the driveway, about a dozen yards up the hill. At first she doesn't recognize him, given he's dressed in full hunting camouflage, but after a moment or two, she realizes it is only Wendell.

He stares at them, as still as Rocky, as if he is as worried about the dog as the dog is about him. In fact, Mara wonders if the old guy isn't growling back. She grabs Rocky's collar and snaps her leash onto the ring with a wave to Jensen. "Hello! Sorry! He's all bark, no bite." she says.

Jensen lifts his hand and returns a light flutter of the hand in return.

Relieved, Mara pulls Rocky along behind her and reaches the end of the driveway. "Hello there, Mr. Wendell. And how are ya'll this evening?"

Jensen coughs and spits. "Fine. Quite a dog you've got there. Are you walking him, or is he walking you?"

"Hard to tell sometimes. We're just killing time until Steve gets back. I completed my business early this afternoon, so I wanted to surprise him by coming home two hours earlier than usual, and wouldn't you know it? He's not even here." Mara laughs.

"He working?"

"No, no. He's taking time off. He must be out running errands, I guess. How's Linda?" Mara says, referring to Wendell's wife.

"She's good. Hey, I meant drive over to give you an invitation, but seeing as how you're all the way down here already, I guess you saved me the trouble. I forgot to mention it yesterday."

"An invitation?"

"Yeah. Linda likes her little parties, don't you know, so we always do a little something for Halloween. It'll be this Saturday. I realize it's late notice, but we'd love to have you."

"Oh, no, that's fine. We'd love to come. It's just that Steve's brother will be in town this weekend. Is it OK with ya'll if he tags along with us?"

Jensen frowns for a second, then spits into the ditch next to the driveway and says, "Oh, sure. Bring him along—and anyone else you want to bring—the more the merrier. You've got kids, right?"

"We do, but they're all in Chicago. I doubt they'd want to spend the weekend before Halloween out here with us."

"I suppose that's true. Well, we've got enough of everything." Jensen nods and turns to head back toward his massive farmhouse sitting on top of a small hill at the end of the sloped driveway. "Party starts at six, but we'll be going all night, or until we fall asleep."

"OK, Mr. Wendell. I look forward to it," Mara says to his back. She watches him for several moments before Rocky pulls her to the side of the road to relieve himself in the dead flowers.

Chapter Eleven

1.

"You want to go to that old guy's party?" Steve says, taking a bite of corn on the cob.

"We can't say no to an invitation from our only neighbor."

Steve laughs. "Yeah, I guess not. But my god, who will be there? The Jensen's are, like, eighty. It's gonna be a bunch of old people."

"Probably!" Mara joins him, laughing. "Anyway, if it's too unbearable, we can always use Max as an excuse. We just tell them he needs to go to Davenport to see his friends."

Steve rolls his eyes. "*Fine.* I guess we don't have to stay all night. But man, I was hoping to take Max someplace fun!"

"In *Maquoketa*?"

They laugh. Steve watches Mara as she takes a bite out of a golden ear of Iowa sweet corn. Even eating the least graceful food in the world, she looks beautiful. She looks at him and her eyes widen.

"What?" she says. "Is my face covered with corn?"

Steve laughs out loud, a hearty sound that feels good in his chest. "Oh, no. I was just marveling, that's all."

"Oh, shut up! You must feel good."

"I do!" He laughs again as if to confirm the fact. "It feels good, though—"

"What?" she says, pausing.

"Oh, nothing. It's just—I don't know—whenever I'm feeling good, there's a part of me that waits for the other shoe to drop. Like I can't enjoy it. It is always in my head. It's dumb, but I can't help it."

"It will take time to get used to normal." One of her arms twitches forward an inch, unsure whether to take his hand or let him be.

As if reading her thoughts, Steve takes her hand. "Thanks, honey. I honestly don't know what I'd do without you. I'm lucky."

"Well, I'm not without my *baggage*, ya know, and you've always been good to me. How could I not be just as supportive?" She leans in, her lips puckered.

Steve kisses her, rubs her shoulder, and moves a hair away from her neck. "I have something I need to talk to you about. After I left my therapy session—"

Mara's eyes light up. "Oh, I forgot! How did that go?"

"Fine. Good. I mean, it went pretty well, I guess. It's rough, talking about feelings and memories—but I guess no pain, no gain, right? After it was over, I had lunch at that coffee shop. The one from yesterday."

"The Last Diner, or whatever?" she says.

"Yeah. So, I'm having coffee and just finished my sandwich when this woman walks in. She's all disheveled and looks homeless, I guess, or dirt poor at least. Anyway, she sits at the counter and orders her food. But after a while, she comes over to my table and tells me this crazy story about her daughter. I guess the girl went missing fifteen years ago."

"What happened to her?" Mara sets down her fork.

Steve takes a deep breath, then tells her all about the conversation with Melly Harmon and how her daughter Jesse went missing, leaving no details untold. He tells her how he agreed to look into the matter and even spoke to the chief of police about the incident. Mara listens, nodding with rising eyebrows. "So, you're investigating for this Mandy person?"

"Melly. I'm just sort of looking into it." He searches her eyes for judgment.

She takes a drink of water. "Is that a good idea?"

A blanket of silence covers the room. "Why wouldn't it be?"

Gently, Mara presses. "Don't you think maybe you should rest?"

"I am resting, I promise. And I'm going to therapy, just like I said I would. And this thing, this cold case, it's nothing. I won't spend more than a day or two on it, OK? Plus, this isn't work. It's fun."

Mara looks into his eyes again. "You think investigating a cold case of a missing girl is fun?"

"Well, when you put it that way—"

They laugh. Mara shakes her head and says, "Look, you do what you want—it's your leave of absence. Just be careful, OK? Don't push it. You needed this time for yourself, remember?"

"I know, I know. If I feel like this is getting out of hand, I will stop immediately. OK?"

She frowns at him, smiling a little. "OK. It sounds interesting, I have to admit. Maybe I'll join you in your little detective work. Help you out a little."

"Really?"

"Yep. We southerners are natural detectives—runs in the genes."

"They do?"

"Mm hm. Just another tidbit ya'll don't know about us."

Steve beams. "That would be great!" Steve's phone vibrates in his pocket. He doesn't recognize the number, but slides the answer icon to the right, anyway. "Hello?"

A shrill woman's voice calls out through the receiver, far louder than necessary. "Hello? Hello, is this Steve? The guy I met today at the cafe?"

"Yes, this is him. Is this Melly?"

Mara looks at him, eyes wide. He smiles.

"Yeah, this is Melly. I'm sorry to bother you at home, but I'm here at the cafe and I talked to a guy who lives here, Bob Baxter. You know him?" She slips into a coughing fit.

When she's done coughing, Steve says, "Uh, no I don't. I'm new here, remember?"

"Oh, that's right. Sorry! Well, Bob came in here tonight and I told him you were helping me look for my Jesse. Bob was one of those boys who said they saw Jesse out there on that dirt road off the Grant Wood Byway—the Old Road, it's called. Anyway, he said he'd meet you at the diner tomorrow afternoon and tell you his story. Tomorrow at one. OK?"

Steve scratches his head. "Yeah, yeah, that's fine with me. I can be there at one."

Melly weeps a little and whispers thanks, though Steve isn't sure it's to him. "OK, bless you, Mr. Spain. Bye-bye!"

"Bye, Melly."

2.

Mara's Phone Video Recording #2 - Tuesday, October 24, 2:17 a.m.

We see darkness, then the camera moves in and out of focus. Leaves and dead grass and chunks of dirt fly across the screen from top to bottom. Mara's slippers pop in and out of frame—first the right, then the left. The camera tilts up and we see the shadow woods approaching.

Mara's voice says, "Where is it? Shit, shit. Steve? Steve?" The camera jostles and Mara curses. We see the tops of the trees and the moon above. The camera tilts downward in a blur of grainy images. "OK, where are you?" The camera pans right and left across the empty woods.

The camera cuts out, then back.

Sound of Mara breathing. At the center of the screen, we see three trees illuminated by Mara's flashlight, though fuzzy with low light visual noise.

Wind blows through the phone's microphone and a bird squawks from above. Mara whispers, barely audible above the noises of nature. "It's right there. Just past that middle tree. It was just there. *Steve, Steve*!"

The camera swings around to Steve standing on the deck, his hands at his sides. He sways, side to side, likes he's sleeping where he stands.

"*Steve*," Mara's voice whispers again. "Are you awake? Shit, Steve!"

He makes no movement, no response to Mara's calls. The snap of a broken stick sounds from behind and once again the screen becomes a blur of dark movement. The image shifts in and out while the automatic iris opens and closes as the phone struggles to adjust its focus.

"Oh, my god. It's right there, between the trees. It's a—it looks like a--" Mara calls into the woods. "Hello? Who's there? Who's out there?" We hear growling in the background, then Mara says, "No, Rocky. You stay up there with Dad, OK? You stay up—"

The camera cuts out.

3.

Mara leads Steve into the house from the deck, bolting the French doors behind them. She rushes around him to the front door to confirm it's locked. Returning to the living room, she stops for a moment, considering. She nods and says, "Better go through the rest. You wait there, Steve."

Steve remains where she left him, next to the kitchen counter a few feet inside the French doors. *What's wrong with him? Is he sleep walking? It's like he's frozen.* Rocky stands next to Steve, his head tilted, watching Mara.

"Come on, boy, help me check the house," she says.

As she descends into the basement, Rocky lopes behind her down the stairs. She checks the locks on the sliding doors in the den. Same for the windows in the office and the second guest bedroom.

As she enters the third bedroom and steps further into the room, she hears the bedroom door close shut behind her. Rocky whines from the other side of the door. Without looking behind her, she takes a few steps back towards the door. A familiar sharp chill hits her as if she's stepped into a meat freezer. She halts just before the doorway, holding her breath. A feeling comes over her she hasn't had since they left the last house.

I'm not alone in this room.

Mara immediately begins shaking, almost uncontrollably. Her eyes clamp shut as she whispers, "No, no, no. Not here. Not here too!"

Eyes open, just barely, she scans the room. The moonlight casts a blue beam of light through the thin curtains, but just past them, she sees something in the corner.

At first, it appears as little more than a shadow—a trick of the light and the dark. But as her eyes adjust, she sees it. A figure, partially obscured by the drapes and the moonlight. Holding her breath and saying a quick prayer, she reaches behind her, eyes focused on the thing in the corner. Her old friend. As her hands fumble for the knob, the silhouette seems to shift. It steps forward, just a little. Her eyes still locked on the corner of the room, she raises her hand past the doorknob to the wall. With a gulp of air, she flips on the light switch.

Nothing. The room is empty, as always. Heart racing, she opens the door and closes it behind her, not daring to turn off the light again. She knows what she'll see if she does.

Her knees shake as she continues upstairs. She finds Steve where she left him, next to the kitchen counter, eyes open but registering nothing. She leads him back to bed.

As she pushes her husband onto the memory foam mattress, he wakes. "Hey, what happened?"

"We can talk about it tomorrow." She removes her robe and slippers, then slides under the covers to snuggle up next to him. "Just stay with me. Let me hold on to you."

"What happened?" His voice is fading.

"Tomorrow. Go back to sleep."

"Was I sleepwalking?"

"Yes."

"Oh."

Across the room, she spots Rocky watching them expectantly, his eyes shifting from one to the other, ears lifted. She snaps her fingers and the old mastiff climbs onto the bed, then circles twice before settling in at the foot on Mara's side. For once, Mara doesn't mind the mastiff hogging the bed.

Chapter Twelve

"Have you gone back?" Dr. Nguyen asks.

She is wearing slacks today. Steve hopes her clothing choice isn't a conscious thing—like she noticed him glancing at her legs one too many times. A surge of embarrassment rushes over him and he looks down at his lap.

"Are you OK?" she says.

Steve looks up. "Uh—yes, I'm fine. What was the question?"

"I asked if you ever went back. To the place on the river where your parents' friends lived."

"The place where my sister died?"

"Yes."

"No. Of course not," he says.

"Why, *of course*?"

Steve shrugs. "I don't know how I'd react to being there again."

"It might be cathartic."

Steve scratches the whiskers on his chin. "Maybe. It's just been a place that—I don't know..." He clears his throat and wipes his eyes.

They sit in silence until Dr. Nguyen finally lets him off the hook. "You mentioned earlier about a cold case? A missing girl?"

Rolling his eyes, Steve says, "Let me guess. You think it's a bad idea?"

She looks surprised by the question. "Not at all."

"*Really*?" Steve says with more sarcasm than he intended.

She places a hand on her chest. "Honest. I have no judgment about it; you've barely mentioned it. *Should* I think it's a bad idea?"

Steve hesitates. "Mara thinks I'll overdo it. Stress myself out."

Dr. Nguyen nods. "And what do you think?"

"I think it would be nice to help this lady, ya know? Maybe give her some closure—it doesn't feel like a stressful thing. Mara's worried about me. She's a worrier. Do you think it's a good idea?"

"That depends," she says.

"That's a very *therapeutic* answer."

She laughs. "I don't mean it to be. My opinion on it depends on certain things."

"Like what?" Steve says.

"On the case itself, for one. Let's say you find out something disturbing in the course of your investigating. How would you react to that?"

"I don't know."

"So there you go. I don't know either. What if you get into trouble? Someone might not want the truth to be known."

"You've been watching too many movies," Steve says, crossing his legs.

"But you see what I mean? There are a lot of variables here."

Steve stares out the window. *How do I talk about what's really going on? She'll have me committed.*

"Is there something else?" she says.

"I, uh—what do you mean?"

"You seem pensive. Is there something else on your mind? If so, now is the time." She tilts her head, looking at the clock.

"I don't know how to discuss it."

"Why?"

Steve pinches his slacks between his thumb and forefinger, sliding his hand down his leg to create a makeshift seam. "I, uh—it's just something weird. Like really weird. Probably sounds crazy."

"Crazy? How?"

"I feel dumb even mentioning it."

Dr. Nguyen narrows her eyes, brow furrowed, not unlike how Rocky might do when he hears a funny sound.

"It has to do with—"

"Yes?"

"The supernatural."

"Oh!"

"Ghosts and demons—stuff like that. Stupid stuff. I shouldn't even mention it; you'll probably want to lock me up. But Mara can back me up!"

Dr. Nguyen's eyebrows rise—she's curious, but doesn't seem surprised. "How do ghosts and demons affect your life?"

Steve swallows. "A lot, believe it or not. It's been going on for some time now, ever since we first bought the last house—the one on Elm Street. That's where it all started. When the previous owners accepted our offer, we laughed and said we hoped it didn't turn into a nightmare. Get it? Nightmare—"

"Yes, Nightmare on Elm Street," she finishes with a kind chuckle.

"Right. Anyway, it turned into one, an actual nightmare. That house had—I don't know—*something* in it. I was never one to buy into that stuff, the occult or whatever. My parents were religious, but I never was. God, demons, heaven and hell. I was all about science and proof and logic, but then we moved into that house." Steve once again checks Dr. Nguyen for signs of shock or disbelief. Her face is a sphinx.

"How so?" Her interest in his story seems, at least on the surface, to be genuine.

Steve looks sideways at Dr. Nguyen over the top of his glasses, drumming his fingers on the arms of the IKEA chair as he considers the situation for a moment. How will she take this story? Will she accept it at face value, or will it become one of her copious notes? Will she use it as part of some exotic diagnosis, or maybe laugh it off as a clear sign he's lost his mind?

"Steve," she whispers, leaning forward in her chair. "I only want to hear your story. No judgement here, OK? We can process all of it later, but for now, I want you to feel safe. Believe me, you're not the first client to relate supernatural occurrences. Hell, I've had some myself. It's pretty normal, actually." She smiles and sits back, folding her hands in her lap. "So, tell me."

"The first part is simple to explain. After my sister died, I had these visions. Really odd visions of things."

"Such as?"

"Crazy stuff. But the main one, I saw repeatedly. This woman would appear to me, bloody and dying. She seemed to be running from someone, you know? Like she was looking for help. One time, my mom stopped at the post office to drop off a letter while I waited in the car. I look out the car window and the woman is limping down the sidewalk toward me, blood running down her arms, like always. She comes to the car window, which I've got rolled down part of the way. It was awful. I just remember her bloody hand reaching out to me, grabbing onto the window to keep me from rolling it up. And just when it felt like she was going to get me, I blacked out, like always."

"Awful. Could it have been a dream?"

"That's what I've always told myself. Dreams are easy to explain, but the other stuff—not so much."

"What other stuff?"

Steve looks at the ceiling, then closes his eyes, stretching his neck from side to side until it cracks. "The first night we were in the old house, we heard a loud scream—like a woman's scream. Ear-piercing kind of thing, you know? It woke us up. Like I said, I was never one to believe in ghosts, so my immediate thought was that some weirdo had gotten into the house, ya know? Like, they broke in somehow, or maybe squatters. It had been empty for some weeks before we bought it."

"So, I went into my gun safe, grabbed my Glock, and opened the bedroom door. I peeked out into the hallway, ya know, like this." Steve mimics himself, sticking his head out a pantomime door.

"And I called out something like, 'You're trespassing! This is our house and I've got a gun!' Stuff like that. But there was no answer and I couldn't hear anyone moving around. It was an older house, built in the twenties, so it had those creaky floors and stairs. If anyone—anyone human—had been walking around, you'd hear it. I checked all the rooms, upstairs and downstairs, all the way into the basement." Steve takes a breath, feeling shaky.

"Go on," Dr. Nguyen says, eyes widened.

"Well. The basement had a small room like a workroom with a really nice built-in workbench on one wall. They set the water heater and furnace in the back corner at the far side of the room. Dust all over the place. I always got the creeps whenever I went into that room. There was this awful smell, like *death*. That's the only way I could describe it. We searched that room for dead animals in every nook and cranny but found nothing. The stench would come and go. Sometimes it went away for a while, like months at a time, but it always came back."

Steve reaches for a paper cup of water sitting on the end table next to him and takes a drink. "The room had one of those hanging lightbulbs where you pull on the chain and it turns on, you know?"

She nods.

"So, I pull on the chain and the light pops on. What I saw was unexpected. There was a *face*. A thin face over there by the furnace." Steve motions toward the corner of the office, picturing the scene before him. "This face. Just staring out at me."

In the corner of his vision, Dr. Nguyen leans forward. "Just a face?" she says.

"It had a body too—it wasn't just a floating head, ya know—but there were shadows in the back of the room, so I couldn't see much of anything else. The light from the swinging light bulb shone on the face. These big round eyes. That's what I remember most. Light green eyes and the whites were dark yellow, like an old bruise. Its teeth were green and decayed and there were strings of hair hanging down on either side of its head. Its skin was slimy and rotten gray like a corpse that's been floating in water..." Steve's voice trails off as his eyes fill with tears.

"What did you do?" Dr. Nguyen says.

Steve clears his throat. "That's the funny part—I did nothing. I stared at that face for a long time. It stared back at me, but didn't make a move. I could hear it breathing and it blinked once in a while. Along with the drool that leaked from its mouth, those were the only signs of life I saw in it. And you want to know the weird thing? It looked like—"

"What?"

"Like it knew something about me. It knew me. I know it sounds crazy. I—and I don't know why I did this—but I turned around and went back upstairs. And that was it. I didn't say a word about it—I told Mara everything was fine. I returned the gun to the safe and went to bed. Didn't wake again until the morning. It was the strangest thing. I didn't tell Mara what I saw it until some months later, after everything else happened."

"Everything else?"

"Yeah. There were other things. Presences." Steve exhales. Despite his initial misgivings, it feels good to talk about this stuff to someone other than Mara or one of her pseudo-psychic acquaintances.

"What other things? Other disturbances?"

"Yeah."

"Such as?" she asks.

Steve sits forward in his seat until his elbows are resting on his thighs, sliding his hands up his face and under his glasses. "Oh, god. It's ridiculous."

"This seems like it's hard for you to talk about," she says.

Steve lets an embarrassed laugh that comes out a bit too loud. "It's just that I feel embarrassed even mentioning it."

"Why?"

"I guess it's been a part of my life for so long. It makes no sense for me to keep it a secret. Especially here with you." Steve looks at her and she responds with an encouraging smile. "It was fascinating at first. There were the usual things you associated with a haunted house. Stuff would move, ya know? Like my keys, for instance. I'd leave them on the table—leave them in a certain spot, you know, and the next day they'd be in the kitchen or someplace else. I know, I know, that could just be my memory. But it happened to *both* of us. We even took pictures of where we left stuff just so we had proof for ourselves that we left the thing where we left it—keys, hats, gloves, whatever."

"Did you ever seek help?" she says.

"You mean like a ghost hunter?"

"Or a parapsychologist?"

"Yeah, we had everyone under the sun in that house at one point or another—anyone with that kind of title, anyway. A team from St. Ambrose was at the house twice. They made videos and sound recordings—cameras all over the damn house. Just like Poltergeist!"

"Fascinating! Did they find any proof?" she says.

"Yeah, I guess. This parapsychologist, Doctor Truman, said it was the most 'fruitful investigation' he's ever done. Picked up voices and some weird-looking stuff on the video. Strange temperature changes too—cold spots, or whatever. I never knew whether they were for real or bullshitters, but Mara seemed to buy into it."

"Did it scare her?"

"It did, and it didn't."

"Meaning?"

How do I explain Mara? he thinks to himself. "Mara gets freaked out by this stuff, but she's drawn to it. She fills her spare time reading book after book about hauntings and demons, or watching those ghost hunter shows on cable. But if I make a single joke about it, she gets mad at me like I might piss off something in the house. Max was the worst. He'd stay with us and call out into the house for a ghost to show itself. That used to get Mara all riled up, but she'd laugh about it. Max is like that. He lightens the mood."

"You told me in our last session Max is coming to visit soon."

"Yeah," Steve says, looking at the clock. "He's coming in this weekend. Friday night."

"You must be excited about that."

"I am. He hasn't been out here since last Christmas, I think."

"That's not very often."

"No, it's not. But that's the way it goes."

"Must be hard when you've only got the one sibling—"

"No, I've got two. My sister..." Steve's thoughts drift as his head suddenly feels cloudy and his vision blurs. The office goes out of focus. "My sister..." His eyes roll over to Dr. Nguyen, who is watching him, concerned. She's saying something, but he can't hear any sound coming from her mouth.

"I, uh..."

And just like that, it's rising in his chest. The anxiety. Panic. Wrapping his torso in a fat band of oppression, making it hard to breathe, cutting off his circulation. His vision turns a deep red, like a wave of blood washing down a camera lens. Steve sits forward in his chair to catch his breath. Suffocation overwhelms him, and he gasps for oxygen.

Dr. Nguyen kneels next to him, her hand on his forearm. "Steve! Steve! Breathe, just breathe. That's good. Fantastic. Deep breaths, just like that. Good."

They stay like this for some time until the episode passes. The blood wave dries from his vision and his hearing returns.

Just as Dr. Nguyen reaches for her phone to call 911, Steve stands. "It's OK. I'm better, actually. No need to call…"

"Are you sure? I really think you should—"

"NO, I'm good. I'm fine." He looks around him, embarrassed and dazed. "I should get going."

"No, stay. There's no rush. Just stay here and keep breathing."

But Steve brushes past her and out the door through the waiting room where he bustles past a young woman sitting with legs crossed, reading an old copy of Woman's Day magazine. She glances up from her reading with a strange express—one that is not quite a frown, and almost a smile.

Chapter Thirteen

1.

By the time Steve returned to Maquoketa, Dr. Nguyen had called four times, leaving one concerned message and a second directing him to listen to the original. As expected, she urged him to take a Xanax, which he had already done, and to call her as soon as he got the message, which he did not. She had cleared a space on Friday morning at ten.

"Okay, we'll see," he mutters to himself.

When he enters the coffee shop, Rose is leaning on the front counter, adding receipts. She looks up and grins. "Well, hello there. You're turning into a regular already."

Steve musters a light chuckle he hopes doesn't sound as forced as it feels. "I'm meeting someone here. Bob Baxter?"

"Oh, yeah, he's in the john. But he's sitting in the back booth, by the old cigarette machine," Rose says, pointing to the back. A coffee mug and a small cup of water sit on the near side of the booth.

"Does that cigarette machine still work?" Steve says, happy for the distraction. The anxiety has passed, but a tingling remains in his fingertips.

"Sort of. Those things are illegal now. But I love the look, so now I load it with little mini works of art by different local artists. Two bucks each, not too bad," she says.

"What an excellent idea."

"Yep. The artists get a buck, we get a buck."

"Next time, I'll bring quarters."

A man in his early thirties emerges from the men's room and looks down the aisle at Steve. He's about five-ten, African-American, sporting a gray sweatshirt and matching sweatpants. Though he can hardly be thirty or thirty-one, his eyes tell of a painful history and endless worry. He approaches and says, "Steve Spain?"

"Yep, that's me," Steve says, extending his hand.

"Bob Baxter," he says, taking Steve's hand and shaking it. He then gestures to the booth as Rose waits across from them.

"Would you like a coffee, Steve?" she says.

"Yes. Uh, decaf though."

"Gotcha," she says, turning to the coffeemaker.

"So, it doesn't look like Melly will make it," Baxter says. "She says she's sick."

"Ah, sorry to hear that."

Rose comes around the counter and sets a cup and saucer next to Steve. "Anything else I can bring you?"

"Nope, this should do," Steve replies and watches her cross back to her receipts. "So, I'm sure Melly told you I'm sort of helping her out a little."

Baxter shrugs. "You're looking into her daughter's case."

"That's right. I've got some time off, so I agreed to see what I could find out."

"She told me. Must be nice."

"What?"

"To take time off."

"Yes. I'm blessed."

Baxter takes a sip of his coffee and glances out the window, looking up and down the street. Tiny beads of perspiration cover his forehead, even though it's chilly in the diner. "I ain't got a lot to tell you."

"You were with the boys who saw Jessica Harmon after she went missing. Right?" Steve says.

Baxter clears his throat and takes a napkin from the chrome dispenser at the edge of the table. He folds it over his fingers and dabs his forehead with it. "Yeah, so we thought. Later we said we'd made a mistake. Didn't Melly tell you?"

"The police chief told me that."

"You already met the chief?" Baxter reaches for his water glass.

"Yep. He said you guys reported seeing the Harmon girl on a gravel road out by the Grant Wood byway."

Baxter nods, swallowing a mouthful of water. "Yeah. But like I said—like the chief told you—we made a mistake."

"That's true. I'm just checking and double-checking, you know."

"Right."

"No harm looking into it with a fresh pair of eyes."

"Yeah, true," Baxter says. Steve senses that he's struggling to contain his composure.

"She is still missing."

"You got that right."

"What time of day was it when you guys saw the girl?"

"Afternoon. We'd been out there for a while. Wasn't dark out yet, but getting dimmer. I recall it was kinda gloomy, you know? Must have been like four, four-thirty. Something like that. We were fixing to head home before long."

"And you were with Joey Milton, Frankie Trillo, Willy Trillo, and Don Loomis, right?"

Baxter glances out the window again, but this time he isn't looking for anyone. It's like his mind drifts off and his eyes follow. "Yeah, I was with them."

"Why were you out there? Seems like a long way outside of town."

"Oh, hell, not that far. Summers, we rode our bikes all over the county—not much else to do when you're a teenager in Maquoketa. But we loved going out there on account of this old stone bridge. There was a creek out that way and we'd catch crawdads and toads or whatnot—tell ghost stories and all that. But it only took us like twenty minutes to get home from there."

"And you saw a girl on that road?" Steve says. A chill sweeps over the skin of his bare arms.

"Yeah."

"Whom you took to be the Harmon girl, right?"

"Right."

"When did you discover you'd made a mistake?"

Still facing the window, Baxter pops a sideways glance at Steve. "What do you mean?"

"You told the sheriff that you guys had made a mistake—that you hadn't seen Jesse Harmon out there on the old road. Right?"

"Yeah, that's what I been sayin'. Was a mistake."

"Right. But I'm wondering when you decided you were mistaken." Steve takes a sip of his coffee but keeps his eyes trained on Baxter's.

Baxter's eyes shift from Steve to the table and back. "Oh, well, I guess it was—it was after we figured out it wasn't her."

Steve smiles and sets the coffee down. "How long was that?"

Baxter exhales. "Shit, I don't know, that was like fifteen years ago. But a few days, maybe."

"OK, good. That's good, thank you." Steve notes a shift in Baxter's disposition. His shoulders relax. "So, a few days later, you guys realized you'd made a mistake. Right?"

"Yeah, that's about right. Though, again, it was a long time ago."

"Oh, I get that, sure, sure. But within reason, it was a few days at most."

"Yeah, I guess that's safe to say."

"Why?" Steve says and Baxter's shoulders tense up again.

"What do you mean?" Baxter slides down in the booth an inch or two.

"What made you believe you were mistaken about the girl?"

"Well, I didn't get that good of a look at her myself. I mean, not really. And Don said he never saw her at all. It was Joey who said it was a mistake. He was the one who said it was Jesse to begin with."

Steve nods. "Did he try to get her attention?"

"Yes. He called out to her and waved."

"How did she respond?"

Baxter's eyes float up to the ceiling. "She—she just stood there, kinda creepy-like, looking at us. Then she shuffled into the woods off the side of the road."

"What did you guys do?"

"We followed her. Joey was shouting her name, real loud. Willy and Frankie ran ahead of us and we split up and searched the area, but couldn't find nothing. So we rode our bikes back to town and told the police."

Steve notices the man's eyes again. There's a slippery honesty in them. "OK. And then?"

"Then? Uh, Joey called me a few days later and said he'd made a mistake. We hadn't seen Jesse Harmon, that it was one of the Tupper girls. And so I kinda adjusted to his story, I guess you could say."

"Do the Tupper's live in that area?"

"Mm hm. Just down the road a piece."

"Do the Tupper girls have blond hair? Do they look like Jesse?"

"Not exactly. But it was getting dark."

"And that was it?"

Baxter looks above Steve's head. "Yeah, that was it."

Steve leans onto the table, his forearms resting in front of him, his hands clasped, staring into Baxter's eyes. "Bob. What are you not saying?"

"I don't—"

"What do you think happened out there on that old road? Why did you come here to meet me today? I expect there must be a reason, or why waste your time? Why keep in touch with Melly all these years?" Steve holds his gaze and Baxter drops his eyes, red and rimmed with tears.

"Just between me and you?"

Steve gives a firm nod.

"It was dark, like I said, and Joey was closer to where the girl was standing than I was. I mean, he was on the other side of the bridge from me, and I couldn't make out her face. But…" He clears his throat and takes a drink of water, then shakes his head and rolls his eyes. "But it never sat well with me, I guess you could say."

"Why?" Steve says.

"It's gonna sound dumb, but I don't think the girl we saw out there that night was a Tupper. I believe it was Jesse Harmon—I believe it in my heart. And I think there's a good reason we couldn't find her when we went looking. I think she wasn't real. She wasn't—*alive*." Baxter's eyes drift from Steve to the window, then down to the table and back to Steve.

"You mean—"

"I know it sounds nuts. Believe me."

Steve squints at him. "You mean—"

"I mean—" Baxter checks around them to see if anyone is listening. "I mean, I think we saw a ghost."

Steve inhales and holds his breath for several seconds before releasing it through his nose. He nods and glances at Rose, who is still across the diner at the front counter, staring at her phone. "A ghost?"

"I said it sounds stupid. But it's what I think."

"No, I understand why you might think you saw a ghost. It was dark and out there in the middle of nowhere. Why would the girl be out there? Ya know? I get it. But maybe it was one of the Tupper girls? Didn't the Tuppers confirm that one of their girls was out there?"

"No."

"They didn't? So why did the police accept that explanation?"

"Shit, if I know. But I talked to that Tupper girl myself. The only one around Jesse's age was Emma. Emma told the cops she wasn't even home—said she was at the library until closing time. Couldn't have been her."

"What about the other Tupper girls?"

"They were all way younger. Shit, we'd never mistake them for Jesse. Not in a million years."

"Did you tell the police?"

"No. But it didn't matter—the cops already knew." Baxter rubs his forehead.

"What do you mean?"

"They talked to Emma and all the other Tupper girls."

"In that case, why did they stick to that story?"

"Beats me. But I kinda figured they must have had some other info. Shit, I was like fifteen. What was I gonna do about it? But as the years went on and they never found her and never had a single frigging suspect, I'd go back to that night in my mind. I had visions about it. Shit, still do. I wish…" Baxter puts his face in his hands.

"What? What do you wish?"

"I don't know. I wish I'd done something. Anything."

They sit in silence for a time while Steve runs over his notes. "Okay, take me back. Take me back to that night on the road. After Joey Milton first saw the girl and you searched the woods. Did you see any sign of the girl?"

Baxter shakes his head. "No. Nothing. Not a trace of her. It was like she disappeared. And we looked all over the place until it was almost too dark to see. We would have found her if she'd been there. If she'd wanted to be found."

Another chill runs up Steve's back. "How about the other guys? You ever talk about that night since then?" Steve says.

"Not really. You know Joey Milton killed himself, right?"

Steve nods. "Yes."

"Frank and Willy I've lost touch with."

"Where are they now?"

"They work at a garage over in Delmar. But I'd avoid them if I were you."

"Why is that?"

"They ain't the friendly types. And with this subject, they get downright mean. Don't take to people snooping around, asking questions and all that. I'd be careful."

"So, what are you saying?"

"Not saying anything. But you need to be careful." Baxter looks out the window and freezes.

Steve follows his gaze. Across the street, a decrepit Ford sits around the corner of an old brick building—the Lunsford Tackle and Bait Shoppe. A reflection blocks the driver's side of the front windshield. "Do you know that truck?"

Baxter swallows, then glances back at Steve. "Don't worry about that. You just be careful." He leans in to whisper. "This town doesn't want that girl found, you hear me? They don't want anyone found."

"What do you mean by, 'anyone?' Are there other missing kids?"

Baxter glances out the window again. "This was all I got to say. I've done my part, OK? That girl on the road was Jesse. I know it. It was dark, and she was far away and all that, but I *know* it was her. I've always known. Haven't said it out loud much, but I know." He checks the window again. "But that's all I can say. The rest is up to you. Good luck."

Steve stares at the man's back as he departs the diner. When he glances out the window again, the truck is gone. He stands, pays for the coffee, and heads to his car. Moments later, he's heading out of town toward the old road.

2.

Steve parks his car next to a small ditch just before a decrepit stone bridge, and turns off the engine. Peering out the windshield, he gathers his thoughts. This case is cold, but it shouldn't be. Four kids said they saw the girl on this very road on the other side of the old stone bridge only a couple dozen yards away. The road is darkening and silent.

"What is it?" he asks himself. "Why am I out here? This happened fifteen years ago. What the hell am I doing out here?"

He pushes open the car door and steps out onto the dusty gravel, his Florsheims awkward on the crumbled rocks. The tranquility of the place is unexpected, and save for a chill in the air. He waits there for a time, staring across the bridge, as if expecting Jesse Harmon to come skipping out of the woods beyond.

He moves to the bridge and looks over the small stone railing. A narrow creek runs over smoothed stones, carrying random leaves away toward the Upper Iowa River and all the way to the Mississippi.

A memory hits him out of nowhere—an icy river and a small red coat floating beneath him under the ice. A pale face staring through the frost at him, eyes wide in terror. Steve almost loses his balance. Placing one hand on the side of the bridge, he gathers himself. Taking deep breaths, the memory recedes.

As his vision returns, his eyes follow the winding creek back into the trees where it winds to the right until yellow and orange leaves cover it. In his mind, he pictures another bridge, much like this one, though in the memory it is bright daylight and the leaves are in their full summer glorious green. Liesl is running and laughing, carrying a toy of his, a Star Wars figure.

As quick as it flashes into his mind, it pops away, leaving him back in the dim gray of the present. However, the reminiscence stays with him—it waits like a rotten smell from an open refrigerator. He sways.

"Easy, now," he says to himself. "Get back to the car before you face-plant off this bridge into the creek. Who will find you if that happens?" Then another voice speaks. If it's in his mind or on the wind, Steve cannot tell.

No one knows you're here...

Searching for the voice, Steve sees only colored leaves descending from crooked branches, dancing across the cold dry ground. He cuts a look back to the creek and notes his heartbeat. It's increasing with each passing moment and a panic hits him all at once—one that further threatens his tenuous equilibrium. Stumbling across the loose rocks back to the car, he lurches onto the driver's side door and pulls himself into the vehicle.

Resting his head on the wheel, Steve catches his breath and waits for the world to slow its whirl before he lifts his eyes to peer out over the shining black hood to the bridge and the woods beyond. For a moment, and only a moment, he thinks he glimpses a pale figure with long golden hair standing maybe fifty yards past the bridge, just at the edge of the timbers. But when his eyes refocus, it is gone.

Steve starts the car, makes a sharp u-turn, and rumbles back down the road, yellowish gravel dust mercifully obscuring the rear view.

Chapter Fourteen

1.

Mara's car rumbles down 241st Avenue as the sky becomes a darker gray than usual. She checks the time on the dash. It's 5:20. Another ten minutes and the street lamps come to life—that is, if there *were* street lamps on this remote road.

As Mara comes around the last bend, she notices a dark green pickup sitting off to the side—two wheels on, two wheels off—just past her driveway across the road, right where Rocky likes to do his business. The truck's tinted windows obscure the view into the cab. Mara doesn't recognize the vehicle, though she rarely pays attention to such things. It must be one of Jensen's crew doing some kind of work on his property.

She turns down her drive to see another car—this one she recognizes. It's an old Mercedes from the 70s, a 240D, and one that's been well-maintained, though you'd never know by appearances. The exterior was long ago sanded down for a paint job that still hasn't happened. However, the interior is in remarkable shape and the engine could run another two hundred thousand miles.

"Nadine," Mara whispers with a grin.

A petite, curvaceous woman with long red hair glides around the corner of the house as Mara cuts off the engine. In her early forties, Nadine is beautiful and wild, an honest to god flower child with a wicked sparkle in her eyes and a sharp cheshire cat grin. As soon as Mara emerges from the car, Nadine envelopes her in a long soft hug.

"Oh, honey, this place is amazing," Nadine whispers into her ear, holding tight to her and kissing her on the neck before releasing her grasp. She takes Mara by the hands and pulls away, spreading her arms to the sides to get a good look at her. "Oh my, you look scrumptious. Have you lost weight?"

Mara blushes and smiles. "A bit. I wasn't trying to lose, but the move was kinda stressful, but we did it. Speaking of scrumptious, don't you look lovely?"

Nadine laughs, releases her hands, and gives a light spin, sending her long frilled skirt flying out around her revealing her athletic legs and giving away the fact she is not wearing underwear, showing off her perfect heart-shaped behind and untrimmed pubic region.

Mara laughs out loud. "My *goodness*, Nadine. You are not a shy one, now are you?"

"Why should I be? It's only what the goddess gave me, don't you know? And I don't mind people knowing I'm a natural redhead."

"Well, I have no further doubts about that."

They laugh together, and Nadine takes Mara by the face and kisses her on each cheek. Mara breathes deep and, grabbing Nadine by the hand, leads her into the house where Rocky is sitting in the hall with one paw lifted.

"Sweet heaven! There's my handsome boy!" Nadine kicks off her sandals and rushes to kneel in front of Rocky. She wraps her arms around his giant neck and kisses his wrinkled head. Rocky kisses her back with one long, wet tongue before shaking her off to pounce on Mara. "Oh, I see how it is! Throw me off for Mom, huh?"

"He's a momma's boy, it's true," Mara says as she ruffles the top of Rocky's head. "But he's still Steve's dog, make no mistake."

Nadine giggles, an airy sound like a peel of bells ringing in the fall air, and she dances into the living room, her perfect little toes barely touching the wood floors. She stops at the back windows and stares out into the yard. The dim light from the outside shines through her skirt and Mara looks away.

"Oh, honey, what a view," Nadine says. "I mean, I knew when I visited last Spring—back when this was just a hole in the ground—that you'd have a pretty view, but I never realized just how wonderful it would be. And the fall colors!"

"They're something, aren't they," Mara says, joining her.

Nadine takes Mara's hand, still staring through the glass. "Hm."

"What?" Mara says, her heart jumping a beat.

A mysterious expression comes over Nadine's face. She's smiling, but her eyes are scanning the woods with an unsettlingly familiar intensity. Nadine turns to Mara and shakes herself away from whatever thoughts had been troubling her. "It's nothing. This is a beautiful home, Mara. You both must be thrilled." She runs her hands up Mara's arms and across her shoulders. She squeezes down on each shoulder and closes her eyes. "You're stressed, aren't you?"

Mara takes a deep breath. "Yes."

"And it's not just the move, is it?".

"No."

Nadine turns Mara to face her back and kneads each shoulder, one after the other, inhaling and exhaling, searching the muscles and tendons with meticulous zeal. She opens her eyes and says, "OK. I'll get my table from the car and give you a proper session—massage and reiki, maybe a little shiatsu too, for good measure."

"No, Nadine, you don't have to do that. I didn't invite you out here to work—I wanted to *see* you, show you the new place, and make you some dinner, that's all."

"Shush," Nadine says, leaning in and kissing Mara on the check. "You need it and I love you. There's no arguing. I can sense the stress in your body and I don't like it. I wouldn't dream of leaving this house without offering you some relief. Understood? Oh, and no need to cook. I brought you something delicious."

Mara smiles. "Oh, fine. I have to admit, I could use some energy work."

Nadine taps the tip of Mara's nose. "Ding! That's more like it. I'll bring in my table and set up. Where do you prefer?"

"Well, I suppose in the downstairs office to the left. Steve should be home soon, so I'll leave him a note."

"Perfect. Now, you go take a hot shower and I'll get set up. I'll find the office."

2.

Nadine listens at the foot of the basement stairs until she hears the brief squeal of water turning on and the crack of the shower door being closed. She stares into the lower family room. To her right is a short hall with two doors on either side—to her left is another similar hall and doorway setup. A door to her left is open six inches. This must be the office.

She carries her massage table into the open door and flips on the light. There is an L-shaped desk hugging the far wall, with a built-in bookcase surrounding it. Aside from a filing cabinet and a small table and lamp, the room is empty, save for an Asian rug in the middle. Nadine smiles and removes the table from its carrying case, then unfolds it and covers it with white flannel sheets. She sets her lotion on the desk then tiptoes back into the living area. Listening for a moment, she hears the water still running upstairs.

Tiptoeing across the den, she peeks her head into the guest bedroom to the right. A window curtain ruffles in a slow but firm breeze. Then, just as Nadine is about to close the door, she notices something in the corner. A misty figure hovers lightly behind the billowing curtain, glaring at her with a familiar malice. Nadine smirks and says, "You again? I thought we had an understanding, you and I. Well, suit yourself."

After closing the guest room, she returns to the den and crosses to the sliding glass door at the end of the room. Drawing the curtain with her hand, she peers into the backyard. Darkness has almost set, making it hard to see past the glare reflected by the basement lights. She unlatches the lock and slides the door far enough to fit her head through the opening. The smell of fall emanates from the forest and she gives her widest smile, closing her eyes with a deep inhale of air. However, soon the smile fades and she levels a deadly stare into the wooded ravine. She thinks about stepping outside, but the sound of movement upstairs stops her.

Mara calls from the top of the stairs. "Be down in a minute, Nadine. You find the office?"

Nadine closes the sliding door silently and skitters back toward the stairs. "Um, yes! I found it—all set up. Come down when you're ready."

She frowns at the sliding door.

3.

Mara is lost in bliss. Nadine's hands, always knowing, always intuitive—intelligent even—roll over her upper back. She can't picture how the woman does it, but she's thankful to be the recipient. "I must watch you do this sometime. I can't understand how you get your hands to do this," Mara says, not sure if Nadine can hear her through the face hole.

Nadine laughs. "Oh, a witch never gives away her secrets."

"That's not fair. I bet you keep the men happy with those hands."

"And women," Nadine whispers with a light laugh that blows a light puff of breath across Mara's ear.

Mara blushes once again, feeling goosebumps rise on her back. She hopes they're not too noticeable.

Answering her fear, Nadine says, "Oh, relax, Mara. These hands know their place."

Mara thinks of protesting or making up a defense, but Nadine's smooth fingers find a tightness in her right scapula she didn't know was there, sending all other thoughts from her mind. She floats in a cloud for a small eternity before she hears Nadine clear her throat as her hands roll fluidly to the back of Mara's left thigh, shifting into long slow movements up and down from the gluteus to just above the backs of her knee. "Mara."

"Yes?"

"How do you like the house?"

"We...love...it."

"Good. That's good."

Something in Nadine's tone pulls Mara out of her revelry and wakes her from the dream-like world she'd drifted into. "Why?"

"Just curious, that's all. Don't worry about it. Relax." With that, Nadine's hands shift into a movement, crossing in and out, above and under each other, together and apart—a kind of dance that drags Mara back into a deeper ecstasy. By the time Nadine has reached her feet, Mara is already asleep.

4.

Steve squeezes the steering wheel as he looks out the windshield at the old Mercedes sitting in his spot in the driveway. He rolls his eyes and pulls in behind Mara's car.

"Nadine," he says. The woman always arrives at the least convenient time.

When he enters the house Steve pays Rocky a simple pat on the head, brushing past him to the kitchen where he sees a familiar redheaded woman standing at the stove, mixing something in a pan. She turns to him and gives an enormous smile, then dances across the room to him and wraps her arms around his neck with an exaggerated flourish.

"Welcome home, Mr. Spain," she says and kisses him on the mouth.

Steve pulls away from her, and she giggles, returning to the stove. She's always had a lack of boundaries, but even for her, this is bold.

"Didn't know you were coming out." He sets his car keys on the counter and checks his phone.

"Thought you could use some company out here in this wilderness. Plus, I wanted to see the new digs. Very nice."

"Where's Mara?" Rocky lopes over to him and sniffs his pants.

"Oh, she's basking in the glow of one of my famous body energy sessions. She was sleeping when I left her. You should try it sometime, Mr. Stuffy-pants."

"I'm not stuffy," he says, looking at the stove. "What's that you're making?"

In the window's reflection, he sees her turn and smile at his back. "Just some of my famous chili, that's all."

"Yum," he says. "I do remember you make a mean chili."

"Why, thank you, honey."

He flinches. "Don't call me that."

"What? You don't want to play house with me?" She laughs again. "What shall I call you then?"

"Steve. Just Steve."

"That's no fun. I prefer honey."

"I don't," he says and jogs down the stairs to the basement. He finds Mara lying on her back, the massage blanket barely covering her body. One leg is exposed to her pelvis and the corner of the blanket only just hides her right nipple. She is fast asleep. Steve feels blood rush through him and he reaches out to touch her, warm and radiant in the aftermath of whatever spell Nadine cast upon her. The woman, as annoying as she can be, gives an amazing massage.

"Love," he says, touching her arm. "You asleep?"

"Hmm?" she says, turning to him. "Oh, hey there. Sorry, I'm just so tired. Nadine worked me good. You need her to do this to you, Steve."

"Yeah. Maybe." He pulls his hand back to his side. "Uh, looks like she's cooking. You should come up."

"OK. Give me a few." She moans and yawns wide. "I'm all tingly." Moments later, she's asleep again, her breathing heavy and slow.

Steve closes the door behind him and returns to the upstairs to see Nadine standing, hands at her sides in the middle of the kitchen, staring at him. She is naked—no underwear, no bra—nothing covering her at all. Her voluptuous body is soft and pale. Her breasts, large and round, sit perfectly in the middle of her chest and a full red bush covers the entire area inches below her navel. She is natural and beautiful like a woodland queen and she stands there unashamed, as if to be an offering.

Steve opens his mouth but cannot speak.

"Hello, honey," she says. "How would you like me?"

"I—what are you talking—"

"Oh, Steve, don't be shy. Just say what you want. Just say what you need from me. I'm yours for the next twenty minutes—that's how long she'll be asleep."

"Who?" Steve says, his voice cracking. His mouth is dry.

"Your wife. Mara. She'll be asleep a while longer, I think. She'll be asleep while we do as we wish."

Steve looks at Rocky, sitting by the French doors watching him, his head tilted as if he too cannot believe what he's seeing. Then Steve realizes Rocky looks fuzzy sitting over there. Everything is fuzzy, like someone has covered the entire world in gauze. "I, uh. Nadine, that's not happening. Put your clothes...back...on."

In a blink, he is back in the downstairs office, standing above Mara, who is still asleep on the massage table. His head swims. That schizophrenic place between dreaming and waking, where nothing seems real and everything seems possible. It's as if not a moment has passed since he stood here before, like something transported him back in time.

"Mara?" he says, looking around at the office. Had he dreamed of seeing Nadine in the kitchen? "Mara?"

She stirs again, her breasts exposed now, and she rubs her eyes, then looks up at him. She smiles and giggles and says, "Oh, hi. Gosh, I'm tired. I can't believe I fell asleep."

"Yeah. You must have been tired."

"I guess. Is Nadine still here?" She says, covering herself with the small blanket.

"I don't know. Maybe?"

"What do you mean, maybe?" Mara laughs. "Here, hand me my robe. She's making us her famous chili. Mm I can smell it. Can't you?"

His head feels like it's swimming. As Mara stands and puts on her robe, he stares down at the massage table and feels nauseous.

"You OK, honey?" she says.

"Don't call me that," he snaps back.

"What?" Mara says, confused. "Call you what?"

Steve holds his gaze on the table and closes his eyes. "Nevermind. Sorry. My head is killing me. I feel dizzy."

She pats him on the back and opens the door, stepping into the hall. "It's OK. I feel a little light-headed too. I'm gonna see if she needs help."

As the sound of Mara's footsteps fades up the stairs, Steve opens his eyes and looks again at the table. There in the middle is a tiny wet spot soaking into the cream flannel sheets.

5.

Steve stares at the bowl of hot chili mixed with broken saltine crackers and melted cheddar. His vision is clearing, little by little. Across the table, Mara savors a spoonful of the spicy chili. Nadine sits to his right.

Nadine says, "Are you feeling OK, Steve? Aren't you hungry? Pretty sure you worked up an appetite, didn't you?"

Steve coughs. "What?"

"Today. Mara said you were running around all day. Aren't you hungry?"

At her mention of it, he realizes he is indeed quite hungry. Starving. "Yeah, I am."

Steve scoops his oversized spoon into the muck and pulls a heaping pile into his mouth. It's spicy and full of flavor—meaty and mushy—and his head seems to clear almost as soon as he tastes the chili. At once, his mood lightens and a warmth spreads throughout his muscles and skin. He smiles and says, "It's wonderful." He laughs.

Nadine claps her hands and laughs with him. "Oh, good!"

"Nadine, did I tell you Max is coming to visit? He'll be here Friday afternoon," Mara says.

"Really? I have yet to meet this one," Nadine says, then turns to Steve. "When was the last time you saw him?"

"Last Christmas," Steve replies.

"You must be excited. He's coming for Halloween?" Nadine sounds a little too interested in this news.

"Yep. His favorite holiday. Hasn't been out here for a proper fall in some years."

Mara says, "It's like ninety degrees in October out there in Los Angeles. Can you believe that?"

"Oh, I believe it," Nadine says. "I lived out there for a few years in the early two-thousands. The heat just about killed me."

"I could never live out there," Steve says. "Too much traffic, too many people. It would drive me nuts."

Nadine asks, "And the heat?"

"Yeah that too."

"Says the guy who moved as far away from people as he could get," Mara says.

They laugh together, even Steve. "Yeah, Max and I are alike in some ways, not so much in others."

"He's coming with us to the Jensen's big Halloween bash this weekend. Hey, you should come too! You'd like Max and I'm sure he'd *love* you." Mara looks at Steve. "What do you think?"

"Yeah, that's a great idea," he says. "He's always complaining of being a third wheel when he visits."

"Sure! I'd love to meet him." Nadine giggles and takes a sip of wine. "So what kind of party do these country folk throw?"

Steve shrugs. "No idea. I guess people from all around come to it, though. But I'm sure you've got plenty of other things to do, it being the weekend before Halloween and all."

Mara says, "Yeah. Don't feel you have to come. I doubt it's anything big."

Nadine shakes her head. "Nope, I have nothing going on at all. I'd love to join you guys for some backwoods Samhain shenanigans. And meeting another Spain boy would be rad as hell."

"Rad?" Mara says.

"Don't make fun of me, little southern miss. You know I'm a total nineties girl."

As the chili continues to work its magic, Steve smiles at Mara—the warmest smile he's given anyone in days, maybe even weeks. She meets his gaze with an equal smile and heavy eyelids. "Oh my," she says through a sudden yawn. "I could go to bed right now and I'd be asleep before my head hit the pillow. I'm so relaxed. What did you do to me, doll?"

"Remember? I have magic fingers." Nadine winks and gives a sideways glance at Steve and a wink.

Steve's smile fades.

"Maybe you could do something for our little visitors," Mara says, taking another spoonful.

"What do you mean?" Nadine says.

Mara covers her mouth to speak. "Oh, we've got something out there in the woods. I'm just sure."

"Really? Like the last house?" Nadine says, her eyebrows raised in the devil's arches.

"I don't know about that. Not like that," Steve says, touching her forearm without thinking. Her skin is almost too warm for the temperature in the room, but there's something else. She feels electric. A jolt runs through him and he pulls his hand away.

She glances at his hand and smiles up at him. "It's not a ghost? Maybe it's a coyote, or what? A bobcat!"

"Do we have coyotes out here?" Mara says.

"Well, sure. You can run across them sometimes when you're hunting. Or early in the morning. In the evening."

"I forgot you're a hunter." Nadine says.

"Not anymore. Used to deer hunt, but I gave it up."

"Why?"

Mara takes a sip of wine. "He tired of it."

Steve smiles at her, appreciating the attempt to save him from an embarrassing story. "No, it's OK, honey," he says to her, then looks at Nadine. "I lost the desire, I guess you could say."

Nadine says, "I suppose it's like anything, right? You do it long enough, it gets boring."

Steve says, "Yeah, but it's more than that. I went out one day with a couple friends and we came upon a buck—big one, twenty points. You don't see them that big around here, too many cornfields and not enough cover. But this place was wooded, kind of like here. This guy had a hundred acres, unfarmed and unhunted for years, so the deer population had run amok, eating up all the vegetation. They were having a huge effect on the ecosystem and starving.

"Anyway, there were deer everywhere, a herd of them, just standing there. I didn't understand what the hell was going on. Why didn't they run? But before I could ask, one guy just let loose with an arrow, then everyone followed. It was like shooting fish in a barrel. No sport at all. But worst of all—the worst part of the whole thing was the sounds. They made these horrible screams I'd never heard before. It was disturbing."

"Even though hunting them was more humane than letting them starve to death?" Nadine says.

"Well, yeah, I guess that was the point for us to be there. But it still felt ugly. Kinda mechanical, if you know what I mean. Deer everywhere—we just had to lift our bows and let loose. No sport. It's just *manage-ment*—which I get, I do. But still—"

"It doesn't feel wild." Nadine puts a warm, electric hand on his arm and squeezes.

"I guess. But that was the end of that hobby."

Mara says, "So, now we buy enormous properties and build houses on them." She laughs.

Nadine takes Mara's hand with her right hand, then takes Steve's in her left, palms up, her fingers spread and wiggling in invitation. Her skin is soft as he places his hand onto hers, and her fingers wrap around the side of his palm, their nails natural but manicured. She squeezes their hands and lets out a long exhale before speaking. "I have something to say."

Mara says, "Yes? What is it?"

Nadine smiles at each of them. "I sense something here."

"Shit," Steve says.

Mara lowers her head. "Are you sure?"

"Yes."

"But this house is brand new. How could there be ghosts?" Mara says.

"I didn't say ghosts, and it's not the house. Nothing has happened in this house—no murders, no suicides, no death at all. The two of you haven't so much as had sex here yet."

Steve glares across the table at Mara, releasing Nadine's hand.

Mara lets go of the other and waves her own hands in protest. "I never said a word to her, Steve. Honest!"

"She didn't. I sense it from both of you."

"The meds I'm on make it hard to—get *hard*," Steve says, feeling the color rush to his face. In his periphery, Mara shoots a look of death at Nadine, crossing her arms and tilting her head the way she does when she's about to give someone a piece of her mind.

"I'm not judging either of you, or your relationship," Nadine says, avoiding Mara's coming onslaught. "Please believe me in that. The point is, I don't believe the presence is in the house. It may enter, but it comes from outside. Out there." She points out the back windows.

Mara says, "What makes you think something's here?"

"I don't think it—I *feel* it. All around us. You can't tell me you don't feel it too. I know you do." Nadine's eyes shift back and forth between them.

"So, what is it?" Mara says.

"Good question, but you'd know better than me. Has something happened?"

Mara looks to Steve with a borderline pleading expression, as if begging to tell her everything. Steve nods and Mara exhales. "Yes, a few strange things have happened. Nothing major, not like the last house, but still—"

"Such as?" Nadine asks.

Mara turns to Steve again with a pleading look. "Honey?"

Steve sighs. "Mara was out of the house walking in the back the other night. Kind of like before."

"Sleep walking?"

Mara says, "No. I mean, not exactly."

Nadine says, "Like before?"

"Yes," they reply in unison.

"But that's not all," Mara says. "We've seen something. I know I saw something out there in the woods the other night—past the tree line. The sound of it woke me up, and I looked out the windows. Rocky was barking and growling like crazy, too. And then what Steve saw—"

Nadine leans into the table, clasping her hands before her. "Steve?"

"Hell, I don't know. With the meds I'm on and all—"

"Those meds don't cause hallucinations," Mara says.

Nadine lifts a hand to quiet her. "Did you see something?"

Steve nods.

"Outside?"

Steve peers at her over the tops of his glasses. "Yeah," he says, hesitating.

"Have you seen anything inside the house?"

Steve looks down at his chili. "Yeah."

"What was it?"

"I don't know." The three words felt like lying.

Nadine says, "Steve, don't feel embarrassed about it."

"I don't," he snaps.

Nadine and Mara both stare at him with looks so piteous it drives him to stand. "Look, I don't know what I saw, OK? I have no fucking clue what's in this goddamn house anymore than I knew what the hell what in the last house! What does it matter anyway? What do any of my fucking problems have to do with anything when the whole goddamn world has gone to shit? I will not sit here and complain. I've got a beautiful house, a wonderful wife, and a life most people would kill for. A founding partner of a prosperous law firm—everything is amazing!" Steve stops, realizing the pity on the ladies' faces has morphed into worry. "Fuck it. I need air. Come on, Rocky."

Out in the cool night air, Steve watches as the Mastiff scurries over the dirty back yard, tail up and nose to the ground. Trotting over to a small tree, he lifts his leg.

6.

"What was that about?" Nadine says, eyes wide with an odd twinkle.

Mara stares at Steve through the window. "You know."

Nadine shrugs. "After all that has happened, he still can't come to grips with it? He can't believe. And he's such an intelligent man."

Mara levels a narrow look at Nadine. The woman is impossible to read—there's always underlying subtext in her tone. "It's hard for him. You know that."

"He's stubborn." Nadine takes Mara's hands. "You must forgive him, Mara. There are things in this world he's not ready to face, or maybe he can't see what you and I see."

"Forgive him? There's nothing to forgive. He'll come around in his own time. And deep down, he knows it's all true, but I think his anxiety makes it hard. It controls him sometimes."

Nadine kisses her hand. Her lips are soft and wet. "He's fighting it. The time will come when he'll give in, but I think it will take something for that to happen."

"What?" Mara says.

"Hard to say." Nadine maintains eye contact, but her eyes seem to focus on something far away, as if following a thought or a memory. Shaking her head, she stands. "Anyhow, I should get out of your hair. I hope you liked the food."

Mara doesn't let go of her hands. "I mean it. Steve's a good man—he's just going through something right now. But when he's on the other side, you'll see, he will come around."

"I don't doubt it one bit." Nadine leans in to her, giving one long kiss that tastes like honey and fresh mint. Mara's heart races and she almost pulls away, but Nadine releases her. "Let me say goodbye to Steve real quick."

Mara feels a twinge of jealousy, but she nods and says, "I need to use the restroom."

7.

The French doors open behind Steve, and without glancing back, he knows it's not Mara. Keeping his attention fixed on the woods, he says, "Sorry about that."

Nadine slips next to him and puts an arm around his waist. He wraps his arm around her shoulders, bringing relief from the chill air like a random warm spot in a murky lake. "No need for apologies," she says, her voice once again like the ringing of bells, warming his heart unexplainably. "It's been a stressful time, packing and moving. Anyone would be a little—off."

"It's not only that."

"True. But all the commotion can't have helped."

"I guess." Steve scans the trees but now only sees leaves and branches and trunks. The woods feel to him as empty as an open grave. "What's out there?"

Nadine leans her head into the crook of his arm, looking into the woods. "Animals and plants and earth and dead things—and something more. I wouldn't venture too far into those woods, certainly not alone. Whatever's out there, leave it be."

"Problem is—it doesn't stay outside."

"Nothing ever does."

8.

Steve closes the front door as he hears Nadine's car rumble away down the dirt road. He wipes his lips and shakes his head. Rocky passes by him and Steve pats him on the head as the dog lumbers through the living room to his XXL-sized bed near the fireplace. The last embers are glowing red and there is a growing chill in the house. Reaching to the thermostat, Steve bumps the heat a notch, then hits the lights and heads to the bathroom.

Once he's brushed his teeth and his clothes are off, he finds Mara lying wide awake in bed, her eyes fixed on the ceiling. He slides under the sheets and lies facing her. She says, "What a strange night."

"Yeah."

"What was in that wine?"

"Beats me. But it's got me all cloudy-headed."

"Yeah, I feel like I dozed off, like I only remember bits and pieces. Isn't that weird?"

"I'd say it must have been the massage, but I feel that way too. What did Nadine put in that chili of hers? I feel like I was just outside with her." Steve grunts a laugh.

Mara says, "Oh, her hands are magic. But she was acting weird, don't you think? Flirtatious."

"She's always flirtatious."

"Yeah, but not like this. This was different."

The cloudiness overtaking him, Steve feels like his eyes might slam shut any moment. "Yeah—it was uncomfortable."

When Mara speaks, he hears the cloudiness her in voice. "Odd thing is…I didn't mind…so much. Isn't…that…odd?"

"Yeah…"

Mara rolls herself over to him and gives him one long kiss, then slides her hand into his sweats. "I think it's time we made something *happen* in this house."

Despite the drowsiness, the bizarre fuzziness of his mind—despite the anti-anxiety meds—a preternatural desire awakens within him. He takes her head in both hands and returns her kiss.

The wind outside blows, whipping around the house with a whistling force. Through the howling, Steve hears a soft voice whispering to him in words he does not recognize. A chant that seems to envelop his mind in a rich haze of euphoria. As the voice continues, a desire rises within him. His hand moves across Mara's neck and down her chest, feeling for a moment her rising nipples through the soft material of her t-shirt. As his hand continues down her body, Steve senses a sensation he's never felt before, electric and wild. Mara's body twitches as his fingers move over her stomach.

As Mara climbs on top of him, images flash through Steve's mind. Images not of Mara, but of their guest. Nadine, nude in the kitchen. Kissing him. Lying under him as dead leaves crunch under her back. Nadine standing over a massage table with Mara lying face down, her fingers exploring under the flannel sheet, glancing back at him and winking. Images flash repeating, overlapping, picking up speed until Steve can think of nothing else. Nothing but Nadine. Opening his eyes, he sees Mara, moving on top of him to some unheard rhythm, her eyes squeezed shut, eyebrows raised, as if the same images are flooding her own mind. Is it his imagination, or is the room bathed in a glowing green light?

Movement draws his attention to the window. Steve thinks he sees the shadowy semi-translucent image of a woman floating on the air outside, her arms and hands outstretched, her hedonistic figure framed by the crooked branches of the darkened woods—her red hair and dress both whipped to the side by the growing power of the October wind. Her bright green eyes glow in the darkness as Steve and Mara move together to a secret, magic rhythm.

CHAPTER FIFTEEN

Steve drives into Delmar, Iowa, at around two in the afternoon. There isn't much in this little town but a Casey's General Store, a post office, a modest school building long ago boarded up and closed, and a greasy garage called Trillo Repair. As Steve pulls to the curb just outside the shop, he recognizes two men, one with short black hair and another with long, almost-blond hair, standing on either side of a rusted 2001 Toyota Camry. The blond is pointing towards the front hood as the other rubs his face, head bowed. Both are in dingy gray coveralls, smeared in old grease. A green Ram pickup sits at the side of the white stone building.

Grabbing a legal notepad and pen, Steve steps out of his car. As he approaches the open garage door, the men look at him. The blond leans against the Camry and the other steps towards Steve.

"Hello, there," Steve says, holding out his hand to the dark-haired man. "How's it going?"

Not taking his hand, the man says, "Not too shabby. Nice car," with a contemptuous tone.

"Thanks. I got it last Spring." Steve sees he has a patch on his chest with the name *Frankie* embroidered on it. "Frankie Trillo?"

"Yep."

Steve turns to the other one. "And that makes you Willy."

"Yep," the blond grunts.

"Nice to meet you, fellas. I'm Steve Spain and—"

"We know who you are," Frankie says.

"Oh, you do? How's that?" Steve says.

"Word gets around. What do you want?"

"I wanted to ask you some questions."

"You a cop?" Frankie crosses his arms.

Willy's eyes shift back and forth between them, then he turns his back to Steve. Obviously, he's content to let Frankie handle this conversation. Steve gets the feeling someone tipped them off to his visit. But who?

"Nope. I'm a lawyer."

"What's a lawyer want with us?"

"Oh, I'm not here on any official capacity as a lawyer. I'm following up on some stuff for a friend."

Frankie shrugs. "What's it about? We don't know shit about anything."

"You remember a girl named Jesse Harmon?" Steve says.

"Of course. Who around here doesn't?"

"And do you recall seeing her outside of Maquoketa some time after she went missing?"

Frankie's eyes narrow. "I remember *thinking* we saw that girl. And I remember realizing we made a mistake. We told that to the police."

"Yes, I know. I've got some questions about that situation."

Willy turns to Steve, a flash of fire in his eyes. "What *situation*?"

"Oh, just the whole seeing her—not seeing her thing."

"We don't know nothing about that." Willy's voice cracks.

"What do you mean? You don't remember that evening, or you remember nothing about it?" Steve keeps his eyes on Willy, but he notices Frankie sizing him up.

"None of it," Willy says. "We don't know nothing about none of it!" Willy throws a dirty rag onto the front fender of an old Volvo and storms off through a door with the word "Office" painted on it.

Steve raises his hands to Frankie, palms out. "I didn't mean to upset your brother. I'm just following up on some information, that's all. Meant nothing by it."

Wiping his hands with a towel, Frankie says nothing but smiles at Steve the way you smile at someone you'd just as soon punch in the face. "What kind of lawyer are you?"

"My firm handles an array—from contracts to taxes to criminal to civil law. But like I said, I'm not here in an official capacity. A woman asked me to investigate a cold case. Mrs. Harmon, Jesse's mother."

"Melly. You know she's crazy as a loon, right?"

"Losing a daughter isn't easy, I'm sure."

"Yeah, well." Frankie shrugs.

"So, that evening."

"Look. Like we told the cops, we made a mistake. Scratch that, Joey Milton made a mistake. He was the one who said it was Jesse. The rest of us didn't see her very good."

"Where were you standing when you saw the girl?"

"On the bridge. Again, it's all in the police—"

"But where on the bridge?"

Steve thinks the guy might hit him. Instead, Frankie says, "I don't like being interrupted. Got it?"

"Yes, sorry. No offense intended. I am efficient in my conversations. Apologies."

"Efficient? More like rude. I bet you say that a lot."

"What's that?"

"'No offense.'"

Steve nods. "Yes, again I'm sorry. You were saying?"

Frankie sighs. "I guess I was standing in the middle."

"And your brother?"

"Shit, I don't know. It was fourteen years ago, for christ's sake." Frankie tosses the towel into a can next to a red tool cart.

"Fifteen."

"What?"

"It was fifteen years ago," Steve says.

Frankie's jaw clenches. "OK. *Fifteen*. I don't remember where my brother was standing fifteen years ago. Got it?"

"Approximately?"

"I guess he was somewhere near me. He's always near me."

"So middle of the bridge, too?"

"Yeah, I guess so."

"But not closer to the woods than Joey Milton?"

"Right."

Steve writes this information on his legal pad, then looks at Frankie. The man's muscles are twitching. "And where was Bob Baxter?"

"Uh, I think he was on the other side of the bridge," Frankie says.

"From?"

"*From*?" Frankie says, looking confused.

"Are you talking about the other side of the bridge, or Joey and the girl?"

Frankie opens his mouth to say something, then straightens himself. "The other side from Joey. Behind us."

"Bob was farthest from the girl?"

"No. Don was."

"Don Loomis?"

"Yeah."

Steve says, "Where was Don?"

"He was back around the bend."

"You and your brother had a better view than Bob?"

"Uh."

"It's OK, I'm not trying to trick you. I'm just getting a picture of the scene, that's all."

"Mister. You couldn't trick me if you tried."

Shaking his head, Steve says, "I don't doubt that for a minute."

"I'm not a fucking idiot." Frankie's face is flushed.

"I never said you were. Please, let me ask a couple more questions and I'll be out of your hair. I know this subject is sensitive."

"Sensitive? Fuck that. It's annoying."

"Even so."

"Feel like I'm on trial."

"You're not. I'm sorry if I'm giving you that impression, but you boys were the last ones to see Jesse Harmon alive."

Frankie's mouth twitches. "But we didn't see Jesse; that was a mistake. It was Emma Tupper. It's in the police report."

"I know it is, but police reports can be wrong. And they can manipulate teenagers." When he says this, Frankie's body tenses, but Steve continues before the guy can threaten him or curse him out. "Even if it *was* Emma Tupper, I would still like to ask more questions."

Frankie exhales and nods, turning away and leaning against the front of the car, giving Steve his profile.

"Which one of you first identified the girl as Jesse Harmon?"

"Joey. He called out to her."

"Right. And then what happened?"

He exhales like a teenager being told to stop using the computer. "Like I said a bazillion times, she went off into the woods."

"How?"

"What?"

"How did she go off? Did she run, walk, skip?"

"She walked, I guess."

"She didn't run away. Like she was afraid of you, correct? She just walked."

"I mean, I couldn't see her facial expression, but she didn't look like she was in a hurry. She didn't seem scared." Frankie scratches his upper arm.

"And then what happened?"

"Then Joey chased after her, screaming her name like bloody murder. And we followed. We couldn't find her when we got into the woods. It was like she disappeared into the mist."

"It was foggy that evening, right?" Steve continues writing on his legal pad as Frankie talks.

"Yeah. The temperature dropped in the afternoon and there was fog rolling around. I remember that was the reason we went there. Don't get a lot of fog like that around here, not in the afternoon anyway, and it was October, so we thought it was kinda spooky. Joey had his Super 8 camera with him and we were shooting a little horror movie we'd been working on."

Steve stops writing and looks up, eyes wide. "A movie?" *Why did Bob leave that part out?* Steve thinks.

Frankie nods. "It was too dark to shoot at that point."

"You were making a movie?"

"That's what I said." Frankie goes rigid for a moment. "Didn't nobody tell you that part?"

Steve shakes his head. "No."

"Shit. Well, that's what we were doing."

"What kind of movie?"

Frankie spits on the greasy floor. "Some zombie thing. Like Night of the Living Dead. Joey was obsessed with that shit."

"Did you guys make a lot of movies back then?"

"Some. Joey was always writing scripts. He thought he was the next Spielberg, I guess. Willy and I weren't friends with those guys—Joey just used us as bad guys because he thought we looked tough."

"Sounds like fun."

He shrugs. "It was, I guess. We got to act like we were cracking skulls and killing people or whatever. Don Loomis was pretty good at gory makeup and special effects. For a dipshit." Frankie laughs. "That crazy fucker used spaghetti as guts, and he could make a head of cauliflower look just like a human brain."

"And why Super 8? That was OG, even fifteen years ago. Why not video?"

Frankie leans on the car again. "Yep. Joey wanted to make *actual* movies—or anyway, that's what he always said. Didn't think video was authentic enough. He'd go through hell to buy film and store it in the freezer. It would drive his old man crazy with all the little cans of film and all the lights and shit all over the house. But they were good sports about it, his parents. *Our* old man—shit, he would've chucked all that out the fucking window. But Joey's family let him lock down the house to shoot a couple of scenes in the middle of the night. Crazy!" Frankie chuckles, looking down at the floor.

"How many movies did you guys make?"

"We were in four or five, but Joey made more than that. Didn't have the money to get most of them finished. I think he shot scenes that popped into his head. His parents have an entire closet full of unfinished movies, I bet."

"So, that evening. You were on the bridge to shoot a scene, right?"

"Yeah."

"Joey was at the far end of the bridge, and you and Willy were in the middle."

"Yep."

"And Bob was on the far end away from Joey?" Steve says. "Don was out by the bikes, around the bend?"

"Yeah, we were supposed to be zombies attacking Bob. Joey wanted to get the shot from behind us so he could see Bob's reaction, I suppose."

"But it was getting dark?"

"Yeah. Joey didn't have any outside lights with batteries and there wasn't an outlet out there in the country, so he wanted to shoot real quick-like before it got too dark. But it didn't matter because Bob said he saw someone in the trees—just after Joey started rolling."

Steve looks up from the notepad again. "Wait. Bob saw the girl first?"

"Yeah. But he didn't recognize her. So, Joey looked at her."

"And then what happened?" Steve asks.

"Joey yelled, 'Hey, Jesse,' or 'Is that Jesse?' And I turned around and saw her too. Later, Joey said she was wearing a white dress, but I didn't see her that good. By the time my eyes focused, she'd cut off into the trees and that was it."

"But you guys ran after her, right?"

"Yeah. We split in different directions. I walked parallel to the road, about ten yards off it, away from the bridge. Walked a mile down that road, then doubled back and waited by the bridge." Frankie stops for several moments, blinking down at his shoes. "The rest of them came back five or ten minutes later, maybe."

Steve writes, then asks, "Who came back first, after you?"

"Willy, I think. But Bob was right behind him. Joey was out there a while longer."

"How much longer?"

"Not sure. Fifteen minutes, maybe. We got on our bikes and headed back to town."

Steve taps the pad of paper with his pen. "And you went straight to the police?"

"Not Willy and me. Cops make me nervous and I didn't want my dad getting a call from them, even if it was for a good cause. He'd think I was in trouble anyway, and that was just as bad. A day or two later, Joey tells me in school he and Bob made a mistake—that he'd seen the Tupper girl, not Jesse. And that was that." Frankie snaps his fingers, then crosses his arms.

"You didn't question him about it?"

"Nope."

Steve clicks the pen and sticks it in the inside pocket of his jacket. "Seems odd."

Frankie pops a sideways look at him. "What?"

"Well, one day you're certain you saw Jesse Harmon, the next you're not."

"Jesus! Get it through your head! Joey saw her, not me. And when the police told us we'd seen the Tupper girl, how was I going to argue with them? I was a teenager."

"But you never wondered? All these years?"

"Nope." Frankie looks away, arms still crossed.

"I sure would have. A thing like that? Pretty sure I'd think about it a lot."

Frankie shrugs. "That's you."

Steve smiles. "Guess so. I suppose that's it for now. Thank you for your time, Frankie."

Frankie stands. "For now?"

"You don't mind if I stop by again—should anything else come up?"

"Like what?"

"Oh, I don't know. Probably won't happen, but if a thought occurs to me. You won't mind answering another question or two, would you?" Steve studies Frankie's expression. He has a good poker face, but Steve sees a tell.

Frankie spits again. "I think I've answered all the questions I want to answer. The rest you can find in that fucking report. If I were you..."

"Yes?"

"Just—wrap it up quick. That's all I got to say."

Without another word, Frankie Trillo turns and heads through the same door as his brother, leaving Steve alone and surprised by the sudden exit.

As he pulls his car around, making a U-turn onto Market Street, Steve glances back at the shop and spots Willy Trillo's face in the office window, watching him depart.

Chapter Sixteen

1.

The Milton house sits at the corner of Maple and 4th, an immense white Victorian style home with a white and gray wood porch wrapping around the east side of the home. It's well preserved but the symptoms of age, and aging caretakers, are clear. Steve figures the house must be well over a hundred years old, if not older—maybe even eighteen hundreds. *Gotta be at least five bedrooms*, Steve thinks.

On his way back from Delmar, he had called Bob Baxter for the Milton's address, hoping they might have information to offer. Bob seemed worried about the Trillos, but Steve reassured him all went well.

Frankie Trillo had been more forthcoming than he'd supposed, given Bob's warning, but there was more to the narrative. Steve had done enough interviews with shifty personalities for their conversation to set off his bullshit meter. Both of the Trillos seemed uncomfortable with his presence, and that alone told him enough.

A few moments after he knocks on the screen door, an older woman in her late sixties or early seventies appears behind the old mesh screen. Wearing a flowered dress straight out of a 1960s Better Homes and Gardens magazine, horn-rimmed glasses, and dyed brown hair pulled up into a bun, Gladys Milton looks like a walking antique. "Yes?" she says.

"Mrs. Milton?"

"Yes."

"I'm Steve Spain. Mrs. Harmon hired me to look into her daughter's cold-case. Do you know Melly Harmon?"

"Yes, we know her. I imagine everyone in Maquoketa knows Melissa. She gets around, in a manner of speaking. Shame about her poor daughter. Have you found anything?" Her voice is deep for a woman and when she speaks, her mouth smacks as if she's just eaten a chocolate chip cookie.

"A little. That's why I'm here, Mrs. Milton. I'd like to ask you some questions about your son, Joey—"

"Joseph," she says.

"Pardon?"

"His name was Joseph—the kids called him *Joey*. I never much cared for shortening names, a handsome name like Joseph. Is your name shortened?"

"Yes."

"With a v or a ph?"

"With a v. I always preferred Steve, but my mom must have thought more like you, Mrs. Milton. She never liked shortened names either."

Mrs. Milton grins, revealing a line of straight but yellowing teeth. "Please, call me Gladys," she says, opening the screen door with one hand, extending her other hand inward. "Won't you come in?"

"Thank you, Gladys."

An aroma like stale pine hits him as soon as he steps into the foyer, like someone left a Christmas tree up far too long. There is also a distinct medicinal odor, not surprising given the age of the occupants.

"Is Mr. Milton at home?"

"Oh, yes. He's upstairs working. I could ask him to join us, but I think he would refuse. Too busy, always too busy," she says, smiling up at the ceiling.

Steve thinks about requesting his presence, but decides against it. "That's fine. I'm sure you can answer the questions I have."

Gladys leads him through an oak archway into the formal living room, furnished with an antique sofa and loveseat, with a large leather chair next to a brick fireplace. The mantle, adorned with wood carvings of what appear to be hundreds of baby angels, encases a stately fireplace at the far end of the room. At Gladys's direction, Steve sits on the sofa in front of a wood-framed bay window and she takes the love seat opposite him. Behind her, another archway leads to a formal dining room with a long ornately carved wood table and seating for ten. "Can I offer you some tea and cookies? We are rather low on refreshments. I haven't been to the market in some days and I rarely entertain anymore. At one time, this house was bustling with activity, but now it's big and lonely."

"No, thank you. This is a beautiful home. How many bedrooms, if you don't mind me asking?"

"Oh, I don't mind talking about this home, not one bit. We have *seven* bedrooms, if you can believe it."

Steve laughs. "Seven! Wow!"

Gladys shares his laugh, leaning toward him with a monstrous smile, wide eyed, her eyebrows arched halfway up her bulbous forehead. "Yes, 'wow,' is right," she says, nodding violently. "But we needed all the room we could get, with five children bouncing around this place." She stares out at the foyer, her eyes glistening. "So many moments. They add up, you know."

"That's a big family. Boys and girls?" Steve says.

"Two boys and three girls. Joseph was the youngest. He came fifteen years after my oldest, Charlene. A surprise to be sure, but we thought of it as a blessing, old as we were. I was forty-one at the time and Ronald was almost forty-seven."

"Sounds like this place was full of life."

"It was." Her eyes drift over his head and out the window, focusing on nothing in particular. Finally, she looks back at him and says, "What did you wish to ask me, Mr. Spain?"

"I wanted to know a little more about the day Joey—sorry, *Joseph*—the day Joseph said he saw Jesse Harmon on the old road."

"But he didn't see Jessica Harmon. He saw the oldest Tupper girl. Oh, what was her name?"

"Emma."

"Yes, Emma. That's who he saw." Gladys crosses her ankles, giving a patient smile that doesn't reach her eyes.

"He first reported seeing Jesse Harmon. Rode back into town, fast as his bike would take him, all the way to the police station to make the report."

Gladys's smile remains, though diminished, almost sunken, like a jack-o'-lantern three days past Halloween. "That's true. But he was mistaken."

"Yes—"

"That's what he said. He said he made a mistake and that he'd seen Emma Tupper out there. It was near the Tupper property, so it made sense. The police confirmed all of this." Gladys clears her throat and stands. "Apologies, but I'd like a cup of tea. Care for one?"

"That would be great, thank you."

Alone, Steve observes the decor. At one time, all the Milton's things were nice, perhaps even expensive, by the looks. But nothing appears to have been updated in ages. Family photos—including photos of all the children—sit on almost every available surface, held in elaborate frames resting on delicate knitted doilies, faded and dull. The hard wood floors could use refinishing and the several oriental rugs spread about are clean, but worn. The same is true for the British-style flowery wallpaper adorning each upright surface.

At once, Steve notices movement coming from above, muffled and low, almost a light pounding. Though he cannot be sure, it doesn't sound like it's in the room above him, but perhaps in a room above that, maybe in the attic.

When Gladys enters carrying a tray with two cups of tea, she catches him staring at the ceiling. "Oh, that's just Ronald working away, as always."

"What's he working on?" Steve says, taking one of the porcelain cups.

"Who knows? He's building something or other," she says with a wave of the hand. "I don't pay it any mind."

"You don't know what he's working on?"

"Wiling away his time with his woodworking, but I don't have the foggiest idea what in particular he's working on right *now*. If I had to guess, I'd say it was a toy boat. He loves boats."

"I see."

Gladys takes a sip. "Where were we?"

"I was asking you about the evening your Joseph claimed to have seen a girl on the old road."

"Yes."

"Did he tell you why he changed his mind about who he'd seen?"

"I don't recall. That was so many years ago. But I believe the police determined that the Tupper girl was out there that day and so they assured Joseph he'd been mistaken. And that was all there was to it."

"Yes, that's what Mrs. Harmon finds troubling. Emma Tupper denied being on The Old Road that day. She told the police she was at the library doing homework when Joseph and his friends were filming at the bridge. And Emma Tupper doesn't have blond hair like Jesse Harmon—she's a brunette. It seems unlikely your son would mistake a brown-haired girl with a blond girl."

"Yes, I see how that might set one to wondering. But you know it was dusk and Joseph described the area as foggy, if I remember. Perhaps the weather led to his mistaken report?"

Steve nods. "Sure, sure. That's possible. But given that Emma Tupper denied being out there, *combined* with your son's initial report, well, that sets my mind to wondering."

"I see. There's no doubt that's an odd set of circumstances. If I were a fan of mysteries, I'd find this most interesting. But I have little taste for this sort of thing, and since my son is no longer with us, I don't see how I can add much to your inquiry."

"How long ago did he pass?"

"He didn't *pass*—he killed himself," she says with a shocking bluntness.

"Yes, I heard that. I'm sorry for your loss. Were there any signs or indications? Depression?"

"Joseph struggled with depression for many years after high school. No one could understand it. He was a smart, talented, charming young man with the entire world at his doorstep, so it seemed. College came easy to him—graduated with honors from Iowa State, headed for a promising engineering career."

"Interesting. I would have thought he'd go into movies."

Gladys's demeanor brightens. "You heard about his filmmaking?"

"I spoke to a few of his friends."

"Then I'm sure you've spoken to that Baxter boy and the Trillo brothers. They were all with him that day on the old road. And Emma Tupper?"

"Not Emma, but yes to the others."

"I see. Movies were his passion, but my husband, Ronald, wouldn't hear of his son going to film school. He insisted Joseph get a degree in something that could support a family. I understood his point, but I think he underestimated the intensity of Joseph's passion. Mind you, my Ronald had nothing but the best intentions for his son, but Joseph was never the same with him after that. There was a coldness between them that lasted until the end. After Joseph's death, my dear husband has never been the same himself. Instead of enjoying retirement, he sits up there in the attic, pining away at the woodwork bench, talking to himself until the early hours. When he finally comes to bed, he barely sleeps. The next day, he gets up and does it all over again—day after day. Guilt does strange things to a man, and to a house." She looks around her.

"I'm sorry."

"Nothing to be sorry for—it's life. Life and living. If you do it long enough, you're bound to come upon a pain you can't abide."

"It's a big house."

"Yes, and empty, too. The only one we ever owned—our first and last house. Cold in the winter and hot in the summer, though we do sometimes get a pleasant breeze. I think about moving into something smaller, more manageable, but Ronald will never hear of it." Gladys gives a startled look. "I'm so sorry. Here we are dredging up the past when I'm sure you have more pressing things on your mind. Was there anything else you wished to know?"

"The movies your son made. Do you still have them?"

"I do, though I've only watched a few myself. Ronald had them developed a few years ago and stored in Joseph's old room. I think he may have watched a few too, but most of them were unfinished. What did Joseph call it? *Rare* footage?"

"Raw footage," Steve says.

"Yes, that's it!"

Movement near the stairs catches Steve's eye and for a second he thinks he sees someone standing at the top, just where the railing and the ceiling converge—the smallest hint of a trouser leg moving out of view to the floor above. "Gladys, would you mind if I looked at those old films?"

"You mean you'd like to go into his room?"

"Yes."

Gladys looks toward the stairs, mouth agape.

"I don't mean to impose, but to be thorough, it might be helpful to have a look at them. Leave no stone unturned, you know."

"I understand. It's just that no one has been in his room for so many years. I suppose there's no harm in letting you go for a look."

The wood floors in the upstairs hallway protest each step with pronounced creaking. Like the first floor, a floral print wallpaper that looks confiscated from a Stanley Kubrick film covers the walls. Red and pink flowers spring forth from emerald stems winding in warped columns up on both sides of the hall, giving the illusion the walls are closing in on you.

Steve steadies his nerves with deep breaths as he makes his way toward a room on the left at the end of the hall, per Gladys's directions. "I will not follow you, Mr. Spain. Since Joseph's death, I have not come close to his room. I trust you'll forgive me."

"That's fine," Steve says.

"I hear strange sounds coming at night."

"Great," he mutters under his breath. When he reaches the door, Steve glances behind him. With a nod from Gladys, he twists the brass handle, which responds with a low groan as he swings the oak door wide and steps into Joey Milton's room.

2.

A saw buzzes from above the ceiling as he scans the dreary bedroom. Ragged cardboard boxes stacked along the walls and upon the twin bed in the corner, give the air of time standing still. A four-drawer dresser sits at the wall next to the door. There is a chill. Opposite the dresser, a window is half open, its drapes flopping in the mellow breeze. Steve thinks about closing it, wondering if anyone ever sets foot in the room, but decides he had better stick to searching for the films.

Gladys calls to him from the hall. "We left the film cannisters in the closet. Joey labeled them. I think the one you want has to do with a dead bridge or something along those lines."

"Great, thanks!" Steve says.

He heads to a door in the far corner, painted white, with a red crystal knob. When he turns it, the knob wiggles loosely in his hand like it might pop out of the socket, but opens the latch all the same. Just as he is about to pull the door open, he hears a sound coming from inside the closet, like footsteps, bare feet shuffling away from the door. The floor creaks. He freezes and stares at the door—eyes wide, heart thrumming in his chest. *Well, idiot*, he thinks to himself. *What are you going to do? Either run away now, or open the door. What did you come here for?* Taking a deep breath and releasing it slowly, he opens the door quickly, knees bent, ready for fight or flight.

Inside, the closet is on the small side, typical for an old house, with one wooden rod holding a few coats pushed off to one side, and several empty wire hangers. Old toys and stuffed animals are stacked in a recessed area to the left, while three pairs of men's shoes, worn and dusty, occupy the area to the right. Directly in front of him, just below the hanging coats, stands a two shelf bookcase filled with cans of Super 8 film. Next to it, is an ancient metal projector and several film spools.

The cans are labeled with titles to various movies—some finished, others unfinished, and still others marked as 'RAW.' Steve smiles as he reads the titles. *The Raven, Ullalume,* and *Telltale Heart* speak to Joey's clear love for Poe, while *Revenge of the Dead, Attack of the Dead,* and *Dead Will Rise* signal a budding fascination with Romero.

"Ahead of his time," Steve says.

One label in particular catches his eye. *Bridge of the Undead—1 of 2.* As Steve pulls it from the bookcase, a quick draft of wind pushes across his face from the right, just past the old shoes. Gooseflesh spreads from the back of his skull down his back. Flustered, he stands, the case in one hand, grabbing the antique projector with the other, then shuts the closet door with an elbow.

As he hurries back across the shag carpet, he hears a knocking behind him and an airy sound like a sigh. Glancing back, he sees nothing but the dingy white closet door, firmly closed.

3.

Back at home, Steve sets up Joey's projector and threads the film through the mechanism, fixing it to a second spool. Rocky wags next to him, uncertain of what's going on, but happy Steve is home. Turning out the lights and flipping the black knob on the projector to ON, Steve squats on the basement floor. The first image cast upon the drywall is a shaky shot of gravel and a pair of feet in black Chuck Taylor high tops. With a whirl, the camera pans up to reveal a dirt road with fall trees and weeds on either side. It's the infamous Old Road. Steve grabs his cell phone and takes a picture of the scene.

Three boys stand on a bridge, the two closest wearing ripped pants and over-sized suit coats with their backs to the camera. A young Bob Baxter, crouching with a large stick, waits at the far side. Steve takes another picture of this scene.

One of the closest two boys turns to the camera. His face, covered in dirty makeup, curls into a smile as fake blood drips from his lower lip. It's Frankie Trillo, which means the blonde boy next to him must be his brother, Willy-much younger versions of the men he met earlier.

The Trillo boys advance on Baxter in an exaggerated stumbling zombie walk. With a slow zoom, the scene fades in and out of focus. Willy and Frankie glance back at the camera just before the view drops to the gravel road and Joey Milton's shoes. The scene cuts out, then back to a fresh shot, once again with the Trillo zombies set up to attack Bob Baxter. This time, as the zombies move, the camera follows them rather than zooming. The scene stays in focus just long enough to get to the action. At once, the Trillos rush Baxter as he swings the stick before him like a lion tamer.

As one, the boys freeze, then a few moments later they relax and turn to the camera. The scene cuts to black for almost five seconds, nothing but scratchy film rolling across Steve's wall, until at last we see the boys once again on the bridge. The Trillos are laughing and Bob Baxter is shaking his head, joining them in the unexplained mirth.

Bob Baxter cranes his neck and says something to the camera. The camera tilts sideways and shifts to the left as if Joey has turned to look at something behind him. Then the view steadies and just as the camera is about to pan further left to reveal the lane behind Joey, the scene cuts off as the last of the film snakes through the projector until it is flapping around the end of the spool.

Steve sits in silence. Was this the moment Joey Milton spotted the girl? The footage cuts off too early to see. Why did it cut off at that precise moment? Did Joey stop filming? Steve examines the tail of the film hanging from the bottom spool. The edge is sharp and slightly slanted. Holding the film toward the overhead light, his heart convulses with one quivering palpitation. Instead of being cut between frames as you'd expect if the film had reached its end, it's sliced diagonally through the middle of the last frame.

4.

Sitting at his usual booth in The Last Cafe on Earth, staring out the window, Steve watches Bob Baxter jaywalk towards him across Main Street, hands in pockets, looking left and right. Throwing the door open, he says hello to Rose, who watches him slide into the booth opposite Steve. "What's up?" Baxter says. "I don't have a lot of time."

"Why didn't you tell me about the films?"

Baxter freezes. "What?"

"The movies—the Super 8 movies you guys made."

"What about them?"

"Don't be shifty, Bob. Why didn't you mention anything about those movies?"

"Why would I?"

"You don't think that's an important piece of information? You guys were filming the evening you saw Jesse, or the Tupper girl, on the old road. Why didn't you mention that?"

Baxter shrugs. "They were just stupid horror movies. Who told you about them?"

"Frankie Trillo," Steve says.

Baxter glances out the window. "You talked to the Trillos?"

"Yeah. I went to their garage this morning. Willy said very little, but Frankie gave me a bit to go on. And after, I met Joey's parents and borrowed some raw footage from that evening. You were making a movie called Bridge of the Undead. Does that ring any bells?"

"Yeah. One of the many we never finished. So what?"

"Did you know Joey was filming the moment he saw the girl?"

"What? Did you see her in the film?"

Steve sits back in the booth and shakes his head. "It cuts off just at the moment the camera pans behind Joey, like the film was cut right there on purpose. Or at least that's what it looks like to me."

"Holy shit..."

"Do you remember Joey filming the girl?" Steve says.

"I remember he was holding the camera, but once we split up to look for her, I don't know what he did with it. Wait a minute, let me think! Joey lost the camera that night. I think he found it again a few days later out there by the side of the road. The film was still in it and everything."

"What?" Steve slaps his palms on the table. "Are you kidding me? Why are you holding this information back?"

"I'm not! Some of this shit I'm just remembering now. Hell, it's been fifteen years, Mr. Spain. I'm so fucked up most of the time, I can barely remember the shit that happened last week."

Steve shakes his head. "Look, nevermind that. The footage was in a can with the words *'one of two'* printed on it. It stands to reason there's at least another can of footage somewhere."

"Yeah, yeah, I get you—"

"But it wasn't in Joey's closet. How close were you to him? Would you have known any hiding places he may have had?"

Baxter rubs his face with both hands. "I wasn't close to him at all—no one was. The guy was a loner. He had *casual* friends, maybe guys who he could ask to be in one of his movies, like me and the Trillos. But none of us were exactly friends with him. And after that night, I sort of lost touch with him. As far as I know, he never shot another movie again."

Steve sighs. He glances at Rose and catches her watching them. When their eyes meet, she returns to whatever she was doing. Steve leans towards Baxter, lowering his voice. "OK. You said Joey lost his camera that night."

"Yeah."

"How?"

"I don't remember, but I think maybe he set it down someplace when we went looking for the girl? He probably forgot where he set it and then it got so dark out by the time we left, he couldn't find it. I just don't remember."

Steve processes the situation for a minute. "Seems logical. Anyway, it's a thought. Still, something about all of this seems—*off*. I can't put my finger on it."

"See? That's what I told you. It's the same reason Melly can't let go of this thing and neither can I. My whole life changed that night on the old road and I can't figure out how or why. Everything went to shit after that day. Everything."

For the first time since meeting him, Steve feels sorry for the guy. For all of them. "Don't worry. I will not give up on this thing. But please, Bob, if you think of anything—anything at all, any memory you might have forgotten from that night—call me. OK?"

"Yeah. But you be careful. Frankie Trillo may have talked to you today, but that doesn't mean you should trust him."

With that, Baxter exits the cafe, taking a right down Main, leaving Steve alone with his thoughts.

Chapter Seventeen

Mara stirs a pot of leftover chili on the stove as she listens to Steve's story. On one hand, she's nervous that he's stressing himself out with all this talk of missing girls and lost video tapes—or Super 8 film, whatever that is—but on the other, it's nice to see him excited about so*mething*.

"I think there's only one thing to do," Steve says.

"What's that?"

"I need to find the missing footage."

"What if there never was a second reel?" Mara says. "What if he *intended* to film more but didn't?"

"But what about the way the film ended? The diagonal edge at the end of the film? It seems like someone cut it at that point."

"Do you know anything about that kind of film? Do you know if it ends with a diagonal edge?"

Steve taps the counter top and sits at one of the breakfast bar stools. "Hm. Yeah, I see what you mean. It ends in the middle of the frame. Why? It looks cut to me."

Catching herself, she says, "True. I'm just playing the devil's advocate. What do I know? And a world where there *is* a hidden second film reel is way more interesting than one where there isn't."

"What's that supposed to mean?"

"It means I'd keep looking."

"You're not taking this seriously. I get it."

"No, no! It's not that. I'm just asking questions, that's all. Mulder needed a Scully, you know."

He laughs. "I guess that's true. And you make a good Scully."

Thank god. "What's your next move?"

"I've got a psych appointment in the morning, but I think I'll go back to the Milton's house and see if they won't let me back in Joey's room, maybe find the other reel. I don't know where I'd find it if it wasn't in his room."

"I have one question that's pestering me," Mara says. "Why didn't Bob Baxter tell you about the filming? Why did you have to hear it from the Trillos? That part is strange."

"Makes me think too. He blamed it on his various addictions, but it's something I'll keep in mind from now on when he tells me something."

Mara hesitates before her next query, but decides she must know. "And how is your anxiety?"

He stiffens, and she thinks for a moment she's said the wrong thing, but he surrenders and says, "It's fine. It has been great getting out of the house. I feel good."

"Good. And last night was fun. We need to do that more often."

"Yes! That was incredible. Nadine should come out more often."

Mara blushes. "Maybe," she says. "Back to the footage. What if there is no missing reel?"

"I went into this whole thing knowing I'd likely never find out everything there is to know. Maybe I'll just tell Melly I couldn't figure out the mystery. That'll be that."

"And what about this house?" Mara can't look at him, but she hears him sigh.

"I don't know."

"Is something going on here? Can we at least talk about that?"

"Is there? Or are we so used to thinking that way we can't get it out of our heads? Maybe—maybe it's my anxiety."

"You think your anxiety is making me see things? You think your anxiety affects *my* vision?"

"It does. How can it not? You live with a husband who can't manage his own emotions. Maybe it's affecting the way you see the world."

Mara shakes her head. "No. I've seen and heard what I've seen and heard. I'm not hallucinating or dreaming. Something is out there, Steve. I don't know if we brought it with us or not. I've heard of situations like that happening—people touched by some entity—when they try to get away from it, they only bring the thing with them."

"If any of that junk is true, those are demons, not ghosts. Our house was haunted, not possessed."

"How do we know?"

"I just—I don't know. I can't keep fretting about this crap every day of my life. It's draining." His face is red, and he seems to be short of breath.

She reaches across the dinner table to him. "I'm sorry. Hey, it's fine. I'm just—"

"No, it's OK."

"No, it isn't. I shouldn't have—"

"No!" Mara flinches at the sudden force of his protest. He continues, "I'm sorry. I get what you're saying; I *do*. There's just nothing to be done about it, you know? And if I focus all my thoughts on a thing I can't change, I'll feel like I'm running in circles, and that's no good. You know? It's no good for you and no good for me. My heart feels like it will punch through my ribs, and it's like someone is pressing down on my chest at the same time. I'm suffocating—on *air*!"

Mara wraps her hands about his shoulders, kissing his neck. "That's dreadful."

"It is."

"What can I do? What do you need?"

"Just peace. Just quiet for a second. It'll pass."

"Do you want your Xanax?"

"No, I think I can manage it. I think I'm good."

"When was the last time you took one?"

"This morning."

"Then you're good for another one if you—"

"No. I'm OK. I can manage. Just need to take deep breaths. Here, you can help me with that."

Mara sits next to him, inhaling and exhaling with him, encouraging every breath.

Chapter Eighteen

Steve wakes, eyes wide, unable to move. *Sleep paralysis.*

Panic rising. Chest rising. That feeling like someone standing on his chest.

His eyes roll as far to his left as they will go. Mara snores next to him. By the round curve of her hip he sees she's lying on her side, turned away from him. A vain attempt to call out to her produces little more than a small cough. Feeling like someone large is sitting on his sternum, he closes his eyes and concentrates on his breathing as Dr. Nguyen taught him in their first session.

Rise and fall. Let it rise and fall. Bring in the air and let it out. Rise and fall. You're fine.

Blocking out all other sounds, all other thoughts, Steve focuses his thoughts on water—a stream of slow-moving water—*his* stream. The one he always goes to when this kind of thing happens. It's Duck Creek in Davenport, a small snake of water running from Davenport through Bettendorf and down to the Mississippi River. This part runs through a wooded area north of the cemetery.

Where Liesl rests.

Fallen leaves litter the grassy banks of the lazy stream or circle in the mellow rapids as they float past on their way to bigger things. In his mind, Steve sees the trees and the bike path just beyond. How many days did he sit on this bank as his mom and dad cried a few hundred yards away over the grave of their lost little girl?

An empty grave, isn't it? Did you ever think of that?

Steve's throat is tightening. The exercises aren't working. Another voice speaks in his mind, distracting him from the exercise.

Where is her body?

He coughs—not loud enough to wake Mara. A liquid fills his lungs, his own spit. He's choking on it, but he's unable to expel the substance.

Shut up, he yells in his mind. *Shut up, shut up!*

A low chuckle rumbles in his brain. Grabbing hold of his focus, Steve returns his mind to his stream and listens to its trickling water as he melds it to the sound of his own breathing. Soon, his chest rises ever so higher than before and the suffocating sensation subsides. He calms.

Then he hears something else, beyond the stream and the sound of his own breathing. The sound is like a footstep made by an enormous beast. It's some distance away. This sound is not in his mind, unlike the water and the breeze.

Another step, and then another.

No, this sound is outside. It's in the woods. With each footfall, a low rumbling shakes him with greater and greater force until it's just outside his window. The pictures on the walls shake and rattle and the window shades clang together and against the glass. It's getting closer now. A high whining sound cuts through the footsteps and in his periphery, Steve sees Rocky standing by the foot of the bed, looking toward the windows.

Closer and closer, the footsteps come, and Steve's breath coincides with each rumbling step. Each step brings more oxygen, but so too does it bring the adrenaline and anxiety, until at last his chest seizes and no more breath will come. With one last effort, Steve lets out a great wailing cry, waking Mara.

His wife turns to him, grabbing his head on each side of his face, calling to him and shaking him, but he cannot hear a sound. The paralysis lifts from him as he drifts into a dark sleep.

Chapter Nineteen

Dr. Nguyen sits facing him, legs crossed. A pen and a pad of paper on her lap, as usual, but her face is unusually grim. She wears a dark pantsuit with a matching scarf, as the office furnace is out. "I think it's important we talk about this, Steve," Dr. Nguyen says.

"I know."

"Do you have any idea what brought on this bout of anxiety?"

"I don't know."

"It isn't your impromptu detective work?"

"No. That doesn't feel stressful at all. It's given me something to keep my mind occupied. The stress didn't come back until later, when I was home."

"Did you take your PRN?"

He shakes his head.

"Why not?"

"I managed without the meds. Mara led me through my breathing exercises."

"But you said you had a panic attack at night. It woke you up."

"Yeah."

"Did you do your relaxation strategy again?"

Steve nods, blinking, feeling like a tear might escape down his face if he's not careful.

"There's a tissue box on the table next to you."

He takes one.

"But your wife had to wake up and give you the PRN, right?"

He nods.

"Have you noticed if being home increases your stress?" she asks.

Steve thinks about the question and wipes his eyes. "No. I feel fine most of the time at home, but maybe something Mara and I talked about set me off. You know how it goes—it's hard to tell what causes an attack." How can he tell her about the sounds he heard? How can he tell her about the things in the forest? *She'll call in the white coats and lock you away. Probably take Mara while she's at it.*

"What were you talking about with Mara?"

"Oh, she—I don't know..."

Dr. Nguyen tilts her head. "Yes?"

"Stuff about the old house and the new house."

She clears her throat and sets the pad of paper and pen on the coffee table in front of her. "If you're not forthcoming, there isn't much I can do for you."

"I know."

"You only get out of these sessions—"

"—what I bring into them. Yes, I know. I'm sorry, I don't mean to be elusive. I don't. Some things are hard to discuss. When I think about saying it—how the words will sound—it's crazy."

"You're not *crazy*, Steve. You suffer from anxiety."

"People might say, what's the difference?"

"You know better."

"Maybe. Anyway, I guess there's no point in hiding it. I'm already on Xanax and blubbering in a shrink's office, so I may as well go all in." Steve looks at her and sees no measure of judgment in her eyes, only curiosity mixed with a hint of concern. "In the previous session, I mentioned the thing in our last house, right? The ghost, or whatever it was?"

"Yes."

"We think we might have…"

"Yes?"

"We think—there's a chance we brought it with us."

There's a moment's hesitation in her response. "Brought it with you? The haunting?"

"Yes."

"You and your wife think this?"

"She brought it up last night. At first, I kinda pooh-poohed the idea, but maybe she's right. Odd stuff keeps happening at our house."

"Odd? How?"

"We've seen things outside in our yard, and in the house, too."

"What kinds of things?"

He looks down at his lap. "Figures. I suppose it's like *shadows* of people. Or maybe apparitions."

"In the house too?"

"Yes."

"But the house is brand new. No one else has lived there, right?" she asks.

"That's what I said. But Mara thinks we brought this stuff with us, you know? Maybe it hitched a ride. That seems more like a possession based on what I've read, anyway. I mean, who's an expert in this crap? If it's even real."

"What did you see inside the house?"

Steve breathes deep. "It was a tiny figure. Long scraggly hair and thin, like Gollum from *Lord of the Rings*, kinda. Just like the thing in our last house—the one in the basement workroom. Hell, might have been the same one."

"What did this creature do?"

"Nothing. It was in our living room, staring at me. I saw it one night when I got up to go to the bathroom. Even Rocky saw it."

"Your dog?"

"Yeah. He was growling out the bedroom door and his hackles were up."

"Was this creature the one you saw in the basement of your last house?"

Steve scratches his chin. "I don't know. In the dark, I could only see a silhouette from the living room windows. It crouched low to the floor, just looking at me. And then..."

Dr. Nguyen leans forward. "Yes? Steve?"

He looks at her, tears now running down his face. "I blacked out."

"You lost consciousness?"

"I guess so. Or at least I don't remember what happened. I lost time. I remember standing in our backyard looking out at the woods. Actually, I was in the ravine, staring at this dead oak tree."

"You were outside? By yourself?"

"With Rocky, but yeah. Barefoot too."

"How did you get there?"

"No idea."

"From the time you saw the creature in your living room to the time you found yourself in the ravine, how much time passed?" she asks, picking up the pad of paper and her pen and writing something down.

"No idea. I was cold, so I must have been out there for some time. When I woke up, it was 2:30 and when I went back to bed, it was 3:05." He glances at Dr. Nguyen, suddenly realizing something he hadn't thought of before.

"How long were you looking at the creature in the living room?"

"Not long. A couple minutes, maybe."

"And how much time passed from the time you awoke in the ravine to the time you went back to bed?"

"Again, maybe a few minutes. I didn't want to stay out there that long. I felt like something was out there coming towards me."

"What do you mean?" she asks.

Steve says, "I felt—a presence out there. Maybe a few. It looked like something had swallowed the entire forest. But what set me off was what I heard. Something was whispering. Like a bunch of people, just whispering."

"What were they saying?"

"I couldn't tell. They were mumbling or speaking an unfamiliar language. Either way, I would not stay out there to figure it out."

"I don't blame you. That must have been frightening."

Steve smirks. She's doing her therapist talk again—placating him. "Yeah, you could say it was scary—goddamn scary."

"So. The total time you can account for is, say, five to ten minutes. Right?"

"Maybe. Something like that."

"That means you're missing at least twenty-five minutes. Twenty-five minutes you can't account for."

Steve looks out the window. It's a gloomy day with rain in the forecast later. It will rain when he picks up Max this evening. "Yeah," he says in an absent tone. "I guess so."

"That's quite a chunk of time to be unconscious. This concerns me."

"Yeah."

"Do you have nightmares?"

"You know I do."

"This ghost, could it perhaps be a dream? A very realistic dream?"

Steve's heart races. "My dreams aren't this real. I have different recurring nightmares. Some have to do with my sister, other with ghosts. But they're never like this."

She studies his face. "What are your dream ghosts like?"

"Not like this."

"Describe them."

Steve takes a deep breath, holds it, then releases. "They're like stereotypes. Airy apparitions. This one even has a long white sheet, like a costume. That one's actually the scariest, believe it or not. Sounds dumb, I know."

"Why?"

"Why is it the scariest?" he asks.

"Yes."

"I don't know. It just kinda hovers there, watching me. Sometimes I'm tied to a chair or chained to my bed. Sometimes I'm frozen in ice up to my knees."

"What does it do to you?"

A sharp shiver runs up his spine. "It hovers there for a while, then kinda drifts toward me. Slow and menacing. But I wake up before it gets to me. And of course there's always the woman—the one with the bloody hands, reaching through the car window—always reaching for me."

She makes a thoughtful sound. "We should rethink your med regimen."

Steve turns to her. He's tried that once before with mixed results. His anxiety was more manageable, but he felt lousy and the sex was impossible. "Why?"

"Isn't it obvious? This goes beyond simple panic attacks. As harrowing as those episodes can feel, they're relatively harmless, at least physically. It is different when a person loses memory and blacks out. You can hurt yourself or someone else. People have burned their homes to the ground trying to cook a meal in a state like that. What if you'd left your dog out there to roam free and something happened to him? You'd never forgive yourself. It might be time to move away from PRNs and onto something regular."

"But this hasn't happened before."

"All the more reason to take it seriously," she says.

Steve wipes a tear from his eye. "We have no reason to believe this will happen again."

"Do you know it won't?"

"What if it's not the anxiety?"

Her eyes, full of suspicion, look him up and down from behind her glasses. "What else could it be?"

"Maybe it's what we think it is, Mara and me. Maybe we are being visited by something unnatural." Her shoulders slump ever so slightly. "No, hear me out. These things—people say they're being visited or haunted by things all the time. It's been around as long as there have been people, right?"

"Yes. Superstitions have been with us for centuries. But now we have something so much better, something that explains all the mysteries of life—*science*. You're an educated person, Steve. You know, there's a rational explanation for everything you've experienced."

"Now wait, doctor. We're not talking about banging walls from old pipes or creaky floors settling here. The things we've experienced, Mara and I—the things we've *seen* with our own eyes—they can't be anything but what they are. Otherwise, you're saying—what? You'd have to say we were both hallucinating."

Dr. Nguyen sits back in her chair, crossing her legs again. "I'm not in a position to make definitive conclusions about any of this, Steve. But earlier last night, you suffered a panic attack. You managed using your breathing exercises, then some hours later, you awaken with sleep paralysis. It's no wonder. I think if you'd taken your Xanax, or if you'd been on a regular medication, what happened to you last night would not have occurred."

"So you're saying I'm crazy."

"That's not what I'm—"

"Yes, it is! You're saying I'm nuts. I'm hallucinating so much I'm seeing things in my house and walking around outside. And this condition must be contagious because my wife is seeing the same things, and it sure seems like my dog is seeing them too. The ghosts in our last house and the dark figures in the woods outside our house, it's all just a part of some collective psychotic break?"

"I'm not judging you. There are other possibilities that I am only pointing out. I'm not there in your home, so I can't say definitively what's going on with you or your wife, but I can tell you there's no scientific evidence for ghosts or possessions or any of the other supernatural occurrences people talk about. The ghost hunting shows on television? If they brought a team of actual scientists along with them during their investigations, they would cancel those shows before half a season. They can debunk every single one of their light *anomalies* or mysterious sounds. So let's keep our theories in the quantifiable realm, OK?"

"You'd make a great Scully," Steve says. There's no point in arguing with her about it. How could anyone understand who wasn't there?

Dr. Nguyen laughs. "I probably would. And I don't mean to dismiss your ideas, but I also don't want to stray away from things within our control. Many situations cause anxiety, and some of them are out of our control. I'm not suggesting that we avoid every stressful situation or relationship. Coping with it and managing it, that's the work. The supernatural is too convenient."

"I guess."

Steve runs his hands along the arms of the chair. They sit like this for three to four minutes, silent, until Dr. Nguyen releases him from his thoughts.

"Do you feel guilty?" she says.

"Guilty?"

"Yes."

"About what?"

"I wouldn't know. But do you feel guilty about something?"

"I guess so. I mean, once in a while I'll think of something dumb I did or how I put my foot in my mouth—"

"Does this happen frequently?"

He laughs. "I feel like it happens more often the older I get. Sometimes I wish I could erase my twenties."

"Did you make a lot of mistakes?"

"Yeah. Mostly with people."

"Relationships?"

He nods. "It's hard to remember what I did wrong versus what they did wrong, you know?"

"I do."

"And sometimes I'm harder on myself than I should be."

"Why do you think that is?"

"No idea."

"Do you think a lot about previous relationships?"

"Uh, not really. I don't sit around and pour over every detail. But sometimes I'll think about something I said or something I did, and I'll wrack myself with guilt. Isn't that weird? A dumb thing that happened decades ago and I still worry about it. That stuff will drive you crazy. But I think I've been a good person in my life. I hope..."

"I imagine each of us feels that way."

"True."

"Do you feel guilt about Liesl?"

Steve shoots her a wide-eyed look. There's no apology in her expression, only a determined stare. "I do."

"Why?"

"I should have done something."

"What could you have done?"

"Jumped in and saved her."

"In the frozen Mississippi? You'd be dead now, too. What would that solve?"

Steve feels like he's in slow motion. "I shouldn't have let her follow me onto the ice. We should have stayed inside."

"You were a child yourself. You didn't force your sister to go out there."

"I told my mom I'd watch her. I told her we'd be OK out there..." The room spins and he squeezes his eyes closed to center himself. When he opens them again, he's no longer in the doctor's office, but standing on a snowy slope. Below him is the Mississippi River, covered in a layer of ice.

Chapter Twenty

Everything around him is white and glowing in a soft blur of winter daylight. There's a modest ranch-style house fifty yards up a short hill overlooking a wide river. But there's nothing else around—only a line of trees some distance away. The rest of the world is brightest white, covered in two feet of snow. Steve's own voice emanates through the memory like an echo. Near the riverbank, a tiny figure appears.

Steve says, "I see her, over there on the shore. I tell her to stay where she is, but she shakes her head. She's got on her red coat with a white knitted cap and mittens with a matching scarf. A raggedy doll hangs from her hand. It's one of those ugly homemade things, sewn together by my grandma."

"Steve..." Dr. Nguyen's voice sounds like it's coming from the other side of the River, or the other side of the world.

"It must be Leclaire to the North. It's just snowy hills and bare trees. Squinting across the river, I can make out a small dark figure, but it's too far away to see what or who it is. Then I recognize her."

"'Liesl,' I say. 'Stay on the shore.' But she shakes her head again and steps onto the ice. 'Mom'll get mad,' I say, but still she ignores me. She runs to a patch of ice and slides about five feet—"

Dr. Nguyen's voice again. *"Steve, listen—"*

Ignoring her faint call, Steve continues. "Liesl giggles and I laugh too, forgetting the danger. Then I run ahead to find my patch of ice and slide across it. Feet slip out from under me, and I fall on my butt, which makes me laugh even harder despite the pain."

"Open your eyes..." Dr. Nguyen's voice floats on the winter air.

"I feel something under me, like a vibration, but I'm laughing too hard to notice what it is. Then Liesl slides again and falls on her behind, just to copy me. She squeals with laughter. I can still hear it, her infectious little laugh."

"But then she stands real quick, and she's looking down at her feet. I stand too and look down at the ice. I see something weird. Streaks of bubbles? And—what the heck is that?"

"Liesl says my name, real serious, like she's scared. 'Stevie,' she says. 'There's water under me.'"

"A baby screams somewhere behind me, but muffled like it's coming from inside the house. It's Max. He's crying his head off. That kid had some lungs. I say to Liesl, 'Just stay there. I'm coming!' Or did I *want* to say that? Funny. I can't remember. But I remember what comes next. I remember that well."

"The baby screams louder until it fills the entire world."

That face. An unfamiliar voice whispers to him. It's not his own voice, and it's not Dr. Nguyen. It sounds like sweet rot. *That face you'll never forget, will you, Stevie-boy?*

"Don't call me that."

Dr. Nguyen's voice sounds far away now. *"Call you what? Steve, listen—"*

"Liesl! Her eyes are wide and filled with tears, like she knows what's about to happen."

"Steve—open your eyes." A light shines from above, unnatural, flashing over the hills and icy river like a massive spotlight.

The voice whispers, *Stevie, she is going under the ice. She's going under the ice. She'll wash away down to the locks, where she'll be sucked down even deeper. You've heard stories about the giant catfish. Remember them? There were divers who saw a catfish in the dark places of the Mississippi—thirty feet long! They won't find her body. And if they did—oh, Stevie, if they did. Do you know what they would have found? Do you have any idea?*

"Liesl stares at me for those last seconds and says—"

You know what she says. You hear it every night.

"She says, 'Stevie, I—' and she's gone. Falls through the ice. Drops into the river. I run to catch her, but she's gone."

The voice laughs, cruelly. *Did you see a red coat through the frozen water, shooting down the river, little hands pounding on the ice as her tiny lungs fill with freezing water?*

"No! I never saw that. I saw nothing like that!"

You sure?

"Yes."

Are you Stevie? Are you sure?

"Yes!"

Lie to yourself, Stevie boy. Lie to yourself.

"I'm not lying—"

You shouldn't be here. You've no business in this place. Leave before I take you and put you under the ice like your sister. Down with the giant catfish. The story of the divers...

"I need her—"

What you seek isn't here.

"What I seek?"

It's behind the wall. Behind the wall—look behind the wall—you missed something, Stevie-boy. Look behind the wall. And remember.

With that, the entire wintry scene dissolves, and Steve finds himself back in reality. When he opens his eyes, he's lying on his back, staring up at Dr. Nguyen, who is kneeling over him with a pair of smelling salts in her fingers.

"Steve?"

"How did I—"

"You passed out. Are you OK?"

"I think so." Steve stands, light-headed and wobbly on his feet, but alert.

"Please, have a seat."

Checking his watch, he says, "I think my time is up. Isn't it?"

"Don't worry about that. Just sit." She stands next to him, patting his arm. "I'm inclined to call the paramedics."

"No, no, I'm fine. I need to rest for a moment. Wow, that was strange. I imagined that day on the river. Was I speaking out loud?"

"Yes. You were telling me all about it. Though it sounded like you were responding to someone else. Were you talking to someone in your dream?"

Steve looks at her, unsure of what to say. "I..."

"Remember, it's important you tell me everything."

Deciding there's no point in keeping it to himself—if she chucks him into a looney bin, maybe it's for the best—Steve nods. "There was a voice."

"Whose voice?" she asks, no hint of surprise in her voice.

"I don't know."

"And this voice spoke to you?"

"Yes."

"In the memory?"

"Yes."

"What did it say?"

"I don't remember word-for-word, but the voice was mocking me."

"You didn't recognize it?"

"No."

Look behind the wall...

"And you don't remember what it said to you? Anything?"

"One thing. I remember one thing it said."

"What was that?"

"Look behind the wall."

A quizzical expression pinches her face into a frown. "Behind the wall? What does that mean?"

Steve thinks. "I'm not sure. But I need to go." He stands and puts on his jacket.

"Where?"

He waits next to the chair, running over every event from the past few days. Finally, a thought occurs to him. "The Milton's. I need to go to the Milton's house again. Something I missed."

"You should stay and rest for a while."

"No, I'm fine. I promise. And I don't want to keep you from your clients. Next week then?" he asks.

"Yes. Monday."

"You got it."

Steve waves goodbye and ignores the woman waiting in the lobby—the one with the bloody hands. She laughs as he exits.

Chapter Twenty-One

"I'm sorry to bother you, Mrs. Milton."

"Gladys! Oh, two visits in two days, and with the same visitor. This is most unusual for our house, I can promise you that. But not unwelcome. How can I help you today, Mr. Spain?"

"I was hoping I could get back into your son's room. I think I might have missed something."

"What could that be?" Gladys Milton's caked on foundation is moist and smeared in places on her cheeks just below the rims of her glasses. Behind the thick lenses, her bulging eyes are bloodshot and her plastic smile reveals two rows of yellow teeth. The hand propping open the storm door holds a wadded tissue in its palm.

"I brought back the film I borrowed yesterday."

"Oh, why thank you. That was fast. Did you see anything that was helpful?"

"Maybe. If you wouldn't mind, I'd like one more look around. I'm sorry if this is a bad time."

She considers him for several moments, her eyes staring through him. Her tone turns icy. "I'm sorry. I don't see what you could have missed yesterday. You didn't look through the bookcase? It has all the films on it."

"I did. There may be more to the film, something your son cut from the footage. He might have hidden it somewhere."

She glances behind her, up the stairs. "I wouldn't know anything about it. I've found nothing hidden in his room, nor anywhere else."

"Maybe the basement or the attic?"

"There isn't much down there anymore. We had a mouse problem and had to get rid of things. I didn't find film in any of those boxes. My husband gutted the attic two years ago to make room for his woodworking. Anything that was up there would be gone by now."

"I see. All the same, I wonder if you'd let me look around his room again—if it's not too much trouble. I promise, after that, I'll be out of your hair forever."

"Oh, now that would be a shame." She looks him over again, then opens the screen wider. "You know your way, don't you? I'd show you up, but my ankles are bothering me today."

"Yes, I remember the way. And thank you, Mrs. Milton."

"Gladys, please. And you're welcome."

"Gladys. Thank you."

The bedroom door creaks and Steve steps into Joey Milton's childhood bedroom. All of Joey's things remain where he left them the last time he was in this room. Part of Steve feels like he's intruding on someone else's life.

As he opens the closet door, he notes the relative silence of the house, compared to the noise of work the day before. Mr. Milton must be on a break from his woodworking. Steve returns the can of film he borrowed yesterday back in its place on the shelf. Shifting onto his knees, he pulls out his cell phone and touches the icon for the flashlight app. Once again, a draft blows through the closet from left to right.

"Where's that draft coming from?" Steve asks himself.

Scooting on his knees into the closet, he reaches to his right, tapping the side wall. A hollow sound echoes in response. With his palm, he gives a light push, feeling the lower section of the wall give a little. Shifting further into the closet, he runs his fingers along the edges of the side wall. His fingernail finds a minuscule lip at the corner. The cut of drywall catches for a second, then releases with a poof of dust. Steve coughs and covers his mouth and eyes.

The dust settles to reveal a crawl space, a few feet wide, leading from Joey's closet to the outer wall of the house. Aged cobwebs fill the space.

He lowers himself and squeezes his shoulders into the opening. Several old toys, Star Wars figures, lie here and there at the end of the nook. Shuffling through the toys, covered in years of dust, he discovers more figures, a few poker chips, several checkers, and a tattered sweatshirt, but no film canister.

"Dammit," Steve whispers.

An irregular area of the wall catches his attention. "A second hiding space?"

To his wonder, it pops out with only a little pressure, revealing a narrow cubby-hole just broad enough to fit his hand. Steve shines the phone flashlight into the opening. More green plastic army men, dozens of dust bunnies, but he notices something metallic leaning against the back. The light illuminates a dirty silver film canister. His heart races. Grasping the can, he retreats from the crawl space. Emerging from the closet, he discovers he is not alone. An older man stands in the doorway, his sparse silver hair shooting out on all sides of his skull. Thick black reading glasses teeter on the end of his nose, constrained by a lanyard fastened to each temple. His white button-up shirt is dusty and smudged with grease, sawdust, and glue, the sleeves rolled up to his elbows.

"Mr. Milton?" Steve asks.

"They're in the walls," Ronald Milton says, ignoring the query.

"Who is?"

"Goddamn creepers. They climb from the walls to the rafters. You can't force them to leave no matter what you do. They'd been mute for a long time—until you happened along." Ronald's eyes drift downward until they land on the film canister in Steve's fist. "What you got there, Mister—"

"Spain. Steve."

Ronald's bloated, languorous eyes drift up to meet Steve's. "What do you have there, Mr. Spain, Steve?"

"Oh, just some film footage. Part of your son's movie—"

"He ain't here."

"What's that?" Steve says.

"Joey. He ain't here."

Steve pauses for a moment, not sure what the old man is talking about. "Yes, I know—"

"He'll be away for some time. He got hung up with demons to wrestle, as I say."

"Yes. Well—"

"Don't believe me?" Ronald looks down his nose at him, biting his lower lip.

"I didn't say that."

"What do you want with his movie?"

"Oh, just curious to see what's on it."

Ronald laughs. "Might wish you hadn't."

"Why is that?"

Ronald cranes his neck to the ceiling. "You ain't from this area."

"No. My wife and I moved here last weekend. But I've spent a lot of time here."

Ronald crosses to him, halting inches from Steve's face, his eyes shifting back and forth, like an optometrist examining for cataracts. "What is happening in that head?" Ronald asks, his eyes magnified by the lenses of his glasses.

"I don't know what you mean."

Stepping back, Ronald says, "Maybe not. Hard to say."

"What?" Steve says, his fight-or-flight senses kicking in.

"So much to do. So many things." Ronald rubs his chin before turning to the door. "Good luck to you, my friend. There are worse things than death, and they're in your own backyard."

Ronald's footsteps echo across the creaky wood floor as he heads out the door. The sounds of his footsteps diminish, then stop. Steve lets out a long sigh, chuckling to himself. However, as he turns to shut the closet door, the footsteps return, growing louder as if Ronald is running towards the bedroom. When he reappears in the doorway, he's holding a golf club in his right hand, eyes wide and mouth open like a silent scream. Before Steve can register what's happening, Milton springs at him with surprising agility for a man his age. He swings the club with one wild lunge, catching Steve square in the temple.

Steve collapses on the wood floor.

Chapter Twenty-Two

Eyes open, then closed, open again. A haze of brown and gold and smothers the room in strange shadows, with only one light source above and a lamp next to Steve. He is vaguely conscious of movement and a dim figure some place in front of him. A dull ache throbs at the side of his head and he can't move his arms or his feet. "Am I paralyzed?" he asks himself aloud.

A voice responds, but he can't make out the words. A male voice, he thinks. Or is it a husky female? It's too muffled to tell. Details focus, bit by bit. Dark wood everywhere, and above, the ceiling is unfinished, only bare rafters. It looks like an attic. The Milton attic.

"Are you there?" a man's voice says, clearer now. "Hello?"

"Yes. I..."

"Ah, there you are. Good, good. I didn't want you dying on us. No, that wouldn't be good."

Gaining more understanding of his position, Steve realizes he's tied to a wood chair, his forearms duck taped to the arms. His forehead appears to be secured by duct tape to something behind him, making it impossible to turn his head more than an inch in either direction. He squints across the room. A man lurks in the shadows, his back to him, stooped over some object. All around the area are unfinished wood toys—trains, cars, boats, and blocks of assorted proportions. Steve moves his mouth to speak, but cannot form words.

There's a woman at the far end of the room. Her thick glasses reflect the lamplight, offering the illusion of gleaming eyes. Her mouth twists into an uneasy grin, her palms clasped at her waist.

"Help..." Steve whispers to her, the sound hardly discernible as a word.

The woman shifts her head with a woeful expression. She adjusts her glasses, then descends the stairs and withdraws from sight.

"Oh, you've discovered your voice, I see. Good, good." The man turns to him. It is Ronald Milton, bearing a long metal device with a sharp edge at its end—some kind of woodworking tool.

"What are you doing?" Steve says.

Ronald tilts his head to the left. "What's that you say? I don't hear so good in my left ear."

"What are you doing?" Steve raises his voice only a little, his head drumming with pain.

Forehead furrowed with an expression you might give someone who's speaking gibberish, Ronald says, "What do you mean?"

"Why am I tied to this chair?"

"Oh, that. I should think you'd know why you're here."

Steve thinks for a moment. "Your son's film."

"That was why you *came* to our house. But why you're tied to this chair? Don't you know?"

"I don't."

Ronald scratches the top of his head with a vexed sigh. "That's odd. But then, maybe it's not *you* answering me. Maybe it's not you at all. Or perhaps you don't know. Maybe it's kept the whole thing from you."

"What—"

"Son, you realize you've got a secret, right? You know what I'm talking about. There's no use in pretending with me."

"Secret? I don't understand—"

Ronald crouches so that his eyes are even with his own, inches away. He taps Steve on the forehead. "What you've got inside you?"

Steve's vision drifts in and out of focus again. "Inside me?"

"Yes."

"What are you talking—"

Ronald thumps him again with his thumb. "What you've got inside this noggin'? Your undesirable visitor."

"My undesirable—what?"

"Visitor. A possessor. A demon, son. Living right inside you and, well, we've got to get him out."

"I don't have any—"

"Now, don't you worry about it one bit, you hear? I have practiced with this kind of thing before. The last time—the last time it didn't go so well, ya see. Now, that I will admit, OK? But I learned from it. A man can learn from his mistakes, so don't you worry. We'll get this demon and yank it out of you if it's the last thing we do, so help me. The breath of God!"

"The last time?"

"Forget about that. This is different. You're stronger than he was—better suited. I think we can get this done, and you'll still have most of your mind when it's finished."

"What the fuck are you talking about?"

Robert crosses the room and takes something from the workbench. A claw, perhaps? "You're possessed, son, sure as the day is long. And I mean to rid you of it. You can thank me later."

"I'm not possessed. I don't need an exorcism!" Steve struggles against the duct tape.

"Exorcism? That's one way to do it. But exorcists—true exorcists—don't grow on trees. And most of the time, it doesn't really work. Takes weeks, maybe months, for that kind of thing. We don't have that kind of time, my friend. No, we do not. The day is coming. It's almost here. Thank the Lord, you showed up at my door just in time."

Steve searches in vain for something he might use to defend himself. "What?"

"It takes years just to get the church to listen to your tale, and even then there's no guarantee they'll endorse it. Many people are suffering for no reason. Sad!"

"I'm not suffering."

Robert takes a small plastic bottle from the workbench, holds it up so Steve can see, and shakes it. It's the bottle of Xanax he keeps in his pocket. "Healthy people don't need medication, my friend."

"Help! Someone help me!"

"There's no use in calling out. No one will hear you through these walls. Dispatching a demon is a loud business, and I am prepared for it. I had the roof sound-proofed a few years ago. So don't you worry, no one will hear your screams."

"Screams?"

"Oh, yes. Pain is the only thing a demon can't abide. Prayers? Holy water? That's all phoney baloney. To rid yourself of a demon, pain is the ticket. Demons aren't used to the sensation. In fact, in their normal form, they don't feel pain at all, or at least not like we feel it. So, when one of them possesses a person, they're making quite a sacrifice, you see? They hate the pain we go through—can't abide it. That's why the early Church used to burn them alive; the best way to drive out a demon. Of course, that method ends up with the vessel dead, and we don't want that, do we, my friend? Of course not! So they have given me this task, appointed by God Himself. It's true. I'm here to help you, Mr. Spain. Can you see that now?"

Steve searches his mind for any idea. "Maybe I don't want to rid myself of the demon. Maybe I want to keep him."

Ronald nods. "Sounds like demon-talk. Oh, I've heard it all."

"Please, Mr. Milton. Please. I have a wife—I have children!"

"There is more reason to do what we must. Don't you see it? You came here for a reason—"

"Yes! I came here for the film. Your son's film!"

"No, the film was only the catalyst. You made yourself come back here. Somewhere in your soul, you knew you needed my help. Hidden film cans? Silly!"

"No, I *found* it! The hidden film cannister—right in your son's closet, hidden behind a false wall. Come look! It's right here in my jacket—right pocket."

A curious expression comes over Ronald's face as he considers Steve's trench coat. He rubs his chin with his hand and crosses to it. Reaching into the pocket, Ronald pulls out the small aluminum film can. "Hm," he says.

"You see? That's the hidden can of film in your son's closet. I wasn't making that up."

Milton stares at the cannister. "Yes. I see. What's on this film, you think?"

"I don't know. But it must have meant something to your son. Important enough to hide it."

"I asked what you *think*."

"Maybe a clue."

"To the Harmon girl's disappearance?"

"Yes. Maybe. Just maybe, the Harmon girl herself."

Milton slides the film back into the coat pocket. "Interesting."

"I think your son may have filmed her. I'm hoping he left a clue behind on that film. After all, he must have hid it for a good reason, wouldn't you agree?"

Ronald stares at the floor—a hint of hesitation, perhaps? "Hm. Interesting. I admit, that is most interesting."

A glimmer of hope rushes through Steve's chest. "*That's* why I came back here. I don't have a demon inside me—I'm trying to find the girl. That's all."

Milton sits on a swivel stool next to the workbench and leans forward, his elbows resting on his knees. "But why do you need Joseph's film? There are people who know what happened to Jessica Harmon, and many more who suspect."

"Who?"

"Oh, the police, for starters. There was obviously more to the story than they told us. Not everyone thought Melly's story was crazy. Some would have you believe the girl disappeared into thin air, but there are others of us who know better."

"Who is trying to suppress the truth? And why?"

"I have my theories. The first place you should have looked was right under your nose."

Steve blinks at him for a moment. "What do you mean?"

"The Old Road. Where my son saw her."

"You mean where he *said* he saw her, but then took back the story?"

"No. Where he *saw* her. Their first report was the truth; I know it. The Old Road separates the Jensens from the Tuppers on the other side of your own property. Those two families go back generations and most of that history isn't pretty."

"How so?"

Shrugging, Ronald says, "There's a darkness out there on the land—your land, too. Maybe that's how you came to be afflicted, maybe not. But everyone knows not to press your luck with that lot. Each year, they invite everyone in town to their July fourth party, their Christmas party, their Halloween party, but no one sane dares to attend. No one but the Jensens, Tuppers, and the good citizens under their sway. I've heard stories about what goes on during those parties and it's not fit for humankind, believe you me. Nothing good has come from that nest of vipers, and nothing ever will. Still, despite all that, I suggest you give them a visit if you survive this day."

"Survive? Can't you see that I'm only interested in finding the truth?" Steve's bound hands are gripping the arms of the chair.

"It appears so. But that changes nothing."

"Why?"

"Your intentions may be your own, or maybe not. But the fact remains, you still have a demon inside you. We've got to get him out before he does something evil. You won't find the girl if you try."

"There's no—"

"Hush, now. I know this isn't easy, being tortured. It's not anyone's idea of fun. I so wish it didn't have to come to this, really I do." Ronald steps across the room to a stack of cardboard boxes, old and beaten from years of storage. He reaches into the top box, pulls out what appears to be a car battery and a bunch of wires, sets them on a small table to Steve's left, and connects the wires to the battery on one end and a square box with a red switch and a knob on the other.

"Mr. Milton. You don't need to do this. I'm not possessed!"

Ronald smirks as he works. "More demon talk. Haven't you wondered why you moved here, Mr. Spain?"

"I've always loved it here."

"Have you?"

"Yes, sir. Since I was a kid."

"You come up here to fish and camp?"

"Yes."

"Catch a lot of fish here, Mr. Spain?" Ronald moves away from Steve.

"Yes."

Ronald watches him from the back of the attic, partially covered in shadow. "Have you caught many fish?"

"Well, I can't remember every fish I ever caught. A lot over the years."

"You're a liar, Mr. Spain. A liar, or at least the thing inside you is a liar. As long as it has hold of you, you'll never find Jesse Harmon. It won't let you. We have to expel it first, then you can sort this mystery out. Ready?"

Ronald crosses to the other side of the attic, near the stairs, then reaches down and returns with a worn leather doctor's bag. He sets it on a second table to Steve's right, then opens the bag and pulls out four soft round pieces of fabric with something metal attached to them. One by one, Milton attaches them to the ends of the wires, then steps closer to Steve, kneeling. "I apologize for this, but I need to open your shirt."

"What are you doing?"

Milton unbuttons Steve's oxford to expose his chest and stomach. He then sticks the connectors to Steve's chest and stomach, leaving one hanging unattached. "Again, I apologize. This will be a little awkward," he says, then unzips Steve's slacks, pulling them along with his underwear down to his ankles.

Gingerly, Milton reaches between Steve's legs and lifts his scrotum, attaching the last connector just below the left testicle. Standing, the old man backs away and retrieves the control box.

"No! No! Please don't do this! Help! Help! Mrs. Milton!" Steve's screams ring out through the attic.

"I'm sorry, Mr. Spain. I am. But this is the only way."

Tears run down Steve's face. "Stop! Just stop!"

Ronald smiles at him, then sets his thumb next to the switch. He takes a deep breath and Steve braces himself, his chest pounding as a wave of panic overwhelms him.

Click.

Nothing. Forehead furrowed, Ronald turns the knob back and forth. "Well, dammit all!"

He hits the thing once or twice with the heel of his hand and a second later, a jolt of electricity runs through Steve's body, sending a flood of pain so sharp and so intense, he cannot make a sound. Waves of electricity pulse through him, flexing his muscles so tight great spasms rise in his chest and stomach. However, the pain emanating from his testicles pulls at him until he feels like he might break through the duct tape holding his head in place.

"Oh, golly!" Ronald flips off the switch, and the pain abates. "I neglected to offer you something to bite down on! I'm so sorry."

Steve's arched back recedes into the chair and a curious taste, something comparable to pennies, fills his mouth. Unable to speak, he weeps uncontrollably.

"Oh dear, your mouth is bleeding. You must have bitten your tongue. I'm so very sorry!" Ronald rushes to him with a rag and wipes the blood that's flowing down his chin. "That was very foolish of me! Please, forgive me!"

"Forgive?"

"I know, I know. But once we're done, you'll thank me. I don't want to do any permanent harm if I can avoid it." Taking another rag, Milton rolls it into a long rope-like coil and places it in his mouth. "There. That will help with the biting." Taking the controls once again, Milton places his thumb next to the switch and says, "Shall we resume?"

Riding a wave of anguish unlike anything he's ever felt before, Steve sits in the pain for what feels like hours. At some point, he thinks he can hear his phone ringing through the rolling agony, but he barely recognizes the sound. Helpless, he suffers through seizure after seizure, until he loses consciousness.

Chapter Twenty-Three

"Steve?" Mara says into her phone. "Why aren't you answering? You've got me worried. Your brother's flight lands in like an hour. Are we still picking him up together? Please, call me."

The woods outside grow darker and a curious silence envelops the land on a pillow of apprehension. Something's happened to Steve. A tingle runs up the back of her neck as she admits it to herself. Rocky whines at her.

"It's OK, bubba," Mara says. "We'll find him."

She looks out the windows, thinking of a million scenarios, each one worse than the next. The only appointment he'd scribbled on the kitchen calendar was his eleven o'clock therapy session. It's not like he could have forgotten about Max—he'd been talking about picking him up just this morning. With Steve's anxiety, any variation in routine sets off alarm bells.

As if on cue, Mara's ring tone sounds out in her hand. "Hey, Max."

"Hey. I tried calling Steve, but his phone keeps going to voicemail."

"Yeah, he's not picking up for me either."

"Well, I made it to Chicago. They're scooting us onto the puddle jumper to Moline now. Should be there a little early."

Mara looks at the clock. "Shit."

"What's wrong?"

"I don't know where the hell Steve is, so I guess I better pick you up myself. It will take like forty minutes to get to the Moline airport, but I'll be there by the time you get your luggage."

"OK, we're boarding now. See you soon."

"See you."

Rocky stands and creeps toward the front hallway, a low growl thrumming in his chest. Mara makes her way to the front door and looks out the peephole, then through the window, finding nothing there. "What is it, Rock?"

The dog whines at her once, then does a one-eighty, returning to his spot behind the sofa.

Mara shakes her head and sighs. A thought occurs to her. She runs into the kitchen and looks at a small business card held to the front of the refrigerator by a Happy Joe's Pizza magnet. She dials the number and waits.

A gentle voice answers, "Hello?"

"Hi, is this Doctor Nguyen?"

Chapter Twenty-Four

1.

A blurry light some distance away flickers above the ruin of a bridge, framed by a halo of gnarled branches. The light wavers in the frosty air for several moments until it drifts away across the bridge and down a gravel road several yards before veering into the brush.

Steve tries following the strange illumination, but his feet won't move—they're stuck in something—arms fixed to his sides. He screams, but his voice seems to die inches past his mouth. Through it all, a curious sensation tickles his consciousness, as if he's asleep and someone's struggling to wake him. But if that were true, why doesn't he wake?

He wanders alone for a while before another light highlights the world to his left. This one is like a lightbulb dangling from a ceiling, brightening a small circle on a plaster floor. A figure emerges from the gloom, striding into the cone of light. It is a man, younger than Ronald, wearing a beat up trucker cap. Steve can barely make his face in the shadow created by the light above, but not enough to recognize him. The man's mouth moves, but no sound comes forth, none that Steve can hear.

The world goes black again.

Some time later, the attic comes back into view as Steve's eyes crack open. Ronald stands above him, looking down on his face as he rubs Steve's shoulder, giving an affectionate smile. "There you are. You passed out on me. I thought I'd let you rest for a while. Might not have been the wisest thing to do, but it pains me to see you suffering. I'm not cut out for this, maybe. And I'm ashamed to admit I dozed off a few hours myself."

Steve groans and smacks his lips in response.

"Are you thirsty?" Ronald asks.

"Yes," he croaks out, his head lolling to the side.

Ronald brings a bottle of water from the other side of the room. Steve opens his mouth and sips as Ronald tips a small stream of water over his lips. "Easy now," Ronald says, pulling the bottle away and replacing the cap. "I mustn't go too soft on you. Remember, we still have to drive the demon out."

"It's out," Steve says.

"Not yet. But we're getting there. This demon is stubborn—we need to double our efforts." Ronald picks up a square wooden box, a little larger than a Rubik's Cube, and waves it above his head. One side of it is open with a metal crank fixed to the opposite side. Ronald asks, "Do you know what this is?"

Steve shakes his head.

"No? Well, in World War II, the gestapo developed several horrific torture devices, perhaps none so awful as this one. Having your testicles injured is one of the most painful things a man can experience. Such a pain will bring him to his knees. Even the slightest of pressure produces an agony unlike any other a man can experience. Imagine the effect when they're crushed."

Steve gasps for breath as his chest tightens.

Ronald continues. "There's dubious evidence for the efficiency of torture on obtaining intelligence from prisoners. Depending on the stakes, a captive might resist many forms of displeasure to keep an enemy at bay. He will lie to buy time for his compatriots or his loved ones. We must take anything learned through torture with the proverbial grain of salt.

However, I'm not here to gain information, Mr. Spain, only to turn out a demon. As I informed you earlier, demons hate pain."

Steve shakes his head. "Please. Please, don't do this."

"I hate causing permanent damage in a session like this, but given your age, you don't need your testicles for anything important. I presume you've had your children, or if you haven't by now, you won't. You're past your child-rearing years, so why does sex matter?"

"You're crazy, you know that? You're fucking crazy. Out of your fucking mind!"

Ronald twists his lips in a grimace, as a shadow moves over his face. His voice, no longer the kind old man, darkens to match his face. "Ah, there it is—the demon speaks. We're getting close."

"I have a wife. I have kids."

"All the more reason to rid yourself of the abomination."

Ronald moves closer, holding the wooden box by the crank. Kneeling, he gives a regretful smile—the same smile a coach might give while cutting a kid from the varsity squad. Taking Steve's scrotum in his icy palm, he lifts it and presses the testicles into the opening, then looks into Steve's watering eyes. "As much as I hate myself for what I'm about to do to you, there's no other choice. As I look at you, I see the evil just behind your pupils, waiting for me to drive it out. You may not believe me now, but when we're finished, you'll thank me for it. You'll love me for it."

"Please, Mr. Milton. Please!"

"Demon, you can save yourself and your host much anguish by leaving this man now. No further harm need come to you or him. Leave this host at once and return to your hell!"

Steve struggles against the rope and duct tape, but Ronald has him so fixed to the chair, he cannot find even an inch of purchase. Heart pounding, blood rising, fingers tingling, he chokes for air. His chest tightens again as panic sets in.

With a screech of wood grinding together against metal, Ronald turns the crank, one-hundred-eighty degree turn, by one-hundred-eighty degree turn. The wall of the little box closes in, pushing his testicles in opposite directions until they line up side by side—and still the walls press on with each turn of the old man's wrist. Tears break loose from Steve's eyes once more and as the pressure intensifies, a ghastly scream bursts forth from his lips.

Every nerve running from his lower abdomen down through his groin and around to his anus flares with fiery agony. One more twist of the knob and the pain becomes so intolerable, Steve thinks his eyes might pop out of his head.

"I call on you, demon! Get out of this poor man's soul! I cast you out!"

Through all the hideous sensations, Steve's eyes catch a hint of movement somewhere behind Ronald. He wonders for a moment if he's hallucinating. But then someone shouts something from behind Ronald. At first, he can't make out what the person is saying, but after several moments, the sound becomes clearer.

"Ronald, step away from Mr. Spain! Put down—uh—whatever you have in your hands and step away. Now!"

Ronald, head bowed, does not remove his hands from the box, nor it from Steve's testicles. The pressure remains constant enough to cause pain as it is. Part of him wishes the old bastard would give that crank and good twist to get it over with and end this intolerable agony once and for all. Milton's knuckles are white with tension.

There is a man in the shadows with two others. They're pointing something at Ronald. *Guns! Yes, that's it. The police!*

"Ronald! This is your last warning! You step away from that poor man or I'll blow your goddamn head off, I swear to god!"

"I can't, Chief. I can't."

"What?"

"Can't!"

"Yes, you can. Just crawl to the left and sit your ass on the floor." The man steps into a beam of light cast by one of the glaring bulbs hanging above them, and recognition floods Steve's mind.

Ronald ignores their orders. "I'm sorry. But I can't let this demon remain."

"The hell you talking about, Ronald? He's got no demon in him. He's just a man, like you or me."

"I don't know about you, Chief Branton, but he's not like me," Ronald says, giving Steve a sideways glance.

"Just step away, Ronald. I don't want to shoot you, but god so help me..."

"It's OK. God will stay your hand, for just a moment more, I think." Ronald looks at Steve, his eyes filled with tears. "Tell Gladys—tell her I love her. I always did." Without another word, Ronald winks at Steve, then twists the crank with all the strength his arthritic knuckles can muster.

The sound of flesh crunching followed by a wave of pain seizes Steve's entire body and he falls into a series of convulsions. Gunshots ringing out in the dusty attic, and the last thing he sees is the lightbulb above him, swinging in the dim room until a black curtain falls and Steve's mind drifts away.

2.

A white light becomes brighter, pushing through the blackness until it is all Steve can see—nothing but white light all around him. Details emerge—a ceiling and walls, both white as winter snow. A remote beeping sound echoes from some place outside but not far away and a metallic voice mumbles something or other about a surgeon this or nurse that. He hears a voice—a recognizable male voice—speaking in a muffled baritone.

"Steve? You awake?"

Footsteps leave the room and the voice says something to someone outside the room. Two sets of footsteps return followed by two heads hovering above him. One is Mara, the other is his brother.

"Max?" Steve says, his voice hoarse.

Max smiles. "Hey, there. Fancy meeting you here."

"Steve, are you OK?" Mara says.

Taking stock of himself, he determines he is OK, though perhaps more than a little sore. Well, most of his body. One area is not sore at all—there is no feeling at all. His middle section feels numb, almost paralyzed, and worry floods his brain. He reaches for his privates, finding them wrapped in a soft gauze.

"Don't touch!" Mara says. "Let it heal."

"Is everything—OK?" Steve asks.

Mara and Max look at each other. Max steps away from the bed and out of the room.

"Oh, god," Steve says.

"Don't worry. I promise you'll be fine and they—they saved one of your testicles."

"What?"

"They had to remove the other. But it's fine—they said you only need one for everything to function like normal. It's all good." Mara pulls a chair closer to the bed and kisses his hand.

"What the fuck?" He glares at the ceiling, running everything through his mind. "And Milton?"

"Dead."

"Good riddance," Max says from the doorway, then crosses to the left side of the bed opposite Mara. "How you doing, Steve-O?"

"Uh, not so good." Steve looks away. The pity in Max's eyes is almost too much to bear.

"I'm sure. But it looks like they're going to let you out of here tomorrow morning. They want to make sure your ticker is OK."

"Where are we?" Steve asks.

"Davenport East," Mara says.

"What time is it?"

"About three," Max says.

"You sure Milton's dead?"

"As a doorknob." Max pats Steve's arm. "You don't have to worry about him."

"And Gladys? Mrs. Milton?"

Mara shrugs. "She was in custody last we heard. Not sure what they will do with her. I assume it depends on what you tell them. The police were here a while ago to interview you. They're waiting for you to wake up."

Steve sighs. "Can I get out tonight?"

Max and Mara glance at each other. Mara says, "I don't know. Why would you want to? It's best for them to monitor you for a while. You've had quite an ordeal, it sounds like."

Max nods. "You just rest, bro."

For the first time since waking, Steve notices Mara's eyes are red and bloodshot, like she's been weeping for hours. Even Max looks like he's been crying. "I'd rather be home with Rocky and you guys."

Mara stares at him for a while, then says, "I guess we can ask them after you talk with the police. But let's not rush into it. Give yourself some time to rest."

A nurse, blond with bright green eyes, pops into the room and cuts in front of Mara to check his IV. "You're awake," the nurse says. "Good. How are you feeling?" Her voice is loud and scratchy, more like a bartender than a healthcare professional.

"Sore. But OK, I guess," Steve says.

"Great. The police are waiting in the hall. Do you feel up to answer a few questions? If not, I can send them away until later."

"No, it's fine. Send them in. But would it be possible for me to leave tonight instead of tomorrow?"

Writing something down on her clipboard, the nurse frowns. "Who said you're going home tomorrow?"

Max says, "The doctor told us that earlier."

Shaking her head, she says, "You only came out of surgery an hour ago. If I were you, I'd take as much time to rest as they'd allow me. I'll be right back with the officers."

Minutes later, Chief Branton and another officer—an older guy with graying hair and a short white beard—position themselves at the foot of the hospital bed. "Mr. Spain, glad to see you're doing OK, all things considered," says the chief. "You need anything?"

"No, I think I'm good for now," Steve says.

"Good." Branton extends his hand to Mara. "I'm Chief Branton. This is one of my officers, Sargent Lane. So, I have a few questions. Won't take up too much of your time. I think we have everything we will need, but can I ask what you were doing at the Milton's house yesterday? Did it have to do with your investigation for Melly Harmon?"

"Yes," Steve says.

Branton nods, getting out a pad of paper and pencil. "I thought so. Because of his son's involvement in the mistaken identification?"

"Yes."

"And who assaulted you?"

"Mr. Milton. Ronald Milton."

"Mhm. Where did the assault take place?"

"Joey's bedroom."

Branton stops writing and looks down at him. The other officer maintains an icy, indecipherable stare. "What were you doing in their son's bedroom?" Branton asks.

"Searching for info."

"Information on Jesse Harmon's disappearance?"

"Yes."

"Did you find anything?"

Steve pauses and looks back and forth between the officers. "Nothing extraordinary."

"They tied you to a chair in the attic. How did Milton subdue you?"

"He hit me over the head with something. Don't remember what it was, but it hurt. I can tell you that." Steve's head throbs and his heart rate speeds up.

"I'm sure. You didn't notice how Mr. Milton got you into the attic, did you?"

Steve thinks. "No. That whole time is blank. But I would guess he had his wife help him—she is a strong-looking woman. And at some point, I think someone else may have been there. A man."

"Really? Did you get a look at him?"

Steve says, "No. And I can't be sure if I really saw another man or not. I thought I saw a guy with a beat up old trucker hat on in between passing out. But, like I said, I can't be sure of it."

The cops glance at each other. Branton asks, "Do you know if Gladys Milton was aware of your presence in the attic?"

"Oh, she knew. When I first came to, duct taped to that chair, she was standing there watching us. She looked—I don't know—troubled, I guess. It was almost like she wanted to help me, but when I called to her, she turned and walked back down the stairs. But, yeah, she knew I was there. She heard my screams. I know it."

Mara covers her face, sobbing, and runs out of the room. Max steps back from the bed and turns to the windows.

Chief Branton shakes his head, incredulity written on his face. "We guessed she had to have known, but she's not saying a word about any of it right now. Still, I think she will before long. There's a guilty look on her face—a sadness. She'll confess."

"Guilt? I hope she chokes on it."

The officers glance at each other. Branton says, "As for the Harmon girl—did you find anything in their house relevant to that case?"

"No, nothing."

Branton says, "Any idea why Milton targeted you?"

"He said he saw a demon in me."

Neither the chief nor Sargent Lane react, though Branton writes something on his notepad. "What did he do to you?"

Steve's voice catches as he speaks. "He hooked up—hooked me up to a car battery and electrocuted me." He notices Mara turn away. "Did that for quite a while. I passed out a few times. Then he—" Tears stream down his face and his mouth refuses to say anything more.

"He used the wood box on your testicles?" Branton says.

Steve nods.

"And that was when we arrived?"

"Yeah."

"Was he trying to do some kind of exorcism?"

"Not exactly. He said pain is more effective—the demon doesn't want to stay in the body. Lunatic."

Branton nods. "I can't imagine what you went through. But I'm glad to hear you're doing OK. I wish we'd gotten there earlier."

"Me too."

"Will this be the end of your Harmon investigation?" The chief's eyes present a feigned disinterest, but the attempt appears deceptive.

"I don't know," Steve says.

"Might be a good idea."

"Why?"

The chief tucks the pen in his shirt pocket and sets the pad of paper under his arm, hooking his thumb on his gun belt. "Well, look what came of it. Some things are better left alone."

Max, leaning against the windowsill, crosses his arms. Glancing at Steve, he says nothing, but his expression seems to say, *just go along with it.*

"What does Milton have to do with anything? I mean, he didn't attack me because I was investigating the Jesse Harmon case. Right?"

Branton clears his throat. "Probably not. But even so..."

A thick silence hovers over the room for a while as Steve processes the unspoken possibilities in the conversation. "Thanks, Chief. I'll give that some thought. You may be right."

Branton smiles and pats Lane on the back. "Come on Sargent, let's get out of these peoples' hair. They've been through enough already."

"Sorry to make you come all the way down here, Chief."

"No worries. We can visit Lane's brother while we're here in the Quad Cities. Have a good day, folks. See you soon, I hope." The officers turn and exit.

"Wow," Max says.

"What?" Mara asks.

Max shrugs. "Just weird. Seemed like he didn't want you to investigate that case."

"Yeah," Steve says.

"Any idea why?"

"None. He wasn't even the chief back when the girl went missing."

"Strange."

Steve looks at Mara. Her eyes are puffy and wet. She takes his hand, her own filled with wadded tissue.

Max glances back and forth between the two. "I think I'll head down to the cafeteria and grab an egg salad sandwich and some chips. I'll be back in a while."

Mara watches him go, then the floodgates open. She lays her head on his chest and sobs. "I'm sorry. So sorry," she says.

"It's OK."

"No, it's not. I'm supposed to be strong for you, but here I am blathering and you're taking it so well. How on earth are you calm after what happened?"

"I think I'm still in disbelief. That, and whatever meds they gave me. It's like I'm stone."

Lifting her head, she takes his face in her hands and stares into his eyes. "I love you, Steve. I love you so much. Please, consider what the chief said. There's something wrong with this case, I think."

"I think so too."

"Then stay out."

Steve kisses her. "How can I?"

"Easy."

"Difficult. Something stinks. I don't know *what*, but now that I've got the scent, I can't let it go. I can't."

"How's your anxiety?"

"That's the weird thing. I'm not feeling it at all. You'd think I'd be a wreck with everything I've been through, but I'm not. Like I said, must be the shock."

Mara kisses Steve's cheek. "Must be." She climbs into the bed with him and they fall asleep together.

Thirty minutes later, Steve wakes with a jolt, short of breath. A throbbing ache burns his groin and his head feels like it's filled with pebbles. Mara breathes under his arm, still deep asleep. Max sits in a chair near the window, staring at his phone. "Hey," Steve says to him, half-whispering so as not to wake Mara.

"Oh, hey. You're up. How you feel?" Max says.

"Like shit."

"Yeah, I bet."

"How are you holding up? Must be tired after your flight."

"All you've been through and you're worried about me?" Max chuckles, shaking his head.

"You know me."

"Sure do."

Steve looks out the window. All he can see is dark clouds, lit by flashes of lightning from a soon-to-hit storm. They sit in silence, listening to the low rumble of thunder rolling overhead and Mara's heavy sighs of sleep. "Do you believe in hell?" Steve asks.

Max gives him a quizzical look. "Hell? Not really."

"Think it's possible?"

"I think it's doubtful."

"Maybe."

Max says, "Why? You're not thinking about something that lunatic said, are you?"

"I am."

"Steve, that guy was crazy. Crazy people say crazy things—it goes with the package, you know?"

"You don't believe anymore?"

"Not since I was a kid."

"You've been in California too long."

"You've been in Iowa too long."

"Maybe. But what if it's true? A fire that burns forever—burning all the sinners for all eternity—never ending pain." Steve's heart jumps with a small palpitation.

"That would take one fucked up god to allow something like that, don't you think?" Max says.

"Wages of sin."

"Wages of sin is death, not eternal torture."

A memory rushes through Steve's mind and he flinches.

"Oh, sorry. I didn't mean—"

"No, it's OK. It's fine. Max?"

"Yeah?"

"We went fishing up here, didn't we? Growing up?"

"We?" Max smirks. "I never went fishing with you guys. It was always you and dad."

"But we went fishing, right?"

"Yeah. Why?"

Steve looks out the window at another dreary Iowa sky. "Nothing."

The room is silent again as the first drops of rain clink on the window frame outside. Mara's breathing remains steady and deep. The window's reflection on the wall projects a rectangular scene of streaming water like tears falling all over the room. "A fire that burns forever—unquenchable."

Max watches him silently as sleep returns, taking Steve back into memories he'd rather forget, both old and new.

Chapter Twenty-Five

Gladys Milton rests alone in the station interview room, handcuffs fastened to a ring at the center of a square metal table. Fluorescent lights give the already bleakly painted room a dreary glow. If there's one thing Gladys hates, it's bad lighting. She rests on her elbows at the table, hands cupped over her forehead to shield her eyes from the glare.

Why are they putting me through this? Don't they know I wasn't the one torturing the poor man? Don't they understand my Ronald was doing God's work? I'll tell them and they'll see. They'll all see when I'm done. I'll make them see!

She smiles to herself as a pair of officers enter the room. One is the handsome Chief of Police and the other is a grim-looking, older man with a face like a fist. The chief takes the metal chair opposite her, setting a folder, a pad of paper, and a pen in front of him. The grim one moves to the far corner and leans against the wall, crossing his muscular arms.

"Hello, Mrs. Milton," the chief says.

"Please, call me Gladys."

"OK, Gladys."

"How long should this take, Chief Branton?" Gladys asks.

"Pardon?" the chief says, shuffling through some papers in the folder.

"I have to feed the cats at some point this afternoon. And there's an awful mess in the attic from my poor Ronald, plus the funeral arrangements."

"Mrs. Milton—"

"Tut! Gladys."

Branton stares at her wide-eyed. "Gladys. Do you have someone to take care of your pets? A neighbor maybe?"

"Oh, dear no. There's no one I would trust with my babies. Why? Will you need me that long?"

The chief throws a quick glance at the grim one. "Uh, Gladys. I'm afraid you'll be here for a while. No charges yet, but—"

"*Charges*? What in heaven for?"

Branson scoffs. "Why did your husband attack Mr. Spain?"

Gladys doesn't care for this man, nor does she like his attitude. There's a distinct air of braggart she doesn't admire in the least. "He saw evil in him."

"What kind of evil?"

"Does it matter?" Gladys asks, laughing.

"Maybe not, but help me understand."

She scans his face. Ronald would tell her what to think of this police chief. "A demon."

"A demon? Your husband attacked and tortured Mr. Spain because he believed the man was a demon?"

The incredulous tone in his voice makes Gladys want to slap his pretty face. But she takes a breath, gathers herself, and exhales. "No, silly. He didn't believe. Ronald *saw* a demon inside him."

"Inside Mr. Spain?"

"Yes."

"How could he *see* that?"

"My Ronald was blessed, I guess you could say."

Branton sits back in his chair, crossing his arms. "With what?"

"A particular gift. One that only Jesus Himself could offer to a man. Praise the lord!"

Writing on the notepad, Branton says, "I see. Did you ever witness this gift?"

"Oh, yes! I saw it firsthand."

"And did your husband ever tell you how he received a gift like this?"

Though the chief is giving his best attempt at sincerity, Gladys hears the doubt in him, the *sarcasm*. That's another thing Gladys detests with all her being—sarcasm. It's the hallmark of a lack of creativity, she always says. "My Ronald experienced something when he was a child, something that changed him forever."

"What happened to him?"

"Nothing happened *to* him. A miracle occurred and through it, Ronald Milton, at the tender age of eleven, was granted sight beyond sight. One day he was playing in the fields near his parent's farm outside Lost Nation. Have you heard of the town of Lost Nation? It's a tiny little blink-and-you'll-miss-it kind of place. Almost no one lives there now."

"I have. It's over near Clinton," Branton says.

"Yes, that's right," Gladys says. "Well, that's where Ronald was born and where he grew up. And it's where the hand of God touched him, granting him the sight beyond sight."

"God touched him?"

"Yes. Jesus."

"How?"

"Well, now, *that* is a story. While Ronald was playing in the fields by himself, there came a rumbling in the sky. At first, Ronald thought it was thunder, but when he looked up, the sky was blue save only for a few wisps of cloud, here and there. No sign of a storm anywhere. But the rumbling continued, growing louder and louder, until it shook the land itself and almost knocked him right off his feet—on his *bee-hind*, as he used to say to the kids. They'd laugh and laugh!" Gladys covers her mouth with a hand as she chuckles at the memory, eyes watering. "Without warning, an ear-piercing sound snapped through the air, loud enough to bust one of Ronald's eardrums, causing it to bleed down his neck and onto his collar. He had trouble hearing in that ear the rest of his life."

"Anyhoo, when he came back to his senses, Ronald noticed something up there in the sky—something that made little sense at all to him. There was a thin gray line stretching from one horizon to the other, east to west, just a sliver, but long and jagged like a tear in a sheet of aluminum foil. A crack—a crack in the sky! And all at once, the middle of the crack opened up and a hand, if you can believe it, a *hand* reached down through it, right down to the ground, all the way through the warm summer air to my Ronald. And with one finger outstretched, that hand pointed at that odd little boy."

"Well, it froze Ronald in shock—in *awe*, you might say, as I'm sure you can imagine. Just standing there, staring up at the hand of God, his perfect little mouth open wide. And that hand, oh that hand! It reached down and touched Ronald right on the face, right at the bridge of his nose, right between his eyes. And then, just as quick as it came, the hand receded back across that summer sky and was gone. The crack too. After that, Ronald changed. He could sense things about people, evil things. Possessions. He could see it and smell it. When he got to be older, he took exorcism as his calling, ridding people of their demons."

Silence dominates the room for several moments. "Gladys," the chief says. "What he did to Mr. Spain was not an exorcism. It was kidnapping—kidnapping and torture."

"He saved him, Chief Branton. That man owes my husband a eulogy."

"You understand what he did was against the law, right?"

"Exorcising demons? Don't know why it should be illegal. He did that Spain a favor."

"Kidnapping and torture are against the law, no matter the reason."

Gladys doesn't like this man. Not one bit at all. So proud, so vain. "If you want to be technical about it, maybe so, maybe not. But try living with a demon inside you, Chief Branton. Try it sometime, and you might pray for someone to come and remove the thing from you. You might even beg, God forbid."

Branton clears his throat and stares down at the pad of paper. "You knew of your husband's activities?"

"Proudly! Though I admit I'm not as strong as my Ronald. It was hard to hear the cries of pain. I'm not a sphinx! And don't you think it didn't take its toll on my Ronald too."

"And you were aware your husband tied Mr. Spain to a chair in your attic?"

Gladys says, "Indeed. I assisted him in the tying."

"Did you assist your husband with anything else?"

"In the actual—*act*? No. I told you I'm not cut out for that kind of work."

"Did you help your husband any other way?"

"I helped Ronald carry the man up to the attic and secure him to the chair. Which was work, believe you me."

"Did Mr. Spain ask you for help?"

Gladys nods. "Yes, he did, I'm sad to say. Just like all the others."

"*Others?*"

This line of questioning has become rather tedious. Doesn't this man know her babies are getting hungry? "Yes. There have been others. Many."

"How many?"

"That's difficult to say, Chief Branton."

At this, the grim officer in the corner steps closer to the table with a wild look about him. Gladys thinks Ronald might wonder about this one too. If anyone had a demon in him, this officer sure looked the part. The chief?

There is a darkness in there as well. She always could feel it, but Ronald could *see*, and that was better.

Branton folds his hands in front of him. "These others. Where are they now?"

"I'm afraid most of them have gone off to see Jesus, praise the lord. A few lived and even grew to appreciate what my Ronald did for them. Even thanked him!"

"And where are the others, Mrs. Milton? The ones who went to heaven? Where are their bodies?"

"Oh, I promised not to tell." Gladys covers her mouth like a bashful schoolgirl. "But I suppose now that Ronald has gone to Jesus, I can give you a hint."

"Please."

She thinks for a moment until a ridiculous, yellow smile unfurls on her lips. "There's more to our garden than meets the eye." Gladys laughs so violently her glasses fall from her face to the floor. She doesn't pick them up.

Branton rushes from the room, the grim one at his heels. Gladys watches them go, and another giggle erupts from her mouth as she wipes away a tear. Ronald would be so proud.

CHAPTER TWENTY-SIX

1.

Mara pulls the car into the driveway, maneuvering it as close to the front walk as she can get it without drifting onto the dirt. Into the review mirror, she says, "OK, hun, let's take you inside."

"I'll help you, Steve-O." Max hops out and runs around to the rear driver's side door.

"I don't need help, guys," Steve says. "I can manage."

"No need to push it," Mara says into the mirror.

"Yeah, listen to your wife," Max says, extending a hand.

Steve grabs his cane with one hand, accepting Max's hand with the other. "Fine. But I'm not in that much pain, and I'm not paralyzed."

"Doesn't matter. We want to help. Plus, some of these rocks are loose, and I'd hate to have you slip and rip your scrotum open." Max lifts and Steve rises from the car seat.

Once inside the house, Mara does her best to hold Rocky back, who is trying his hardest to attack Steve with slobbery kisses. "Easy, Rocky, you'll pull my arm out of its socket! Calm down!" The mastiff ignores her, dragging Mara down the hall.

"Ha! He's a good listener," Max says.

"Yeah, he doesn't pay attention to Mara at all." Steve manages a stiff, slow walk with the cane in one hand, keeping his other arm around Max's shoulders. "This will take getting used to. I feel like an old man."

"You look like one too." Max laughs.

"I guess so."

"Just kidding. I can't believe you're handling it so well."

"It's OK. It's still like a dream right now with all the meds they've got me on. I'm sure in a few hours I'll be a wreck."

Mara watches Steve. Remembering the kids had wanted to talk to him once he was home, Mara dials their oldest daughter. On the first ring, she picks up, saying, "Hey, are you guys back?"

"Hi Charlotte. Yes, we just got home. Your dad is plopping himself down in his chair right now. Want to talk to him?"

"Yeah. Danny and Viv are here too," Charlotte says, referring to their fraternal twins.

She hands Steve the phone, then signals for Max to join her on the deck. He follows as Steve says into the phone, "No, no, don't you worry. No need to take time off. I know the weekend before Halloween is busy for you guys. Just come down the next weekend."

Outside, Mara pulls a cigarette out of her jacket pocket and lights it.

"You're smoking again?" Max says.

Mara shakes her head. "No. I just needed one today, so I picked up a pack while ya'll were at the hospital."

"Well, shit. Give me one," Max says.

She snorts and hands him the pack along with the lighter. "God, I wish these things weren't so horrible for you," Mara says, exhaling a stream of smoke. She'd forgotten how glorious the feeling is as that smoke fills your lungs, though the taste is stronger than she'd remembered, a byproduct of three years smoke-free.

"I could smoke as a profession."

Mara laughs. It feels good to laugh at something.

"How do you think he's doing?" Max asks.

She glances through the French doors. "He's smiling now. I guess that's something. I'm sure talking to the kids will help a little."

"Are they coming this weekend?"

"No, they're all struggling young adults with side jobs working the bars. Weekends, Charlotte tends at a busy place on Rush Street—makes good money for only two or three nights a week. Steve didn't want them to drop shifts and maybe lose their jobs."

"That's dumb. It's their dad."

"Oh, the kids would have come for sure, but Steve insisted they just come down next weekend. I think maybe he wants the rest. And he hates people fussing over him, which the kids would sure do."

"I guess that makes sense."

They puff on their cigarettes for a while in silence. "You like our forest?"

Max nods. "Yeah. It's gorgeous here. Kinda creepy, too, which is nice."

Mara laughs. "I knew you'd say that."

"Maybe it's just me, but I get no weird vibes from the house. But these woods? Spooky for sure. I expect it's easy for woods to look creepy in October."

"No, it's not just you." The trees creak and groan, swaying as the afternoon breeze picks up. Mara shivers and ties her red sweater closed. "We've only been here a few days, but I sense something. Some strange things have happened since we moved in."

"What strange things?"

"Sleep walking again. We've both done it this week."

"Shit. Really?"

"Yep. Plus, I swear something is out there in those trees. You can feel it when you're down there, like you're being watched. My friend, Nadine, warned us to stay away from them. But how can we? It's our property."

Mara takes another drag of her cigarette as she watches Max scan the woods with his vivid blue eyes.

"You think something followed you here?" Max asks.

"That's a loaded question."

"Yeah."

"But what's out there feels different," Mara says, nodding to the trees. "Whatever was in the last house was dead. I wasn't sure it even knew we were there. But this—whatever is out there in these woods—feels like a conscious presence."

"Could it be someone harassing you?"

"Out here? Who'd do that? Our only neighbors are the Jensens, and I'm sure they wouldn't bother us like that."

"Yeah, I guess."

She takes another drag and shakes her head, laughing at herself. "Stupid. Sounds so absurd. Maybe we're crazy."

"There's always that," Max says.

"Hateful."

"Maybe you two just bring this stuff out. You know? Some people can be magnets for things. Maybe if a place, or in this case an area, has a spirit there—maybe you guys draw these things to you."

"Why would that be?"

"Shit, I don't know. I'm just spit-balling—I don't even know if I believe in this crap. But Steve has dealt with loss in his life, you know."

Mara nods. "Liesl."

"Liesl."

Taking a drag on her cigarette, Mara considers Max for a moment. "You never deal with this haunting stuff, though, do you?"

"Nope. Never."

"Why Steve?"

Max shrugs. "Hell if I know. But I wasn't there when it happened. I was inside the house with Mom and Dad. Heck, I never knew Liesl, except for pictures and home movies. I was just a baby when she was—when she drowned."

"True."

"Steve carries a lot of guilt about that day," Max says, putting his cigarette out in a small glass ashtray balanced on one of the deck posts, then lights another.

"He carries a lot of emotions about that day, not just guilt."

"I'm sure that's true. Mom and Dad tried to make him see it wasn't his fault, that he had nothing to do with it, but he always felt blamed by them. I guess he read a lot in their tone."

Mara puts out her cigarette and crosses her arms, shivering in the cold air. "What do you mean?"

"Liesl's death changed everything—how he regarded every interaction in his life, especially with our parents—it was all perceived through the prism of her death. If they reprimanded him about a thing he did, or if they displayed any kind of irritation with him—regular parent-teenager kinds of stuff—he'd take it the wrong way. Every teenager thinks his parents hate him. You know how it is."

"Oh, I sure do."

"And most teenagers feel that way because—well, because they're teenagers. Teenagers are assholes. They grow out of it, but for Steve it was different. He had a *reason* to think his parents hated him, at least in his own mind. Some nights, he'd cry in bed and say Mom and Dad hated him because they thought he killed Liesl. It was awful. I'd try to tell him it wasn't true, that Mom and Dad loved him as much as they loved me, but I was seven years younger than him. He didn't want my advice, and I didn't understand how to express it very well. I didn't have to live with the thoughts he lived with."

Mara knows all of this, but it helps to hear it from someone else. "That makes sense. But what about the ghosts? They weren't just in Steve's mind; I heard them too. And whatever is happening here, it's happening to both of us."

"I'm no authority, but maybe they're drawn to him. I don't know."

They stand on the deck for a while as the trees sway in a chilly breeze.

2.

"No, I'm fine, Danny. I promise you I'm fine. Just a little tender down below," Steve says into the phone. His son sounds far too concerned.

"Dad," says Danny. "If you need to talk, just call, OK? And get an iPhone, so we can FaceTime!"

"I will—well, maybe not the iPhone—but yes, I'll call if I need to talk."

"Promise?"

"I promise." Steve's phone vibrates with an incoming call. "Hey guys, I'm getting another call. I'll call you back in a day or two, OK?"

His three kids yell their I-love-you's into the receiver and Steve switches to the incoming call.

"Dr. Nguyen?" he says.

"Hello, Steve. I'm glad to hear your voice," Dr. Nguyen says. "How are you doing?"

"I'm OK. Better than you'd expect." He glances through the French doors and sees that Mara and Max smoking and talking. *A cigarette sounds good*. "Tender, but not too bad, believe it or not. Mara told me you helped save my life."

"No, it was Mara. She called me looking for you. I told her where you said you might be heading. I am sorry to break confidentiality, but I thought it was important. You understand my reasons, right?" There's a nervousness in her voice.

"Oh, don't worry about that, Dr. Nguyen. That never even crossed my mind. I'm so thankful you told her where I was going. Believe me about that."

"Oh, good. It worried me."

"Just because I'm a lawyer doesn't mean I'm always looking for lawsuits. I know right from wrong."

She laughs. "Good. How are you doing, emotionally?"

As if on cue, Steve's eyes fill with tears and the floodgates break. He sobs into the phone for a while, as Dr. Nguyen listens. Mara and Max are still talking outside. Steve stands and takes the phone into their bedroom, closing the door behind him. He lies down on the bed and stares at the ceiling. "I—I don't know. Shit, I was doing fine until just now. Maybe shock is wearing off?"

"Could be. Or maybe you've been trying so hard to be strong for everyone. You bottled up your feelings. Feelings won't stay bottled up forever with what you've been through."

"I thought I might die."

"I know. I think we should meet as soon as you're able to move around."

Looking out the bedroom window, Steve sees something in the tree branches just outside. "Yeah..."

"Hello? Steve?"

"Yeah, I'm here..."

"Are you OK?"

"Have you ever felt like someone cursed you?" He knows something's out there in the branches of the nearest oak tree. Something almost visible.

"Is that how you feel? That you're cursed?" Dr. Nguyen asks.

The thing outside hides behind the thick and crooked arm of a branch. It's concealed by leaves. "Wouldn't you?"

"Given all you've been through, it's understandable to feel that way."

"I guess so."

"Can I ask you a question, Steve?"

"Yes."

"Do you feel like hurting yourself?"

"No."

"Good. You're safe?"

The thing in the tree, the thing that is and isn't there, can read his thoughts—a presence grows in *his mind.* "I guess."

"We can meet on Saturday, if you can get here."

A gust of wind pushes the top of the oak to the left, revealing empty space where the thing had been. "It disappeared," he says.

"What did you say?"

"Sorry. No, that won't be necessary, Dr. Nguyen. It can wait."

"Are you sure?" Her concern is endearing.

"Yeah. I'm good. Thanks for calling."

"Please, call if you need anything. And let me know when you'd like to set up an appointment, OK?"

"Yeah..."

Steve clicks off the phone, his eyes fixed on the empty oak branch.

Chapter Twenty-Seven

Don Loomis sits behind the controls of a beat up Bobcat in the backyard of Ronald and Gladys Milton's house. Though it's only fifty-six degrees, sweat soaks into his dirty John Deere cap. The Chief surveys the yard at the corner of the house.

Don eyes the side of the house. *The place could do with some paint and about ten grand of work. Would be a sweet old house if they put a little into it,* he thinks.

But the condition of the paint job isn't what's got him sweating. At the southern end of the house, the chief of police is speaking to an officer and an old guy who looks familiar, but whose name he can't quite place. Lou stares at a piece of paper in his hands. The chief motions for them to follow and he leads them past Don and to the back corner of the house, pointing into the backyard.

Don knows why they're here, of course. He knows what they're about to find, but he's got no choice but to play dumb. *Nothing connects me here.*

After several moments of pointing and talking, Branton motions for Don to bring up the Bobcat. Lou meets him halfway and motions to cut the engine. Stepping up to the side, Lou says, "Hey, you're never going to believe what that asshole did."

"Who? The chief?" Don says.

"No, Milton! Goddamn idiot killed a bunch of folks and buried them in the garden. And guess who gets to dig that shit up?"

"Are you kidding me?"

Lou shakes his head. "Wish I was."

"And I'm supposed to dig them up with the Bobcat?"

"No, just get the holes started. Don't want the bucket to tear them up. Dig about three feet down, then we'll go in with shovels."

"The hell I am! Digging up dead bodies ain't in my job description, Lou! Don't they have a team for this? Forensics, or some shit like that?"

"Do you think this is the NYPD? *We're* the goddamn forensics team. And I don't like this any better than you, but I'll be damned if I'm going to turn down the pay they're offering. It's almost double our usual."

"I don't care if it's a million dollars. I ain't stepping foot off this Bobcat."

"Fine! You stay in the Bobcat and let us do the dirty work if you're so scared of a bunch of old bones."

"Damn right, I will."

Lou steps off and heads back to the others, muttering as he walks away. "Pain in my ass, Don! A fucking pain in my ass!"

Don sometimes thinks he's a fool for sticking with Lou's little construction company, but the old turd pays pretty well now that he can only do half the things they're hired for. Once he retires, Don will buy him out and run things himself. *Will I keep the name?* Lou's Construction Co. ain't fancy, but it's known in the area and comes with history and all kinds of return customers. Still, Loomis Contracting has a ring to it. He needs time to think about it.

The chief motions for Don to bring the Bobcat to the backyard. He shouts over the noise of the engine. "See those flowers?"

"Uh, yeah," Don replies, as if to say, *No shit, Sherlock. They're right in front of me.*

"Start there. We'll tell you when to hold off, OK?"

"Gotcha."

Don drags the bucket across a small section of rose garden. Branton waves for Don to back off, then he and the other officer drop into the hole and begin pulling back dirt with their bare hands.

Watching them struggle with the dark Iowa soil, Don almost feels guilty he isn't down there with them. Lou is too old to be doing stupid stuff. Just as Don hops down to grab a shovel, he hears a loud cracking sound followed by a sharp curse.

"I think I hit something," Lou says.

Branton jogs to him and, setting his shovel on the ground outside the hole, kneels and digs with his hands. The other guy joins him, saying to Lou, "You should climb out now. Let us handle this, Lou."

"You got it," Lou says.

Don can't quite see what they're doing, aside from their shoulders rolling right and left as they paw through the dirt. Branton stops and whispers something to the other guy—something Don can't quite hear.

"Whatcha got?" Lou asks.

"Not sure," Branton says. "But I think it's a rib. Maybe a pair."

"Jesus H—" Lou says.

The other guy calls to Don, "Hey, could you grab my flashlight from that big sack over there?"

Don trudges over to a burlap sack by the back corner of the house and pulls a long black LED flashlight from it, then returns and hands it to the guy. The light reveals that the men are standing on a half-buried skeleton. Quickly, they step to either side of the ditch. From his vantage point, Don can see several more ribs, the front of bony hips, and parts of each thigh bone.

"That crazy son of a bitch," says the other guy.

Branton surveys the rest of the yard. "How many more will we find?"

"Want to call the station? Get more guys out here?"

Branton wipes his hands on his pants. "No. Not yet."

The man looks at the skeleton. "Yeah. We should see what we got."

The chief wipes a layer of black dirt from the bones, but after several moments, he digs with greater urgency. Eventually, Branton stands and spits. "Fuck me!"

"You got to be kidding me," Lou says.

"Wish I was, Lou."

There is nothing but dirt above the shoulders of the skeleton. The head is missing.

Chapter Twenty-Eight

The sun moves through the sky, painting the trees with a golden hour glow. The variation in light drags Steve out of his daydream. So absorbed was he in thought, he didn't notice Max scrolling through his phone on the seat opposite him.

"Max," Steve says.

"Yeah?"

"Do you believe in God?"

Max turns to him, mouth agape. "God?"

"Yeah."

"I don't know. Why?"

"What do you mean you don't know? You never think about it?"

"I think about it. Mom and Dad had us in church three times a week. How could I not? I still don't *know*."

Steve runs his fingers along a welt on his chest where Milton had electrocuted him. It's inflamed and tender to the touch, but not as terrible as he would have expected. He presses his finger into it until he winces. "I get that. What about the devil?"

Max scoffs. "What about him?"

"Believe in him?"

"No."

"Why?"

Max says, "An evil dude leading people down a path to infinite suffering? For eternity? You're telling me a guy lives on earth for ninety years and does some bad stuff and some good stuff, like everyone else, but then has to pay for his sins for *infinity*? Have you ever considered infinity? It's hurts your brain! Time never ending, just going on forever. Now imagine enduring untold suffering all that time."

"I know," Steve says.

"Say you live to eighty. When you're talking about infinity, that's statistically equal to zero. Within a dozen years, you wouldn't remember a single thing you did to get sent to hell. No way. I think as soon as we die, we experience enlightenment and understanding. We see where we fucked up in life, then move on to whatever comes next. That's my idea of the afterlife. We all wake the fuck up and realize what bastards we were when we were human. Sure, maybe there should be some kind of retribution for evil fucks like Nazis or those KKK dicks, but the eternal, agonizing pain—gnashing of teeth and all that stuff they taught us in Sunday school? I don't buy it."

"Just because it's tough to grasp doesn't make it untrue," Steve says, though he sounds like a devil's advocate even to himself.

Max sits forward on the sofa, shaking his head. "It's all manmade, that hell shit. They came up with the concept of hell to keep people from brutalizing each other back before there was enough civilization to do it through laws. Existential fear is a damn powerful regulator—a lot more compelling than angels and resurrections, that's for sure. Religion needed a boogeyman."

"Earlier, you mentioned you didn't know what you believed. Sounds like you believe nothing."

"Oh, I still have a reasonable doubt, thanks to all the religion drummed into our heads every Sunday and Wednesday. Don't worry about that. But I don't see enough evidence to call myself a believer, and based on some of the so-called Christian nationalists I've seen out there, I don't see the benefit."

"Yeah, well, that's a weird offshoot."

Max scoffs. "If you ask me, it's all weird."

"So, you're Agnostic."

Max blinks at him. "That is the definition, I suppose. Though even that sounds sort of decisive, doesn't it?"

They sit together in silence for several minutes, each lost in thought.

Steve inhales and says, "Where's Mara?"

"She ran to the market."

"Good. Help me to the basement, would you?"

"Why?"

"I have something to show you—something I need to look at."

"What?"

"A film."

"Can't we watch it up here?"

"Not this one."

"What the hell kind of film are you showing me?"

"A Super 8."

"Super 8?"

"Yeah, one of those old home movies."

"I know what they are, but why? How? You have a projector?"

"Yep—in the basement."

"You have one of Grandpa's old movies?"

"No, it's from a boy who used to live in town. He fancied himself a young filmmaker."

Max shoots him an incredulous look as Steve scoots himself to the edge of his seat. "Wait. Does this have to do with the little detective work Mara was telling me about? Your Maquoketa mystery? The missing girl? The shit that got you into this mess in the first place?"

"Yes."

"Your wife ordered me to keep you away from that diversion."

"She did?"

Max offers a slow, emphatic nod.

"I guess you're going to fail that task," Steve says.

"Why would I go against Mara?"

"You're my brother—blood is thicker than water, and all that. Plus, I need to watch this footage, otherwise everything that happened at the Milton house will have been for nothing. You see?"

"No." Max rolls his eyes. "But I'm curious about it myself, so I'm willing. She'll call me hateful for encouraging you."

Steve laughs, which leads to him some discomfort. "She'll call you that either way."

"True. You're sure you can make it down there?"

"Yep. I've got my cane and your shoulder. We'll just have to take it slow."

"Going down isn't the problem. How will you fare getting back up? I'm not carrying you."

"I'll be fine. Slow down, slow up."

"Fine."

One step at a time, they make their way down the two flights of steps to the basement. Milton's film projector still sits on the downstairs coffee table, facing the blank patch of wall.

"You guys planning to paint this place, or do you like the look of drywall?" Max says.

"We'll get to it when we get to it. Is your house painted?" Steve asks.

"No bookstore owner can afford to buy a house in Los Angeles, smart ass. But I bet I pay as much in rent as you pay in mortgage for this frigging *estate*."

"Right here," Steve says, grunting, and Max lowers him onto a large leather easy chair. "Grab that reel of film next to the projector and pop it into the top, then wind it through to the other reel."

"Yeah, I recall how to do it. They still had film projectors when I was in high school, but it's been a while." Once the film is in place, Max turns out the lights. "Ready?"

"Ready."

Chapter Twenty-Nine

The rickety shopping cart clangs through the grocery store, its right front wheel spinning round and round. Mara searches for supper as she talks to Nadine on her cell phone. The eyes of curious customers follow her, as she does her best not to acknowledge them. Is it the fact that she's new to town, or have they all learned about the events of the previous night in the Milton house?

"So, now he's home, resting. Praise the baby Jesus."

"Is he in pain? He has to be in pain still, right?" Nadine asks, sounding strangely emotional.

"They've got the pain controlled with some potent meds. Emotionally? I don't know. I guess he's still in shock. He's acting peculiar."

"How do you recover from something like that, you know?" Nadine says.

"I guess he's doing OK, all things considered."

"How are you?"

Mara pauses as tears roll down her face unexpectedly. "Oh, god. I'm crying. I think this is the first time I've cried since last night. Wow." Leaning onto the front of the cart, Mara weeps in the middle of the pasta aisle.

"Oh, honey. It's OK. It's just hitting you now. Let it out."

After almost a minute of sobbing, Mara senses people watching her. She takes out a tissue from her handbag and wipes her eyes. "I'm in the middle of a grocery store."

"Who cares? You think those hicks haven't seen a wife crying before? Pish!"

Mara laughs.

"I'm supposing that hick Halloween party is out of the picture for you all, but why don't I come out tonight, anyway? You can use the company and the help. I've got nothing else to do."

"Yes! That's a wonderful idea. Max is here, and you know I'd love for you to meet him."

"Is he single?"

"Single enough." Mara laughs. "Maybe keep him company while I'm taking care of Steve."

"Sounds perfect! What time?"

Mara reaches for an avocado and checks it for ripeness. Setting it in the cart, she says, "How about seven? I can warm up some of your chili and make a pie. Sound good?"

"Yes! The chili is exactly what Steve needs, trust me. Give that to him, you hear? I'll see you later, hun."

"OK, bye."

Mara puts her phone away and heads toward the checkout line. As she is just about to reach the conveyer belt at register number two, a woman stops her. She's maybe in her fifties with ragged hair and dirty jeans. Her eyes are wild and red. "Are you Mrs. Spain? Steve Spain's wife?"

"Yes. I am." Mara asks.

"I'm Melly Harmon."

At first, the name means nothing to her, but as the knowing manner in the woman's voice hits her, recognition sets in. "Oh! Melly! Yes, I know who you are."

"How is your husband? I feel so responsible. It's my fault what happened to him."

"What do you mean?"

"It's because of me they attacked your husband."

"No, no. That's not true. It was just some senile old man who thought Steve had a demon in him."

Melly freezes for a moment, her eyes flitting back and forth across Mara's face. "He wouldn't have been in that position if it weren't me. As bad as I want to find my daughter, I would never have wanted that to happen to your husband. Just awful."

"Thank you, Melly. But it didn't have to do with your daughter's case. It was just a random awful thing that happened."

"You don't believe that. Do you believe what happened to him was a fluke?" The wild look that had been burning in Melly's eyes has turned icy cold.

"What do you mean?" Mara asks, stepping closer to avoid being overheard.

"The Milton's have been here as long as anyone in town, maybe longer. They had to be connected somehow. You think your husband's investigation and his kidnapping are a coincidence? As sorry as I am that someone hurt him, he can't stop now. I mean it. Someone thought he was getting too close to the truth!"

"Who?"

"I have suspicions."

"Tell me. Tell me, or leave me the fuck alone. Because I don't have patience for any more games. Some fucking lunatic almost killed my husband last night, so no more puzzles. Who did this?"

"I don't know for sure. But the goddamn Tuppers and Jensens. They know something—they *know*, I tell you."

"The Jensens? Why them?"

Melly looks around. "There's too many prying eyes here. Meet me at the diner when you're finished. Make it quick."

Chapter Thirty

The film flips through ten seconds of overexposed frames before a clear image emerges. The scene is a gravel road, surrounded on both sides by the thick fall foliage. As the camera pans to the right, Steve yells, "Right there!" As he attempts to get up from his chair, a sharp pain stabs him in the groin and on either side of his chest, dropping him back onto his seat.

"What?" Max asks, reaching to steady him.

Steve points to the wall, the veins popping from his forehead. "There, in the bushes! You see her? You see?"

"Wait. Yes, I see. Holy shit."

There, maybe twenty yards down, just off the side of the Old Road, we see the face and shoulders of a girl—a teenage girl. She stares at the camera, which shifts and shakes as Joey Milton himself must have recognized her. The film is blurry, but it looks like the girl is smiling. After a moment or two, she steps into the woods, lost from view. The camera jerks right, then left, a blur of images rushing across Steve's basement wall. The camera settles on the road again, now empty save for gravel and dying plant life.

The image cuts to a shot of the bridge. The Trillo boys and Bob Baxter are standing there, each of them staring past the camera in the direction where the girl had been. Frankie's mouth moves as if he's speaking.

Steve says, "It looks like Frankie Trillo is saying something. Something like—'Jesse? Was that Jesse?' Does it look like that to you?"

"Maybe," Max says.

The film cuts to a shot of some woods, darkened and underexposed, shadows and visual noise encroaching at the edge of the image. As the camera moves along an overgrown path, the scene cuts in and out a few times.

The frame jumps and we cut to a small cabin, nestled in a grove of trees and obscured by an overgrown thicket. Made of rotting wood, it leans to the right. Its white paint, what's left of it, is chipped and soiled from years of neglect. Dead vines hang from the frames of the visible glass windows, which are hazy with dirt and dust. The roof, covered in dead leaves and crumbling shingles, appears to be mostly intact.

The camera goes to the ground, and the image cuts black. When the image returns, it's darker outside, as if some time has passed. The cabin comes back into view as someone adjusts the focus. Though noise and grain from the lack of light muddle the image, we can make out the cabin walls, though now its windows glow with illumination as if someone's inside. The light in the window dims, and the silhouette of a figure passes by the nearest window.

"Go back!" Steve sits forward in his chair, ignoring his pain. "Feed it through again, please. Back it up!"

"What?" Max says.

Pulling his phone from his pocket, Steve says, "Just do it. I need to see that cabin again. I wish we could pause it, but I'm afraid it would burn through the film."

"We could have it digitized, you know." Max switches the reels and threads the film through the projector again. "There has to be someone in the Quad Cities who can do it. Hell, if we had the right projector, we could do it ourselves—just hook it up to your laptop."

"Or we can play it again and I'll record it on my phone," Steve says.

"Ah. Yes, welcome to twenty seventeen." Max slaps himself on the forehead as he finishes re-spooling the film. "OK, ready?"

"Yep."

Steve holds his phone towards the wall and records the entire two minutes, ten seconds, of film. Then, as Max removes the reel from the projector and places it back in its canister, Steve watches the video again on his phone.

"How does it look?" Max asks.

"Great, actually. Better than I would have thought." Steve pauses the video on the girl standing at the side of the road. "Max, can you go upstairs and look in my nightstand? There's a brown divided file in the drawer. Grab it for me."

Moments later, Max returns with the file. Turning to the first tab, Steve finds the photo of Jesse Harmon that Melly gave him. He spreads his finger on the screen and holds the phone next to the photo. "Does this look like the same person?"

Standing over his shoulder, Max says, "Could be. Didn't these kids tell anyone they'd found the missing girl?"

Steve explains how they reported the sighting but then withdrew their report and claimed they'd seen Emma Tupper, and not Jesse.

Max says, "Hm. Have you seen the Tupper girl? Did they look alike?"

"Not really. Emma has dark brown hair; Jesse's hair was blond. This girl in the video is blond, right?"

Max nods. "No doubt about that."

Steve sets down the file and continues the video on his phone. When the cabin pops up, he taps the phone screen to pause. "There! Look! Right there! Holy shit!"

Max leans in as Steve points the screen at him. "What am I supposed to be looking at?"

"Look in the window! The one next to the door. Right there," Steve says, pointing at a small window, partially obscured by dead vines. "See it?"

"No, what?"

"Right there in that square of glass!"

Max's face tightens. "Holy shit."

"Yeah, it's a face. A girl's face."

"Sure looks like a face. Can't tell if it's a girl, but someone is looking out that window."

Steve presses two buttons on either side of the phone. "I'm taking a screenshot of this, and one of the girl on the road, to compare." Scrolling back to the beginning, he takes another screen shot, then crops both images to sit side-by-side on the phone screen, pinching his fingers on both sides, zooming in to better show the faces. "What do you think?"

Max compares the ghostly faces. "It's hard to say—the window is so dirty. But it *could* be the same face. The features are similar."

"Are you kidding me? They're identical! That's the girl standing in the weeds on The Old Road. Next, Joey is following the girl, recording it on his camera. They split up and looked for her separately—the Trillo's and Bob Baxter confirmed all of that when I spoke with them. But Joey's only got so much film, right? Those Super 8 film canisters only allowed for like three or four minutes of filming. So, he cuts in and out while he's walking, filming a few seconds at a time. Then he comes upon the cabin and there she is—the girl from the road."

"Maybe. I'm at a disadvantage here, but I admit it all sounds reasonable. Still, it's been how long? Fifteen years, or whatever? If that's her, where is she?"

Steve tries not to be annoyed by Max's hesitation. Maybe it's best to have a little devil's advocate now and then to keep him honest, hone his theories, separate the ridiculous from the probable. "I guess that's part of the mystery."

"OK, I agree. That girl on the road looks like Jesse Harmon. I've never seen this other girl, Tapper, or—"

"*Tupper.*"

"Tupper. But if this isn't her, why did Joey lie?"

"See? Now you're thinking. Was he forced to lie?" Steve says.

"Crazy."

"People around here might know more about this than they're willing to talk about."

"Like who?" Max asks.

"The Jensens and the Tuppers, for starters. Maybe the Trillos know more than they're saying. Wait." Steve rifles through the file again and finds his notes from the interview with the Trillo brothers. "Here. Frankie told me Joey Milton was the first to identify the girl as Jesse Harmon. But in the film, it looks like Frankie is saying, 'Jesse? Is that Jesse?' We can't hear if Joey said anything himself, but it sure looks like Frankie was thinking the same thing at that moment."

"Yeah, I noticed that too." Max moves to the sofa and sits. "Let me see your phone." Steve gives it to him. Flipping the photos back and forth, Max says, "I can't tell much about this face, the one in the cabin window. It looks like a girl, but I can't make out the hair or anything else. This other one, the girl on the road, she's obviously blond. She looks like that picture of Jesse Harmon—maybe a little thinner, but with the same features. If the Tupper girl is brown-haired, it's definitely not her." Steve watches his brother work through the million thoughts running through his mind. Max was always a smart kid, open to information. "Where is Emma Tupper now?"

"Des Moines, from what they told me."

"You have any way to contact her?"

"No. But I'm sure someone in town knows her info. And if not, there's always the internet." Steve takes his phone back and looks at the cabin photo once again. "I need to go out there again and find this cabin. There's something more here."

"Hey now. I'm on board with this detective stuff, so long as it stays in the Rear Window realm, but there's no way you and I are going out there in your condition. You need your rest and Mara would kill us both. Plus, it's getting late in the day for stumbling around through a bunch of undergrowth."

"No, I get it. The cabin can wait a day or two. Besides, tonight we have plans."

Max looks at him, one eyebrow raised. "What plans?"

"The Jensen Halloween party. It's an annual tradition, and they invited us."

Max collapses back onto the sofa, throwing his arms in the air. "You just got out of the hospital after being tortured by a lunatic all night. There's no way Mara will let you go to a goddamn party. And how are you not crying in bed from shock and anxiety?"

"I'm afraid Mara's got no choice. I don't know when I'll have this opportunity again—it's perfect, actually." Steve stands, leaning on his cane. "And as for the anxiety—well, I guess there's no better remedy than a near-death experience."

Max groans. "Good grief! What opportunity? You think you'll never see these people ever again? A little town like Maquoketa?"

"Maybe not all of them at once. All these people we've been talking about, the Tuppers, Jensens, Chief Branton—hell, maybe even a Trillo or two—if my theory is correct, all of them will be at this party. In fact, I'd bet my life on it."

Max's eyes light up. "Oh, shit."

"Yep. So, I've got no choice but to swallow my pain and rally. I'll just have to use all my charm on Mara. Now help me get up those fucking stairs."

Thirty-five minutes later, Mara enters the house carrying a load of groceries and sets them on the counter. Rocky lumbers over to her, tail wagging furiously. When she turns from the counter, she sees Steve and Max sitting in the living room, looking suspicious. "What's going on?" Mara says.

"Honey, don't be mad. But I want to go to the Jensen's party. I know I should rest, but I think I have to be there. It feels like they know something, or at least *someone* at that party will know something about Jesse Harmon. I can't explain it but—"

"I agree," Mara says.

Steve freezes. "You do?"

"Yes. I think we should go."

"Thank you," Steve says.

"But before that happens, I want you to get some rest and some of Nadine's chili in you. That's an order."

"Yes, that's what I need." Steve nods and glances out the window.

The gray figure he'd seen earlier is back, watching him through a patch of orange leaves.

Chapter Thirty-One

There are twelve holes in the ground behind the Milton house, with twelve decaying bodies missing twelve heads.

Don watches from the Bobcat, sipping a cup of hot cocoa his wife was nice enough to bring to him. There's no way of knowing just how many bodies lie buried in the yard. Old Ronald was busier than Don had realized.

"Goddammit, Ronald."

Chief Branton stands near the house, speaking into his cell phone as one of his officers takes pictures of a body in the hole nearest to him. None of the Maquoketa officers have seen anything like this, and it shows. One officer, Tammy Henry, is sitting on the back stoop with her head in her hands, trying not to vomit.

Then there's Lou. Don hadn't realized how annoying that man could be—standing next to all this death, with his hands on his hips, like he's inspecting a backed up septic tank. Lou saunters through the graveyard to Branton, then listens to the private conversation until the chief turns and walks away.

"This is a clusterfuck," Lou says, approaching Don. "I tell ya, Don. I ain't seen nothing like it."

Ya think? It's a yard full of dead bodies, you old dipshit! "Yeah, it's a mess," Don says.

"Looks like the feds are coming to town."

"Why?"

"Don't know. Just overheard Branton arguing with some agent out of Waterloo. Sounded like they've got similar shit going on in other states. Branton was saying, 'I don't give a fuck about Illinois or Wisconsin. Blah, blah, blah. This is my jurisdiction,' and whatnot. Jesus H. Christ! FBI, here in Maquoketa. You believe that?"

"Other states?" Don's vision blurs; his headache is back. "What does that mean?"

"Hell if I know. I suppose we're about to find out," Lou says, pointing a thumb at the chief who is coming their way.

Branton says, "Looks like you can head out, guys. We have to shut it down for now."

"Why is that?" Lou asks, feigning ignorance.

"The feds are taking over."

Lou scrunches his face, as obvious as can be. "They can do that?"

"If they think it's an interstate crime, they sure can."

"Milton did this in other states?"

"It seems like he took his show on the road. Guess I'll find out when they get here," Branton says.

Don asks, "Mr. Milton killed all these people?"

"Sure looks that way. Keep this between the three of us, but Gladys spilled the beans on the entire operation. I guess Ronald fashioned himself as some kind of demon hunter. He used to kidnap people and torture them in the attic—said it was the only way to get rid of the evil. Can you believe that?" Branton looks out over the hole-filled backyard. "I guess he lost a few along the way."

Lou says, "I would never have guessed in all my days."

"You have him locked up?" Don asks.

Branton grimaces. "No. He's dead. I can't say too much just yet. But you know that couple that moved to town? The ones who built a house on Jensen's property?"

Lou says, "The Spains? We worked on their house."

"Ah, that's right." Branton leans in, peering behind him to check that no one is listening. "Well, old Milton had Mr. Spain tied to a chair up there in his attic, going at him with a car battery and some kind of nut-crusher."

"*Nut*-crusher?" Lou says.

"Yeah. Ronald had the guy's nuts in a vice and crushed them like a couple grapes."

"Holy shit!" Lou says.

"I guess one of them was so bad they had to get rid of it. Doctors saved the other, so at least there's that. But the attic looked like a goddamn torture chamber—electrodes and everything."

Lou covers his mouth with his hand. "Why did he go after Spain? He seemed like a nice enough fellow."

"Hell if I know. I guess Milton thought Spain was possessed. Crazy old fool." Branton puts his hands in his pockets and stares over his shoulder at the backyard. "A hell of a mess."

Don's eyes blur and the old headache throbs again, pushing against the sides of his brain so hard it's all he can do to stay upright. His stomach rumbles. *Nothing connects me here. Nothing but Gladys Milton, that is...*

Lou asks, "So, who are all these bodies?"

Branton shrugs. "Not a clue, not yet anyhow. It'll be some time before we know much. *Anyway*, you guys head home; there's nothing else for you to do here. We appreciate the help."

"OK," Lou says. "I guess you've got a long night ahead of you."

Branton laughs. "Sure as hell do. Probably won't be out of here until morning. Looks like I'll miss the Jensen party tonight. You going?"

Lou says, "Ah, well, that's a shame, Chief. But, no, I'm not big on gatherings and Halloween ain't my thing."

Branton nods. "How about you, Don?"

Don thinks about it for a moment as the throbbing pounds harder and harder, threatening to bust through his temples, spraying gray matter all over the chief's shiny badge. Don wants to say, *No, I should stay in tonight. Stay home with the family. Watch scary movies on Netflix.* Instead, he says, "I might have to do that."

Chapter Thirty-Two

1.

Steve closes the bedroom door and drops his aching body to the bed. Though his body, wracked with bruises, burns, and lacerations, aches in a muted agony, his emotions are steady. Reaching into his pocket, he finds the small bottle of pain pills, drops one onto his palm and slaps it into his mouth, dry-swallowing it whole.

Within minutes, he's asleep and dreaming of a place and time long ago, when the world changed for him.

2.

Darkness, then light.

He's standing on a wide frozen river. Sunshine reflecting off the snow and ice, blinding him. Steve squints and shields his eyes with his hand. It's biting cold outside, despite the blinding sunlight.

A modest house sits atop a slope to his left, its roof piled with snow, icicles hanging from its gutters. Glowing with a warmth lost on the rest of the world, the house stares down at Steve like a disappointed parent.

"Steve," a faint voice says to him.

Startled by the unexpected call, he spins to see a little girl in a claret-colored coat with a sky blue scarf and cap, squinting at him through the chilly air. On her face sits an uncertain expression, either a smile or a grimace. Is she greeting him or reacting to the wind? Her arms dangle at her sides, lifted by the thickness of her winter coat. Her heavy stockings can't be keeping her warm in this weather, but they had just come from church, so maybe.

A cracking noise erupts between them, followed by the faint sound of trickling water. Steve's feet vibrate on the ice-covered river. Looking down, he noticed hundreds of bubbles flowing below the ice under his boots. Alarm bells ring out in his mind. A baby's crying reverberates from inside the little house on the hill. Steve says, "Liesl!"

A throbbing sensation hits him square in both temples, as if being banged in the skull by an ape with two stones. Eyes blurry, he tries to look around him. Inexplicably, the show has changed from white to crimson, like the world is a slice of red velvet cake.

The sky is red—the world is red. Everything is bloody and dead. But how can this be?

Gazing at the ice below her little boots, Liesl cries, "Stevie!"

"Yeah?"

"It's—"

"What's happening?" he asks, cutting her off.

Clearing his mind, he realizes it's him. His vision is fading into a field of crimson and his own voice sounds like it's on the other side of the river. Then panic seizes him as the cracking sound intensifies. An intricate web of shattered ice spreads out in all directions from Liesl's feet.

Steve rushes to her, ignoring the danger of the breaking ice, and grabs his sister by the shoulders with both hands. "Liesl!" He screams, but his words are far away.

"Steve!" Liesl's face contorts in a peculiar horror as she stares into his eyes. "Wake up!"

Steve jolts awake in bed, his heart battering the interior of his chest like a spoiled toddler. The sudden movement sends a lightning bolt of pain through his one remaining testicle all the way through his gut into his shoulders and neck. He swings his legs from under the covers and tries to gain his equilibrium. He must have slept a couple of hours. His phone screen says it's six-thirty, and the sky outside has turned a dark shade of gray.

The clobbering headache, a remnant from the dream, continues in the waking world and he picks up his cane. As he stands, something catches his awareness. A hint of movement in the corner of his left eye, just beyond windows—something outside. A thing is moving in the backyard. Hobbling to the windows, he peers into the early night.

There!

Below the deck, about a dozen yards, almost to the tree line, a thin creature with long dirty hair, naked and gray, scampers on all fours into the woods. Steve makes a move toward the bedroom door, but a sharp pain in his groin rejects any thought of pursuit.

Impossible. I'll never catch it, he tells himself. *Never catch that thing, not like this. Not broken and tortured. Let it be.*

Mara calls from the living room, "Honey, you up?"

"Yep. I'm up."

CHAPTER THIRTY-THREE

1.

Mara Phone Recording #3, Saturday, October 28, 7:03 pm.

The camera jostles back and forth, flashing trees and gravel, then back to trees. Off camera, the sound of heavy breathing and muffled laughter. The scene cuts out.

Camera cuts back on, revealing Max's face from below. The light from the phone makes him squint in the dark.

"Damn Mara, that light."

Mara's voice says, off camera, "Sorry, this phone doesn't have great night vision. And here is your beloved uncle, Max. Say hi to the kids, Max."

Max arches his eyebrows and attempts a ridiculous imitation of Jack Nicholson. "Well, hello kids. It's a goddamn spooky Halloween!"

"It's not Halloween yet," Mara says.

Max smiles. "Fine! It's a spooky *almost*-Halloween—pre-Halloween weekend."

Mara laughs. "Yes, it sure is. Tell them where we're headed."

"Oh, that's the topping on this cake. We are right now walking down this dirt road to a back-woods Halloween shindig!" Max hops around, playing an air banjo. "Partying with the hicks."

"Hateful! They're not hicks." The sound of Mara's laughter as we watch Max's routine. "They're wealthy."

"Oh, I'm sure they are. *Iowa* wealthy, anyway."

"Hateful!"

The camera leaves Max, cutting across Mara's face, and to her left to show Steve, his face a mix of frustration and pain. "And here's your father. Why he insisted on hobbling down the gravel road on his cane is anyone's guess. Say hi, Dad."

"Hi kids," Steve grunts. "Happy Halloween."

In a whirl of darkness and faint colors, the camera points ahead of them. The gravel road stretches out before us, winding to the right and out of our sight. The screen goes black for a moment, then flips around so we once again get a selfie-shot of Mara's face.

"Nadine is meeting us after a while—she's running late. So kids, I know you're worried about your dad, but trust me, he's OK. If you want to come down next weekend to see him, that's fine. He's doing great, all things considered." She looks to her left. "Right hon?"

Steve's voice off-camera says, "Never better."

"So, ya'll just get through this week, and come on down next—"

We hear a sound of rustling trees and crunching leaves in the background. Mara's head turns to her right. She stops walking. "Did you see that?" Mara asks.

Max's voice, off-camera, says, "No. I heard something over there, just off the road. A deer maybe?"

"Maybe," says Mara, her voice unsteady. "I'm just so dang jumpy." She looks back into the camera. "Anyway, I hope ya'll are good. Love ya. Bye!"

The camera cuts out.

2.

The Spains come around a bend in the road, revealing the entrance to the Jensen property. A long dirt drive runs up a sloping hill to a large two-story farmhouse at the top. The upstairs windows glare down at them, shining with an incandescent glow like a pair of eyes. Attached to the left side of the house is a three-car garage, beyond which lies a gravel parking lot. Opposite the garage is a massive metal structure, a modern barn painted white with a black framework to match the house.

As they make their way up the half-acre hill, they see half a dozen rows of chairs filled with people, all facing them, as if waiting for the Spains to arrive. Most of the women are in sweat shirts, sporting either University of Iowa or Iowa State University—black and gold or cardinal and gold. All the men and several of the women sport misshapen red baseball caps with the words *Make America Great Again*, emblazoned in cheap gold or white embroidery.

"Holy shit," Max says, his voice low. "*Actual* MAGA hats! In person!"

Steve laughs through the pain of trekking up the drive. "Sorry, brother. But you ain't in California no more."

"Can we go home now?" Max says with an exaggerated mock fear.

The host of elderly pay them no mind, remaining seated in their lawn chairs, staring into the night sky as if awaiting a fireworks display.

As they approach the side of the house, Steve notices a younger man—younger than the people in the chairs, anyway, maybe in his thirties or forties—across the driveway, leaning on the garage with his arms crossed over his chest. His John Deere cap, pulled down over his eyes, conceals his identity in shadow.

"Well, this is quite a party," Mara whispers as the three of them huddle together.

"Just like Hollywood," Max says.

Steve laughs, then grimaces in pain. "Stop making me laugh."

"Can't help it. But I'll try, for your balls' sake—or should I say ball?"

Steve winces again as he coughs out a laugh.

"Stop it, hateful," Mara says, slapping Max on the arm. "Hey, maybe we should split up. Might be easier to spy that way."

Steve nods, but before he can respond, the front door of the main house opens and out steps Wendell Jensen, dressed in his usual brown slacks and a flannel shirt. "Well, hello there. I'm surprised to see you all out here tonight. Surprised, indeed."

"Oh, we wouldn't miss it for the world," Mara says with a wide grin.

"But Mr. Spain, I heard you had quite an ordeal. Are you sure you're OK being out here?"

"Well, I'm here anyway. I thought it would do me some good to get out of the house. This is my brother, Max. He's here from California, visiting."

Wendell looks at Max, his eyes widened a little. "You don't say! Southern or Northern?"

"Southern," Max says. "Los Angeles."

"Welcome! So happy you could make it." Wendell points at Mara. "Didn't you tell me you had fourth coming?"

Mara says, "Yes, my friend Nadine. She'll be here before long."

"Excellent. In that case, Mrs. Spain, you don't mind if I steal your husband for a little while, do you? I've got a wonderful old bottle of Bourbon in my study I'd love to share with him." Wendell smiles at Steve. "Might take the edge off your discomfort."

"Be my guest." Mara raises an eyebrow at Steve.

Wendell says, "Perfect. You two go on around the back. We've got food, all kinds of beer, and several offerings of wine and alcohol. Pop too, if you're not drinkers." The older man motions to Steve, extending his other arm toward the house.

Steve kisses Mara on the cheek. "Have fun, guys. I'll be out soon."

The house is buzzing with activity. To the right is a formal dining room with a long oak table covered in food and Halloween decorations, surrounded by a dozen or more guests of various ages, though most are older than fifty, chatting and eating, or drinking. To the left is a cozy living room with dark paneled walls and a stone fireplace dominating the room.

Before him is a long hall leading past a grand staircase with a cherry wood bannister.

When they enter, conversation subsides as the party-goers observe the newcomers. Wendell says, "Friends. This is our new neighbor, Mr. Steve Spain."

Steve leans on his cane and waves towards the rooms on either side of the entryway. The guests smile at him like statues, frozen where they stand. Steve clears his throat and says, "Happy Halloween."

Still, the other guests give no response, so Wendell takes him by the shoulder and says, "Come. My study is just down this hall."

Like the living room, dark wood paneling lines the walls of Wendell's study, with complementary furnishings and a deep red and blue oriental rug filling the space. Two high-backed leather chairs sit facing each other in the middle of the room, just in front of the massive mahogany desk. A dwindling fire burns at the opposite wall.

"This is quite a room," Steve says. "I'm jealous."

"Why thank you. I always wanted a study like this, ever since I was a boy. When I inherited this old house, I made sure that was the first thing I built into it. Used to be a nursery, if you can believe it."

"Down here on the first floor?"

"My father wasn't much for screaming babies. Made my mother stay down here with the chaos. Please, have a seat." Wendell motions to the far chair and moves to a cabinet, from which he produces two rocks glasses and a crystal bottle filled with a brownish-red liquid.

Steve sits as Wendell hands him a short, fat, glass. "Interesting," Steve says, swirling the liquor in his glass. "You say it's a bourbon? A little on the red side. What kind is it?"

"We make it ourselves."

"You have a distillery?"

"That, we do. I call it bourbon because that's what it most resembles in flavor, but it's something altogether different. Not sure what anyone else would call it, but my grandfather referred to it as a whiskey."

"What's it made of?"

Wendell shakes his head as he pours two fingers of the bourbon in his own glass, then sets the bottle next to Steve and takes the seat opposite him. "Oh, that's a secret. It's been in my family for generations—all the way back to Germany, if you can believe it. Don't be shy; give it a try."

Steve wiggles his eyebrows as he lifts the glass to his lips. "That rhymes."

Wendell smiles back at him with a twinkle in his eye.

The first sip surprises Steve with a remarkable explosion of taste. It's smooth and oak-laden throughout the initial burst of flavor, like any quality bourbon, but there's something else in it, something unusual. His lips tingle with electricity and the inside of his mouth burns from the intensity of the alcohol. "Wow," he says. "That's—*something*."

"Good?"

Steve smiles. A joy fills him—joy and warmth. He finishes the rest, then pours another three fingers. "Oh, yes. Amazing!"

"We're proud of it."

"Germany, you say? I didn't know Germany had their own whiskey."

"Beer and wine are what they're known for. My family invented this whiskey."

Steve stares through the glass with a satisfied grin, holding a mouthful for a moment. He swallows. "Well, it sure is good."

"I'll send you home with a bottle." Wendell sets his own glass on a small table to his right. "So, how are you feeling?"

"With your whiskey, I'm feeling much better." Steve laughs. "Given the circumstances, I'm OK." In the back of his mind, he realizes he can no longer hear anyone else in the house. Still, he senses their presence, as if the lot of them were still in the dining room and living room, standing still like statues, listening to their conversation. The thought gives him a chill.

"I'm amazed you made it tonight. Terrible thing that happened to you."

"Yes."

"Didn't know Ronald well. The two of us never got on, I guess you could say. But I didn't figure him for a murderer."

Steve sets his glass on the table as he feels the room lurch just a little. *Stay focused. This is what you came for.* "Well, he didn't kill me, thank god."

"That's a blessing. So, is that the end of your impromptu investigation?"

Steve takes another sip, looking sideways at the old man. "You know about that?"

"Everyone knows about it. Maquoketa is a small town, Mr. Spain. Word gets around." Wendell's glasses reflect the fireplace flames, obscuring his eyes from view.

"I guess that's true. But as for your question, I don't know why I would end my investigation—I'm too stubborn. Plus, what happened to me had nothing to do with it. Milton didn't care about the Harmon girl."

"Oh? He told you that, did he?"

"Yes."

"Did he say why he tortured you?"

Steve pours another two fingers. "Yep."

"And?"

"He was crazy."

"I doubt that was his reason for smashing your balls."

Steve winces and takes another sip. "He told me I have a demon inside me."

Wendell folds his hands in his lap. The flames of the fire flicker with increased intensity reflected in his eyeglasses. "Ronald always had his flights of fancy. In fact, the two of us butted heads. And that wife of his—well, she was often a pain in my ass. Odd bird. Please have one more. I think you'll find your pain is gone with just another pour."

Steve does as he's told, spilling a bit of the bourbon on the table as he sets the bottle down. "Oops," he says.

"Careful."

"So, yeah. Crazy old Milton. To the Miltons!" Steve raises his glass.

"To the Miltons." Wendell does the same. "And their flights of fancy."

Steve coughs. "Do you think I'm possessed?"

Wendell smiles and looks toward the door. "Why did you come here tonight, Mr. Spain?"

"Like I said, to get out—"

"I'm aware of what you *said*. I want to know why you came here. The truth."

Steve pauses and looks at his empty glass. *How many have I had?* Everything around him, the entire room, is fuzzy. "Why do you think there's something more to tell?"

Wendell laughs, then looks back at him. "I imagine you're a fine lawyer. Questions with questions. But you and I both know why you're here tonight. Came to our little Halloween party even after all of that horror. You and I both know why."

Steve swallows. "I'm not sure what you're getting at, Mr. Jensen. If you think I'm accusing you of killing the Harmon girl, that's not it."

"Are you?"

"I have questions, but I don't see you as a suspect any more than anyone else in town."

"I doubt that's true. But you have questions? Please, ask away."

"Why did everyone lie about Jesse Harmon being out there on the Old Road that night—the night Joey Milton and his friends said they saw her? You and the Tuppers swore up and down it was one of their girls, not Jesse."

"And why do you think we were lying?" Wendell asks more calmly than he should after the semi-veiled accusation.

"Joey Milton's film."

"What about it?"

"I watched it. All of it."

"And something on that film led you here? I'm sure the police inspected Joey's films, didn't they? What could they have missed?"

"There was a missing reel, one Joey Milton had hidden away in a secret compartment in his closet. I was just about to leave the bedroom when his dad clobbered me over the head with something."

"Well done."

"So, you will excuse me for wanting an answer—," Steve says. Without warning, the room shifts before him. A dry burning blazes in his throat and he doubles over in a spasm of nausea.

"Are you OK, Mr. Spain?" Wendell asks.

Pressure rises in his abdomen and it's all Steve can do to keep from heaving the contents of his stomach all over the floor. "I, uh—I'm fine. Just a little—what did you put in this drink?"

"It's an old family recipe—an old family spirit."

Something in Wendell's voice gives him pause. Steve belches and the room rights itself again. He sits back in his chair. Though his vision comes in and out of focus, he no longer feels like vomiting. "I'm OK. Must be the drink and the meds they gave me."

"I apologize. That hadn't occurred to me, mixing drinks with medication. Can I get you a glass of water?"

Steve belches again. "No. I think I'll be fine if I can get the room to stop moving."

Wendell watches him in silence for what feels like an eternity. An awkwardness hovers in the room. "Do you suspect me, Steve?"

Taken aback by the directness of the question, Steve fumbles over his words for a moment. The drink, if nothing else, has dulled his razor sharp mind. Thoughts and words are slow to form. *How many drinks did I pour?*

Then it starts—his heart—thumping in his chest. Pulse rising. His forehead, sweating. Eyes watering. The old feeling that someone is standing on his chest. The sharp pain, just above his ribs, giving a dead-on impression of a heart attack. *Not now. Please, not now! Dear god not now!*

"Are you sure you're OK, Mr. Spain?" Wendell asks, the flames covering the entire front of his lenses. His voice sounds distant, like he's in another room. "You're having trouble breathing. Do you need to lie down?"

Steve waves him away. "No, I said I'm fine! Mr.—Mr. Jensen?"

"Yes?"

"Did you—do you know more than you're telling me? About Jesse Harmon?"

Wendell smiles. Nothing about his demeanor shows a modicum of surprise. The flames in his glasses wave forward and back, almost beckoning. "Why do you ask?"

"On the Milton film—the one that was hidden—there is a shot of the girl they saw on the road that evening."

Wendell remains still. "You don't say?"

"Yep. There sure is."

"And this girl. Could you see who it was?"

"Yes." Steve takes another sip.

"And it wasn't Emma Tupper. Correct?"

"No. The girl in that film was Jesse. I'm certain of it."

"Are you saying the boys lied when they changed their story?"

"Maybe. At least Joey Milton changed his story, of that I'm certain. The other boys claimed they didn't get a good enough look at her to put up an argument. The Milton boy was the one."

"Why on earth would they do that? Do you think they killed her?"

"No. I think someone made Joey lie."

Wendell finishes his glass. "You think his father may have done it? Could she be one of the bodies they've found in the Milton back yard?"

"*Bodies*?" Steve says, almost choking on a sip of the unusual drink.

"Mm hm. They've found more than a dozen bodies buried behind that old coot's house, some from other states, apparently. The FBI has been called in. Did you know that, Mr. Spain?"

Steve hesitates. "No, I didn't."

"Could be that Harmon girl is under one of Gladys's award-winning rose bushes."

"I don't think so."

"Why?"

"My gut tells me something else happened, Mr. Jensen. I don't think Milton's activities had anything to do with Jesse. I think someone had a reason to make Joey Milton lie about the girl he saw on the road that night. And they scared him bad enough he had to hide the footage he took of her."

"And you think that someone was me?" Wendell sounds amused.

"On the film, she leaves the road onto your property. Then there's a shot of a cabin in the woods—those woods out there beyond your fields, I assume." Steve points out the window on the other side of the study. "On the last shot of that film, there's a face looking out from a window in that cabin. I think it's Jesse, though it's hard to see for sure. Is there a cabin on your property, Mr. Jensen? Across the field—in those woods near the Tupper place—close to the Old Road?"

"There is," Wendell says, standing. "Mr. Spain, you've done great work. I'm sorry to string you along like that, but I was most curious about your little theories. As incorrect as they might be, *overall*, there is a hint of the true story in them. You're almost there, and you don't even know it. You're close."

Steve puts his hand over his chest and takes several deep breaths before speaking. "What do you mean?"

"You're close to solving the mystery, Mr. Spain. The journey is almost at an end. But allow me to lead you the rest of the way—you seem to be in some discomfort. Anxiety is such a nasty affliction."

Steve wipes his forehead with his palm. "Lead me where?"

"To what you're here for." Wendell crosses to him, offering a hand. "Come. I'll show you."

"Show me what?"

"The truth."

Chapter Thirty-Four

The half-empty keg slowly fills the red solo cup. Tipping the cup to keep the head from rising too fast, Max sighs. Nearby, a pack of older women, all of whom have the same thick glasses as almost everyone else at the party, sit gossiping at a picnic table. They appear to be observing him. Max almost forgot what it was like to live in a small town.

Just as Max finishes filling his beer, a thin, handsome woman in her seventies, with dyed brown hair, calls to him. "Young man."

Turning to her as he takes a sip of beer, Max says, "Yes?"

"What's your name?"

"Max Spain."

"You from around here?" the woman asks. The other women continue staring at him, their faces devoid of expression.

"No, I'm from California."

"Did you come all the way from California to our little party?" Though it sounds like a joke, the woman's deadpan delivery conveys no humor.

Max laughs and takes a seat at the picnic table opposite the foursome. "No, I'm here with my brother and his wife, Steve and Mara Spain. They live just down the road—"

"I know who they are," the woman says. "He's a lawyer."

"Yep."

"Well, Max, I'm Judy Rasner, and this is Lucille Jensen. And at the far end of the table—that's Abigail Tupper."

"Pleasure to meet you, ladies."

"What's she do for a living? The wife," Judy says.

"Mara? She works for a cell phone company."

This bit of information causes and new wave of muttering amongst the women. Judy says, "Bah! These kids and their phones! Why can't anyone converse nowadays? In person?"

"Oh, they do. But now they have other ways to talk too." Max figures there's little point in arguing this subject. It's obvious none of these ladies can relate to the current generation, but he hopes it will warm them up and lead to other conversations.

Abigail says, "I was at Red Lobster in Davenport with my grandkids and there was a family sitting at the table next to us. Would you believe all of them were on their phones? The kids *and* the parents! It's no wonder families—good quality families—are just dying off. It's a shame, just a shame. I think Trump should make everyone go back to regular phones and TVs, if you ask me."

"I think he uses technology as much as anyone, based on his Twitter habits," Max says. Again, not a conversation he wants to pursue, but here he is.

"Tweeter, Twitter, Friendbook, Instaface, or whatever they're called, it's all the devil," says Lucille Jensen. She's got dark gray hair and horn-rimmed glasses framing icy blue eyes with milky pupils. She's tiny and frail, with wrinkled skin hanging from her bony arms. Her crooked fingers clasped on the table in front of her, she appears to be looking above Max's head as she speaks as if she were blind.

"Oh, Lucille. You think everything's the devil?"

"And so I do. And so it is. Take that Milton fool, for instance. What he did to this young man's poor brother? The work of the devil!"

At the far end of the table, Abigail Tupper, a tall, heavyset lady with gray and strawberry hair, says in a husky voice, "Ronald Milton wasn't a fool. He had a gift."

Max raises an eyebrow at this. "Oh, did he? What kind of gift was that?"

The woman says, "You're Spain's brother. You must know what I know."

"The man claimed he could see demons," Max says. Seeing all the women nodding almost as one, he asks, "You ladies believe it?" Looking around the table, nothing but blank stares answer him.

Mara slides onto the bench next to him. Judging from the curious smile spread on her face, she's been listening to a good part of the conversation.

"This is my sister-in-law, Mara," Max says, then motions to each woman. "Mara, this is Judy Rasner, Lucille Jensen, and Abigail—Tupper?"

"That's right. Excellent memory," Judy says.

"Pleased to meet you," Mara says.

"Oh, well, don't you have the sweetest Carolina accent," Judy says. "Which one?"

Mara looks confused. "Which?"

"Which Carolina? I'm guessing South!"

Mara winks at her. "You got it. Born and raised."

"I knew it!"

"How do you like the new place?" Abigail asks after an annoyed glance at Judy.

"I love it," Mara says. "We both do."

Judy says, "Oh, those woods, though. Don't you find them frightful? I'd never go down there."

"They're magical, I think." Mara's face twitches, betraying an unspoken thought.

"*Magical?* That's one way to put it. You ever see anything in those woods?" Judy asks.

Mara asks, "Like what? Deer? Squirrels?"

Judy shakes her head. "No, dummy! Anything unusual."

"Um. I think Steve saw a bobcat last week—"

"No, not bobcats. I mean ghosts!"

Abigail slaps the table. "Judy Margaret Rasner! Quit your damned paranoid shenanigans!"

"It's OK," Mara says. "I don't mind. Sometimes I feel like there's something out there. That's why I say those woods are magical. I see shadows walking around, like gray mists, if that doesn't make me sound like too much of a loon."

"Not at all, honey."

"They're babies!" Lucille Jensen says, calling out loud enough to silence half the party.

Judy and Abigail roll their eyes. "Oh, Lucille," Abigail says, looking at the fields beyond the yard.

"It's true," Lucille says.

Max glances at Mara, then back at the ladies, his mouth hanging open. "Babies?" he asks.

"Yes. The ghosts of babies are haunting your ravine."

Mara says, "*Whose* babies?"

Max runs through the possibilities in his mind. Perhaps a hundred years ago, whooping cough or small pox killed a bunch of babies in the area. Maybe they were buried back there in the wooded ravine behind Steve's house. Crazy idea, but creepy too. But before the theory can evolve beyond a macabre notion, Lucille brings it all back to earth.

"Abortion babies. That's where they hid them, you know."

Mara bites her cheek to keep from laughing in the woman's face. She takes a drink of wine and says, "I'm sorry. What are you talking about?"

"Oh, don't pay her any mind. She is crazy as a loon, this one," Abigail says.

Judy says, "Shame on you, Lucille, frightening our guests with such rubbish!"

"It ain't rubbish! It's the truth. The things in your woods—they are the ghosts of all the aborted babies that there ever were in the state of Iowa. Maybe even some from Wisconsin and Illinois. Who knows?"

"Oh, shush!" Abigail shakes her head and takes a drink of whatever she's got in her cup.

Lucille slams a bony, arthritic fist on the picnic table with more force than Max would have expected from such a fragile-looking woman. "Don't you shush me, you *Tupper*!" she says, as if being a member of the Tupper family was the most hurtful insult as she could think up. Then she scans her frosty eyes around the table, scowling with disgust at each person. "I tell you now. The place is foul because of all the little babies murdered by their mothers."

A woman's voice interrupts the miserable conversation. "Mara?"

A woman with long red hair approaches their table, in a short green dress with black leggings, a long hunter green coat, and jet black Doctor Martens. She is a shocking presence compared to the others. None of the gray hairs out back pay any attention to her at all. None but Judy, that is.

"Oh, my, would you look at that one?"

One of the other ladies makes a shushing sound.

"Hey," Mara says, getting up and rushing to her friend. "Nadine! I'm so glad you made it."

"How could I not?" Nadine says, hugging Mara but looking over her shoulder to Max. Releasing Mara, she says, "And you must be Max."

Max rises and extends a hand to her as he joins them. "Yep. I'm Steve's brother."

She says, "Yes, you are. Didn't know the Spains made so many handsome men."

"Just the two," Mara says. "But this one's single."

Max blushes as Nadine approaches him, her hips swaying—her large green eyes, equal parts innocent and sinister. Her skin is alabaster and her breasts are as large as her hips are wide. She moves into him, wrapping her arms around his shoulders in a lingering embrace. She smells like honey and mint. "So good to meet you."

"Good to meet you too." Max's face flushes as he awkwardly pulls away from her.

"Where's Steve?" Nadine asks, scanning the area.

"Oh, he's with Mr. Wendell. I guess they're trying a special bourbon, or some such thing," Mara says.

"Didn't invite me," Max says with mock injury.

Nadine laughs and looks at Max's drink. "I guess I need to catch up with you guys. How many have you had?"

Max says, "Just this one. We just got here ourselves. They have a full bar with just about everything you can ask for—liquor and wine—or there's a keg, too. What can I get you?"

"Nothing," she says with a smile. "I can get my own drink. Be right back." She drifts to the drink table as Max watches her.

Mara says, "Cute, huh?"

Max nods. "Cute is not the first word I'd use. She's beautiful."

"She gets attention everywhere we go."

"I bet. It's like she's a walking goddess of fertility."

"You two will hit it off," Mara says, rolling her eyes. "Just be careful."

"Always."

"I'm gonna see if I can find more Jensens or Tuppers. Anyone who might help me get the information Steve wanted. It's time to snoop."

Max says, "OK, sounds good. I'll keep Nadine company."

Mara laughs. "I'll say it again—be careful. She's a vixen."

"I'm counting on it."

As Mara leaves into the back of the house, Nadine returns with a plastic glass of red wine. She steps next to Max, staring out at the elderly party-go-ers.

"Enjoying yourself?" Nadine asks.

"It's a blast," Max says, laughing.

"Nothing beats partying in Maquoketa."

"Yeah, well, we're here on a secret mission."

"Oh, yeah?" She turns to him, eyebrow raised.

"Yep."

"Would this mission have to do with Steve's investigation?"

"Could be. But if I told you, I'd have to kill you."

Nadine shakes her head at the dumb joke and Max feels another rush of embarrassment. "Have you discovered anything?" she asks.

"Nope. Just been talking to those three ladies. You missed quite a con-versation," Max says, motioning to the picnic table.

"I see. Find out anything interesting?"

"They tell me that my brother bought a house on an aborted-baby burial ground. Say that fast three times."

"Oh, my."

"That's what I said."

Max stares at Nadine, mesmerized by the symmetry of her face, the softness of her skin. Though he's only had half of a beer, he feels a strange, almost dizzy, sensation.

She looks at the drink table and says, "I doubt we'll uncover anything useful with this bunch. Why don't we do a couple shots? What do you say we liven up this wake?"

"You got it."

She takes him by the hand, leading him to the drink table—the skin of her palm hums with electricity. Max almost jerks away from the shock of the sensation, but he tightens his grip and follows.

Chapter Thirty-Five

Mara finds the house curiously empty.

No footsteps echoing in the foyer, no dishes clanging in the kitchen, no muffled voices speaking anywhere on the premises. The formal dining room to Mara's right, decked in Halloween decorations, offers evidence that a good number of guests had recently occupied the room. Paper plates, wadded up napkins, and half-empty beverage containers cover most of the flat surfaces. Various treats—store-bought and homemade—and dozens of potluck dishes, half eaten, cover the formal dining table like a mountain of temptation.

To the left, a fire dwindles in the living room's flagstone fireplace. Half-empty glasses sweat on the coffee table and end tables throughout the room.

Mara peers up the wood bannister staircase. A yellow light flickers from the hallway to the right. She calls, "Hello?" The reverberation of her own voice is the sole response.

She moves through the dining room, taking a brownie on the way. The kitchen looks like the living room, half-used. A pile of dishes rest in the right hand sink, while an equal number dry in the left rack. A sliding glass door at the far end of the room lies open a full six inches. To her left, she hears the sounds of voices and laughter coming from the backyard, and Mara realizes the sliding door must open off the side of the house.

A path leads from the doors across the side lawn to a gate in a wood fence. *Did everyone leave out this door?*

Mara conducts a cursory exploration of the rest of the house—downstairs and upstairs too—but finds no one about. She finds the cellar door locked, both at the handle and at the top. Returning to the side door, Mara thinks about fetching Nadine and Max, but decides it might cause suspicion. Instead, she locates a glass and a bottle of wine and swallows a few mouthfuls before heading out the sliding door and down the path toward the woods.

The path leads down a long sloping hillside between two fields. To her right, rows upon rows of dried out grape vines hang from fences, and to her left a fallow field lies covered in dead plants that look a lot like the hops she and Steve saw at an IPA brewery in Galena last summer.

She follows the path for at least a half-mile, seeing not a soul the whole way. The moon offers enough light to make her way through the forest. A few discarded Solo cups are the only signs that the party-goers came this way. As she continues, the forest gets thicker, and the moon offers diminishing light for the path. Fear gets the best of her, and she nearly turns back when she hears voices some distance ahead.

As she comes around a cluster of bushes, an enormous shadow appears before her. Mara crouches, peering through the branches to discover a structure, a small cabin, half-obstructed by dead brush and young trees. Is this the same cabin Steve showed her? The one from Joey Milton's film?

She moves closer, careful to keep hidden behind the brush. Voices sound through the rickety walls and broken windows—men's voices speaking loudly. They're familiar voices. One is older.

Steve?

Just as Mara stands and is about to call through the window, she hears movement behind her—crunching twigs and leaves.

"Max?"

No reply issues from the shadows of the twisted timbers. Mara returns her attention to the cabin. Something tells her to keep hidden, though she can't say why. As she shifts closer to the window, the voices become clearer. It almost sounds to her like Steve is arguing with someone. Wendell, perhaps? Next to the dirty window, she puts her back to the wall to listen. Unfortunately, with the breeze drifting through the tree branches, she can't make out a word of it. Just as she moves to take a peek into the cabin, she hears crunching leaves directly behind her. She freezes. Someone is breathing on the other side of the dead brush.

Alarms bells ring out in her head, but before she can move, a gloved hand covers her mouth and drags her away from the cabin.

CHAPTER THIRTY-SIX

Max laughs for ten minutes straight. Not from a joke or a witty line Nadine may have given him, but from simple joy—a joy he hasn't felt in his whole life. It overwhelms him. Her green eyes seem to glow brighter whenever she looks at him, which swells his chest with desire and—could it be—love? Strange as it seems, the intensity of his feelings for her rolls through his body as she pours another shot with a wink and a kiss on the cheek. Her lips are wet and firm, and when they depart his cheek, they leave behind an aching.

Something catches his eye through his blurring vision—a man standing at the corner of the barn, arms crossed, his John Deere cap pulled low. The same man they saw earlier.

"Who's that guy?" Max asks, his words slurring.

Not looking, Nadine says, "Who cares?"

"He keeps staring at me—us."

"Wonder why? We're the youngest people at this party. Why wouldn't he?"

"He looks weird."

"You know where you are, right?"

Max laughs again, harder than warranted by the joke. Nadine's voice tickles something in him. "Stop," he says. "You'll make me piss my pants."

"Oh, that sounds like fun!" Grabbing him by the midsection, Nadine tickles his hips with her nails.

"OK! OK! Stop! I need to find the bathroom. You wait right here. You got it?" Without thinking, he leans in and kisses her full on the lips. A second later, he yanks his head back and says, "Oh crap! Sorry, I didn't mean to do that."

"It's fine," she says with a raised eyebrow and a Joker-grin. "You should have asked first, but I wanted to do that too." Nadine winks and leans into him with a long kiss that buckles his knees, nearly sending him to the ground.

A rush of adrenaline washes over him and he pulls away, waving his hands. "Whoa! You must be a magician because that's just fucking—crazy! *How* do you do that?"

"I never tell my secrets."

"Save that thought. I'll be right back."

"You got it, Max Spain."

Max turns to leave, glancing at the metal barn. The guy in the John Deere cap is still there, but he's not watching Max any longer. He's staring intently into the fields near the side of the farmhouse. Apparently seeing something that Max cannot, the man crosses the backyard toward the fields.

Nadine interrupts his spying. "I thought you had to use the bathroom."

Max nods, shrugs, and stumbles around the near side of the house and through an open sliding glass door into the kitchen. He pauses for a moment, catching a familiar scent—a perfume—as if someone had just been here. *Flower Bomb?*

"Mara?" he calls into the house, realizing with all the Nadine fun, he'd almost forgotten about his sister-in-law. "Hello?"

He crosses the kitchen, walks through the dining room, and to the foyer, looking into the living room. The place is deserted, though only recently, judging by the state of the food and drinks. *Bah, they must be outside with all the MAGA people staring up at the frigging sky.*

Down the hall, he finds the bathroom. He urinates for what feels like ten minutes, his head bowed so his chin rests on his chest, staring at the perfect stream of clear liquid running into the toilet.

Max washes his hands and stares into the oval mirror above the sink. His eyes are bloodshot and droopy at the corners. "What the hell is in these drinks?"

Suddenly, as his mind clears a little, he remembers something. *Where's Mara?* He can't put his finger on it, but something feels wrong.

"Wait a minute," he says into the mirror. "I'm not drunk. This—this feels like someone drugged me."

"Find Mara," a voice speaks into his mind, startling him.

Heart racing, he washes his face with cold water, slapping his cheeks, then dries off and opens the door. His heart jumps as he finds a figure in the doorway—Nadine, her green eyes glowing that peculiar green. This time, it's not his imagination. They're actually glowing, like two magic emerald lights, piercing his heart.

"What do you say we get out of here? Head back to Steve and Mara's house? They don't need us here, Max." Her words are innocent enough, but her tone speaks of certain activities they might do together in his room. Unsolicited visions flood his mind of Nadine's naked body against his, her voice moaning and giggling with pleasure.

"Uh—yeah." Once again, Max's mind fails him. He can't remember what he's supposed to do. Nadine takes his hand, leading him back through the house and out the front door.

I'm forgetting something again. What is it?

The rest is only patches of consciousness—walking down the gravel road, Nadine touching him, kissing him, coaxing him. The thrill of her presence warming his soul, blinding him to all other thoughts. Stumbling down the gravel driveway. Inside the house—tumbling down the stairs.

"Hey how did we get inside? Where are they? Steve and Mara?" he asks, over the waves of anticipation.

"The door was unlocked, silly. They're already in bed." Nadine's words wash over him with anesthetic charm.

"They left the door unlocked?"

"It's Maquoketa."

"Oh, yeah. But how did they beat us home?"

Nadine laughs. "How much did you have to drink, Mr. Spain?"

In the bed, all the images he'd seen before come vibrantly true, though he wonders if all of it is nothing but a wild dream. Her body moves with his and a warm electricity seems to spread to every atom of his body. Max reaches out his shaking hands to her, taking her face between them. She's the most beautiful thing he's ever seen. Without realizing he's doing it, he prays—not to God, but to *her*. Nadine.

"I am yours, and in you, through you, with you, I can do all things. You are my god, and I devote myself to you. From now and forever." Max hesitates, shocked by his own words. He tries to say something else, but repeats the prayer again. "I am yours, and in you, through you, with you, I can do all things. You are my god, and I devote myself to you. From now and forever."

To Max's wonder, Nadine's eyes burn in a bright glowing light, turning the entire guest room into a deep sea of lush green. A surge of euphoria overpowers his mind. She looks down at him, her eyes flickering in terrible flames.

Max finds he's now shouting with all the strength he has. "My soul! It's yours!"

CHAPTER THIRTY-SEVEN

Wendell opens the cabin door and stands aside for Steve to enter. The trek down the hill and through the woods took every ounce of Steve's diminished energy. Though Wendell offered as much support as he could give, it was still slow-going for the mile-plus hike.

Steve surveys the shabby one-room cabin. Though he's never been here before, something about the place feels familiar. Burning candles encircle the room in three ascending rows, lining the walls in soft yellow light. A film screen stands at the far end of the one-room cabin, the kind you'd see back when teachers still showed films in school. An antique projector, similar to the one Steve borrowed from the Miltons, rests on a wood table in the middle of the room, its cord plugged into a small box sitting next to it, with a spool of Super 8 film fed through its mechanism.

"What's all this?" Steve asks.

"It's a film projector."

"I can see that. Why is it here?"

"We know you've been searching for this film. It's here, safely hidden for years right here in this cabin. Waiting for tonight, or rather, waiting for you, Mr. Spain."

A low thrum rattles within his chest. "For me?"

"Yes. This is the last piece of your puzzle—the last clue to your mystery. I have to say, though I always knew this day would come, it's surreal to be here now. I had wondered if I'd live to see it."

Steve leans on his cane. "What the fuck are you talking about, Jensen?"

"Do you remember coming here before tonight?" Wendell walks to the projector.

"To this cabin? No. When would I have done that?"

"Maybe fifteen years ago?"

"Fifteen years ago? My family had a cabin up here—sold it about ten years ago. But it wasn't on your property. I don't recall ever stepping foot on your land until the day Mara and I came up here to buy the house."

"Your new house."

Steve's heart picks up its pace again. Sweat beads form on his forehead. "Yes."

"Your last house. The last house."

"What are you talking about?"

Wendell puts his hands in his pockets and laughs. "Ah, that's right. You wouldn't remember. I'm getting ahead of myself."

Exhaustion threatening to overwhelm him now, Steve leans against a wall next to a window. A sound outside grabs his attention, muted and soft, like a low moan. "What was that?" He looks through the hazy window, but only sees shadows from the surrounding brush and trees, shifting and waving in the moonlight. "Is someone out there?"

"Oh, just forest sounds—you get a lot of those out here. There are many things in these woods, Mr. Spain. But you have nothing to fear from any of them." Wendell touches the projector.

"What's on the film, Wendell?" Steve says.

"You really don't remember this cabin?"

"I've never been here in my life."

Wendell glances up at him, light from the candles reflected in his glasses like the fireplace earlier, only less dramatic. "You asked what's on this film. Did you know Joey Milton made a third film?"

"No, I didn't. What's on it?"

Wendell smiles. "Everything you want to know. The key to it all."

Steve steps closer, fists clenched. "They key?"

"The last piece of the puzzle."

"The truth?"

"Every bit."

"Show me."

Wendell nods with an expression that might pass for sympathy. He reaches down and flips the switch. In a flash of light and a puff of dust, the old projector lurches to life, casting a faded black-and-white image onto the screen.

Exterior. We see the cabin in its earlier days, still covered in vegetation, but in better shape than it is now. Someone is standing in the window to the left of the door. A cut to black for several frames, then back again. It's night, most of the image hidden in darkness, the only source of light a hazy window, glowing yellow. We move toward the cabin's entrance. The door opens, seemingly on its own, allowing us to enter the rickety space. The camera cuts out, then back in, to reveal a girl lying in the middle of the cabin's wood floor. She is encircled by five figures dressed in robes from head to toe. The central figure, whose robe appears to be a lighter color than the others, stands above her head.

Bound by the wrists, the girl lies peacefully on the wood floor, adorned in a white dress with red flowers, like the girl in Joey's secret film. The camera zooms onto her feet, then pans across her body to her face. Steve gasps. *It's Jesse Harmon!* She does not turn her face away, but stares into the lens with a smile. When tears fall from her crystal clear eyes, they appear not as sorrow or fear, but joy. *Could it be? Joy?*

"What the fuck!" Steve covers his mouth with one hand, leaning with all his weight on the cane with his other. "Where did you get this?"

Wendell signals for him to wait with a wave of the hand.

The camera pulls back slightly, but remains focused on Jesse. Near her head, a light robe drops to the ground. A man's bare feet step into the frame. Jesse stares at the person above her, and her smile widens. *She's happy!*

Now the camera pans upwards across bare legs, over the man's naked body, until at last it reaches his face and stops, focusing—focusing. Steve doubles over and vomits on the cabin floor, then losing his balance, he tips over onto his backside. The face! The man on the screen! *What the fuck is this? This is impossible!*

"Yes, Mr. Spain. It was you." Wendell's voice drips with pity.

The face on the screen—the man in the light colored robe—now nude, standing above Jesse Harmon. It's Steve himself.

"Impossible! This is impossible!"

Wendell raises a hand once again. "Wait."

The camera cuts out, then back. Now we see a wide-angle shot offering a view of the entire room. In the film, Steve holds a long golden dagger before him. He places it near his lips, kissing the hilt and praying. Then, with both hands gripping the dagger and hoisting it above his forehead, he kneels just above Jesse's chest, and brings the blade down upon her, piercing through the skin and bone. Blood spouts from the wound like a fountain, baptizing Steve in crimson. He reaches his hands into the opening in Jesse's chest, filling his hands with blood, wiping it on his face, his arms, and chest. It cuts now to a closeup of Jesse, lingering on her fading eyes as the last bits of life release from them. The smile on her face remains, frozen in death, eyes wide, staring hideously into the camera.

Back to the wide shot. The other figures raise their hands to the ceiling. They chant some unintelligible prayer in unison. Steve Spain, dripping with blood from his sacrifice, bends to a knee and kisses Jesse's lips.

The dark-robed figures kneel, heads bowed, palms offered in supplication, as Steve stands before them like a demigod. The film runs out, flapping on the projector.

"Fuck no! No!" Steve yells, squeezing his head between his hands, unable to rise from his knees. "This is an abomination! It's not true. I know who I am!"

"Yes. *Now* you do. You know who you are." Wendell gives him with the same sympathetic stare, stepping in front of the projector screen, white projector light flashing against his body. "This is you, Steve Spain. This is who you are. But we are not here to judge you, Mr. Spain. No, there is no judgment here. We are only here to help you."

"Help... me? Oh, God! What is this!"

Reaching out a hand to him, Wendell says, "Poor Ronald Milton was right all along, Mr. Spain, crazy old fool though he was. You have something in you—something that makes you forget things. Something that makes you do things. But we can help you, my friend."

Steve scrambles onto his feet, using the cane for leverage, backing away toward the cabin door. "Help? How can you help? It's a lie!"

"We can relieve you of this pain, Mr. Spain. Withdraw this thing from you."

From outside, he hears a sound, first from some distance, then coming closer and closer—a group of people chanting in unison. Candlelight flickers in through the windows.

Steve hobbles out the door, only to run headfirst into a man in a black robe just outside.

"Mr. Spain. We're so glad you came." His voice is deep and muffled under the silken fabric.

"No! Get away!" Steve's voice cracks with pain and fury.

"But don't you see?" says the figure. "Don't you see now?"

"No! I know who I am!"

"Yes, at last you do!"

Several robed figures emerge from behind the far side of the cabin, continuing their chant. But they remain at a distance, facing him.

"No! That's a trick, some nasty trick! That's not—it can't be!"

Wendell appears in the cabin doorway. "You know it wasn't a trick, Mr. Spain. Search your memories."

Steve stumbles toward The Old Road, but his cane gets stuck in a patch of mud and he falls to the grass. He lies there, weeping. "The man in the white—in the white robe. It can't be me. It can't—"

"But it is," says the large black-robed figure. "Let us help you!"

Steve brings himself to stand again, holding his cane before him like a sword. "I know the truth! You're trying to blackmail me! Well, it won't work. You hear me! I'm a fucking lawyer! Back! Get back!" He swings the cane from side to side, backing away from the gathering congregation.

Wendell approaches. "We will not harm you. Come with us, Steve. It's time!"

"Stay the fuck away or I'll bash your fucking heads in, you lunatics! You think you can edit some kid's movie and make me think it's real? I'm a goddamn lawyer! I'll sue your asses off for defamation!" Backing away, Steve keeps swinging the cane.

Wendell and the host of robed figures do not follow, but stand together, shoulder to shoulder, arms reached out to him. "We will wait for you, Mr. Spain. We will wait for you! Let us help you!"

Turning on his heel, Steve ignores the pain ripping through his body, and runs as best he can all the way to the road.

CHAPTER THIRTY-EIGHT

"Quiet," a man's voice hisses, his gloved hand still covering Mara's mouth. "Stay put. Someone's coming. If you want to save your husband, keep quiet."

As her eyes adjust to the dark, she makes out a cap with the John Deere logo on it—it's the man they spoke to when they arrived at the party.

Footsteps sound to her left. She twists her head toward the sound. Four figures are running through the woods twenty yards away, all clad in black. After they pass, the man grabs her by the jaw and turns her face to him.

"You don't want those people finding you, trust me. And your husband—well, he's not himself."

"Who are you?" Mara says through the firm grip.

"Don Loomis. You know me."

Mara thinks. "Don Loomis? You built our house. With Lou—what's his name?"

"Yes, that's me."

"Why are you doing this?"

"I'm saving you. Those folks who just strolled by? They're after your old man."

"Steve? What do they want with him? Oh, no."

"What?" Don asks.

"The investigation. The Harmon girl. Steve was too close to something." She stares into the sky. The milky way crosses high above her like a glittering bridge of stars moving over the universe. "Steve was right—these people in robes, the hidden film, Ronald Milton—it's all tied together. They're gonna kill him."

"I don't think that's what's happening."

"Why?"

"Ronald Milton believed your husband had a demon in him."

"Yeah, Milton was crazy."

"Milton wasn't crazy! He had a gift. If he said he saw a demon in your husband, that means it was true. The people in the robes believe it too."

Don shoots a wild eye up the hill, then stands, craning his neck. "There's more coming, I think. They've got flashlights—probably searching for you. We need to get out of here."

Mara takes the opportunity, jumping to her feet and balling her fist. She swings wild but hard, with all her strength, catching Don with a lucky shot in the nose with the entire force of her bony knuckles. She feels something snap under her fist as the blow lands home, and a sharp pain shoots through her forearm. Don stumbles back, a stream of blood gushes forth. Touching his nose with his right hand, he pulls it back and looks at his bloody fingers, astonishment flashing across his face. Mara turns and races up the hill toward the Jensen house, hoping someone there can help her. If nothing else, she's got to warn Max and Nadine.

As she flies out of the timbers and onto the path between the cornfield and the fallow field, she sees a group of people walking with flashlights. They're calling her name. "Mara! Mara!"

"Help!" she screams as she runs. She can hear Don chasing behind her, his strained breathing growing louder.

A man's voice screams into the night from the area of the cabin, some ways behind them now. *It's Steve!* Mara stops and turns to look. Don is ten yards away, running fast, but she doesn't care. She takes a step to avoid him when a gunshot rings out and Don's forehead explodes. His lifeless body crashes to the ground, his momentum sliding the body forward before coming to a stop just before Mara's feet.

"Mrs. Spain! Mrs. Spain!" Two chubby, identical-looking women rush to flank her, one of them holding a pistol. "Oh dear, oh dear! Are you OK, Mrs. Spain?"

"Jame? Jamie?"

"Yes! Oh, thank heavens that scoundrel didn't get to you!"

"Oh, thank you! Thank you!" Tears stream down Mara's face as she hugs them both. "We have to find Steve! I heard his voice near that cabin."

"Cabin?" says Jame. "What cabin?"

"Down the hill in the woods. There are people in robes down there. They're attacking Steve! We have to go."

The others with Jamie and Jame step to either side of Mara, taking hold of her arms. Jamie says, "Oh, dear. I'm so sorry, Mrs. Spain. And you were such a good customer. Mama said you had great taste."

Jame says, "Heavens, sis! Just get it over with."

Jamie looks at Mara with pity. "I'm so sorry."

Exhausted and confused, Mara asks, "Sorry for what?"

Jamie lifts the gun until the barrel is even with Mara's eyes, and says, "Please, honey. Come with us."

Chapter Thirty-Nine

The house is silent when Steve enters, exhausted and racked with pain from the miles of stumbling through the rough terrain. He closes the door behind him, locking it. Rocky rushes to him, tail wagging. Steve pets him for a moment, thinking of what he saw—what just happened.

It can't be. It's all a lie!

To the back door, he checks the locks. The only illumination comes from the outside sky and the digital clock on various appliances and electronics throughout the kitchen and dining room. Down the slope of the backyard, just outside the tree line, are several figures, all gray and translucent. They make no movement, but remain frozen there, watching him. One catches his eye—a tiny figure crouched in front of the others. It sways side to side. The hair on Steve's scalp rises and he pulls his attention away from the window.

In the bedroom, Mara's figure lies under the covers. Relieved, he rests his forehead on the door frame. "Thank god."

"Come to bed." Mara's sleepy voice is barely audible over the cracking of her throat.

"In a minute. I'm going to check on Max."

"Come to bed, hun."

"A minute."

Downstairs, Steve peeks into Max's room. It's empty save for the bed-sheets balled up at the foot of the bed. The window is open. A voice whispers into his mind, *Maybe he went for a walk in the woods. Maybe he's restless after a night with Nadine. You know how exhausting she can be.*

Steve rubs his face. "Sleep. That's what I need. Lots of sleep."

Yes, sleep. That's what you need. Go to bed with your wife.

Upstairs now. Steve peels off all his clothes as he hobbles into the room.

"Come to bed," says his wife's voice.

To bed. Sleep...

Removing his clothes, he slides into the sheets and, facing her, plants his skin against hers. She is naked too, and somehow her body feels different—plump, curvaceous. Electricity tickles him and she turns to face him, a shadow of a form in the complete darkness. She says something that he can barely make out.

"What?" he says.

"Shh," she whispers. "Quiet, relax."

She kisses him, and Steve touches her face. It's fuller and softer than Mara's.

"Wait!"

Before he can pull away, something clamps down on his wrists, and Nadine brings herself into a kneeling position at his side, whispering words he can't quite hear.

"Nadine! Get out of my bed—"

He cannot seem to form words. His arms extend in either direction to the corners of the bed. Robed figures appear at either side of the room—at least a dozen, perhaps more. Two hold his arms at either side of the head-board while two more hold his ankles at the opposite corners of the foot. Nadine continues whispering as others bind his limbs to the bedposts.

Mara! Mara! he can't speak the words, his mouth will not move.

"Shh," Nadine says, touching his lips with her finger. "Mara will be here soon."

One by one, a dozen candles ignite around the room and Steve sees Nadine, her green eyes glowing, kneeling next to him. She smiles, caressing his face with the backs of her fingers. "Soon, my love. We shall be as one again. The two of us, forever."

One figure steps forward, offering a hand to Nadine. She accepts it and lifts herself from the bed to stand in front of the windows. A stream of blood drips from her thighs onto the bed as she steps to the floor.

Another robed figure, this one dressed in red holding an ancient leather text in his hands, moves to the foot and speaks, "Glory to the night. Glory to the day. Our time is here, at last. You've a demon inside you, Mr. Spain. One we've waited for many years. Tonight, I will separate you from him!"

"Praise The One," the others chant.

The figure in the red robe opens the book. "And so it was the Great One came into this earth and lived among us and became one of us. Praise The One!"

The others repeat after him. "Praise The One"

Nadine looks down at Steve, her green eyes glowing like two planets. "Soon, my love. Soon."

"And so he grew mighty in the innocent's flesh. Praise be The One."

Steve wants to scream at her, to call her a slut, a witch, a crazy person, but he can't. The words will not form. Though he tries to fight, his body will not respond to his own commands. Panic sweeps over him. His heart races, pounding in his chest so hard Steve thinks it might break a rib.

"Sh. Relax. Soon, my love. Soon." Nadine's touch calms him, tickling his skin with minute sparks of electricity.

As the reading continues, Steve feels as if his spirit has changed. As if his body might not hold his soul—getting lighter and lighter—almost like air. *This is it? Is it true? Did I have a demon inside me this whole time?*

Steve can feel it now. It roars just under his consciousness.

Nadine whispers into his ear. "Remember the first sacrifice. Liesl."

"Liesl?" A wave of weariness rushes over him.

The room moves in and out of focus, then dissolves. Steve's mind drifts onto the winds of time. Far away, he goes into darkness until light fills his vision and he passes into memory. Silence.

He's back in the memory—a memory of an awful day. A wintry afternoon on a river of ice appears before him. Liesl, his sister, stands across frozen water, only a dozen yards away. The sound of cracking ice cuts through the silence, as it always does.

Liesl looks at him, "Steve?"

He rushes to her, grabbing her by the shoulders. This time he will save her—this time they will leave together and she will not fall. She will not drop below the ice. Never again will he remember her small body sweeping down the river, all the way to the lock and dam with the monster catfish waiting there to devour her.

"I've got you!"

Liesl stares into his eyes, and he sees—*fear*. Yes, fear. Something else controls his hands now—someone else. His vision turns red.

Helpless, Steve watches as his own body stomps on the ice under Liesl with the heel of his snow boot. Repeatedly, he stomps and stomps, all the while holding firm to Liesl's shoulders, squeezing them with all his strength, as she struggles to break away from him.

She cries out as the ice breaks away under her feet. Her eyes filled with terror, she says, "It's—"

Before she can finish the words, the demon in Steve's body pushes Liesl down through the crack in the ice, letting the river draw her away. Her little red coat flows under the ice beneath him, and down the river.

The memory vanishes, and he's left in a black void, floating aimlessly for what feels like an eternity. His mind drifts in and out of consciousness. Eventually, visions pop into his mind. He sees flashes of his bedroom—Nadine kissing him, the robed figures chanting together, reading from the text.

"You killed my sister," Steve says to the thing in his mind.

It replies, *"Yes."*

"Why? You didn't have to do that."

"But I did."

"Why?"

"It was the only way."

"To do what?"

"To bring you to this night."

"You miscalculated. Those people are exorcising you. You've lost, and it was all for nothing."

At this, this voice of the other laughs. *"Exorcising me? From you?"*

"Yes," Steve says. *"They'll rid me of you! Go back to hell!"*

More laughter. *"I am not from hell. And those people in your bedroom—they aren't casting me out of you. No, they are not, vessel."*

Panic sets in, as if he too is being pushed under a river of ice. *They are not exorcising the demon—no, not the demon at all.*

A hand slaps Steve's face hard and firm, then again, then again, until Steve feels his arms straining, breaking the cords that bind him.

Naked and filled with an immense power, Steve's body rises to its feet in one stiff movement, arms raised in the air. For a second, neither Steve nor the entity within him have control. He looks down at the makeshift congregation as the rising power fills his veins. There is nothing in the world like this feeling and for a moment, just a moment, Steve stops fighting. Instead, he drinks in the unfamiliar sensation, swimming in it. He wants to laugh and scream out into the night and run through the trees until he burns through every inch of every mile of the county. Steve reaches out—

But before he can seize it, a force hits him in the gut, and he doubles over, retching. His eyes glow red and the bloody vision returns. The room illuminates in crimson and green. The congregants, bathed in the lights, continue chanting, though the words sound foreign. Quickly, the creature inside him takes the opportunity. He pushes Steve below, and taking control of the body, runs out of the bedroom. Like a flash of red light, the body tears through the living room, past Rocky's sleeping body, and out the front door into the first pinkish rays of daylight.

Just before the body reaches the gravel driveway, it stops. The demon pushes harder against Steve's consciousness. A presence—an unwelcome visitor. It pushes against his will, thrashing soul against soul, until, with one last scream into the sky, Steve's own spirit is finally forced beyond the boundary of his skin. His spirit, no longer tethered to an earthly form, ascends from the body until it hovers several feet above the property, floating on the crisp October air.

Staring at the earth below, Steve sees the harrowing image of his own body staring back up at him, smiling in triumph but with perhaps a hint of sympathy. His eyes are glowing red.

"Thank you!" the thing in his body says, then turns its attention to the house.

It waits.

Chapter Forty

Steve floats above the yard for some hours, observing his former body below. The October sun, now angled low in the east, but rising, slices through the trees, casting a golden glow like a seldom used Instagram filter.

No one emerges from the house, but a good number of people arrive through the morning, giving the body a wide berth as they enter the house. License plates from far and wide tell the tale of a large conspiracy. Steve is aware of these comings, but none of it matters. He can only stare at his former body, wondering if it will ever move again. More hours pass and still the body remains unmoving, unaware of Steve's spirit watching from above.

Or perhaps it is well aware, but has no reason to care.

The body jerks as if it awakened from a dream. Its head lolls back, eyes closed at first, until the lids open and Steve stares into those red shining eyes. With a hint of a smile, the face looks once again to the mouth of the house—Steve and Mara's last house—and, and enters with not another glance at the sky.

There is a movement at the side of the yard, just behind the tree line. A shape appears from the woods. It's small, little more than a wisp of gray smoke, but in the form of a girl. Features materialize in the puff of fog—a maroon dress, hair pulled back into a thick braid, hands clasped behind her back. Soon, recognition forms. She's pretty and fair of skin, with tiny patches of freckles over her nose and across each cheek. Smiling at him, the girl opens her mouth to say something, but blows him a kiss.

"*Hello,*" Steve says.

"*Hello,*" the girl replies, her voice like chimes ringing in the autumn breeze.

"*What are you doing here?*"

"*I'm here because you're here.*"

"*You're with me?*"

"*Always.*"

"*Do I know you?*"

"*Of course you do.*"

"*Do you know me?*"

"*Of course.*"

"*What's your name?*"

"*Guess.*"

"*Are you Liesl?*"

"*Yes.*"

"*You're my sister.*"

"*I am.*"

An unwanted memory enters his thoughts. "*I'm so sorry.*"

"*For what?*"

"*For what I did to you. That day on the ice. I remember.*"

"*If you remember, then you know it wasn't you who killed me.*"

"*But.*"

She smiles, sympathetically. "*It wasn't you. And that thing in your body isn't you either. What he did to me, and to Jesse, and to many others. None of it was you.*"

"*So, Milton was right.*"

"*He was.*"

"*Could he have saved me?*"

"I wouldn't know."

Singing voices drift through the air from the house, soft and melodic like a solemn hymn. The trees surrounding the property sway with the melody.

"I would tell you not to follow those voices," Liesl says. *"But I know you won't listen."*

"Why shouldn't I?" Steve asks. *"It's my house."*

"Not anymore."

"I'm dead already. So why not go in?"

"It may hurt you."

"Too late for that."

Liesl shakes her head. *"Some injuries are worse than others."*

"Could I hurt worse than I already do?"

"Yes."

"Still. I must see for myself."

"I know. When you are ready, meet us in the woods."

"Us?"

"Yes, there are others. We've been waiting for you. When you have seen what you want to see, come to us."

With only a thought, Steve's spirit flies through the doorway of his former home. The chorus of voices rise to a crescendo, then wane, up and down, in and out of hearing, repeatedly. Though the volume of the hymn fluctuates, its power grows.

Inside the great room of the house, a host gathers near the dining table. Jensens and the Warners, Rose and Rob from the diner, Chief Branton, and a host of others Steve doesn't know. The bodies of Bob Baxter, Gladys Milton, and Don Loomis hang from the vaulted ceiling just above the fireplace. Rocky lies next to the sofa, his head on his paws, watching. The dog seems to notice something. Could he know the spirit of his former master? Perhaps. But Rocky only returns his head to the wood floor with a great sigh.

Nadine stands in the middle of the room. Her eyes shine in bright green like a pair of alien planets. A long black dress covers her from head to toe, with a thin black veil pulled back from her face—a wedding dress. Nadine takes the demon by the hand, kissing him on the lips, and leads Steve's former body to the dining table.

Tied to the table is a naked body. A woman. Her long brown hair cascades along either side of the dinner table, floating off the edges like a chestnut waterfall. It's Mara. Eyes wide with tears, she sees the demon in her husband's body. She struggles to say something, but the gag in her mouth makes speaking impossible.

Steve tries to call to her, to tell Mara that it's not him—it's the demon—but she cannot hear a word he says.

The body raises a finger to its lips and smiles into her brown eyes. Mara fights to shake her head, but the strap across her forehead is too tight. Blood trickles down her temples.

Wendell Jensen crosses to the demon, offering a long carving knife and a fork, the same utensils Steve used to cut so many meals at Thanksgiving and Christmas. How the kids' eyes had sparkled on those joyous occasions.

The Demon kisses Mara once on the lips, then cuts through the skin of her right breast as if through butter, her cries muffled by the flock's call to prayer. As the congregants burst into song, the creature raises the meat to his mouth, tearing his teeth into it. The demon offers a bite to Nadine, who follows his lead.

"Come! Take part, faithful host. I shall reward you with some measure of my blessings. We will begin a change in this world that will shake the foundations of the earth. Now is our time, mine and my beloved goddess, together again and forever. Have cheer in your hearts, dear servants! Here in this house—this last house of the world!"

The worshippers form a line, plates in hand. Steve turns from the horror and in a flash he is outside behind the house, just before the forest, his new crystalline form taking shape as a host of other gray figures approach.

Some time later, a thin gray figure emerges from the house and descends the hill towards him. As she comes nearer, Steve recognizes his wife through the misty figure. They stare at each other for a time, then turn to the back of their house.

Clasping hands, the spirits have one last glimpse of a future that never will be. They turn and glide into the woods, observable to any passing mortal as nothing but two wisps of fog drifting through the forest on a gray October morning.

Matthew Speak grew up in Bettendorf, Iowa, within sight of the Mississippi River. He earned a degree in Theatre Arts and a pre-law certificate at St. Ambrose University, in Davenport, Iowa. Eventually, he moved to California, where he appeared on stage and in a few short films before seeking his teaching credential at California State University at Northridge. Besides writing, he is a co-host of the Cinescare Horror Podcast. He lives in Burbank, California, with his family and their beloved dog, Rosie. Mr. Speak is the author of The Bettendorf Tales, including Devils Glen and Crow Creek.

The Bettendorf Tales:

Devils Glen

Crow Creek